"I just finished reading R.I.P. Chief Taylor by Glynn Amburgey. I really enjoyed it. The twists and turns Glynn takes the reader through in this book lead to a very exciting ending. Also, as a proud father of two adult sons and being an avid car enthusiast, those aspects of Dave's life in the book drew me in."

Pat Perez, former Sheriff, County of Kane, Illinois

Mike,
Enjoy book!
number two!
Thanks
Glynn Amburgey

R.I.P
Chief Taylor

by Glynn Amburgey

JUKE BOX BOOKS LLC

A special thanks to my wife, Donna, for the tireless effort to edit this book so that readers are not subjected to my spelling errors and sentence structure failings.   She is truly my love.

I would also like to acknowledge the family members, friends and the West Carrollton High School class of 1967, and specifically the band members, who allowed the use of names and other attributes for this book. I appreciate all of you and hope you are pleased.

Cover art design contributed by Artist: Joseph M. Getsinger
www.jgetsingerarts.com

ISBN: 979-8-6838346-0-9

Juke Box Books, LLC
St Charles, IL

To Brigit, Jennifer, Nieka, Codie, Kirk, Lyn, and Jewl,

As Dave says, "It's all about kids."

Chapter 1

*W*ow, we're doing great, Dave thought as he reviewed the latest financial report. *I guess I really am doing a great job for the county.* It had been just over two years since he was elected sheriff of Lincoln County.

Dave's first election came after his predecessor died in his lake house. Uncle Will, as Dave called the former sheriff, had been the best friend of Dave's dad since childhood. Will had convinced Dave to join the department. He had worked his way up to patrol sergeant. When Will died, the political party was convinced that the Harbinger name was so well known in the county that Dave would be a shoe in for sheriff. Turned out they were right. The opposition party didn't run a candidate against him.

Dave had been elected to complete Uncle Will's term after his death. There had been a little over two years left in that term of office. Dave was now running for election for his first full term. The March election was only about a month away. But since the opposition party had once again not fielded a candidate against him, Dave was felt little stress over the election.

"Cheryl," Dave raised his voice so his assistant could hear him. "Could you please ask Craig to come to my office when he has time?"

"Of course."

Cheryl Smith was extremely efficient. She was in her mid-fifties and had worked in the Sheriff's office her entire career. The former sheriff had promoted her to her current position about twenty years ago. It seemed she knew everyone and was always on top of what was going on, both in the office and in town.

Major Craig Jackson was head of finance and administration for the sheriff's department. After a few minutes he came into Dave's office.

"What can I do for you, Sheriff?" Craig asked.

"I was looking over the quarterly report and noticed that we still have a lot left in the budget. Am I doing that good a job at keeping expenses down?"

"Good catch. But before you switch the vehicles over to Cadillacs be advised that there was an accounting glitch in the current report. A revised report will be on your desk in the morning."

"Accounting glitch? Does that mean someone entered the wrong numbers?"

"Kind of, but more accurately someone hit the print key before the previous quarter numbers were transferred over.

If you look at the expense totals for last quarter you see that they are greater than this quarter."

"So, the amount left in the budget is lower?"

"Correct. I think we are about the same as this time last year."

"Okay, I'll wait for the new report. Thanks, Craig."

Dave's phone rang as Craig was leaving his office.

"Dave Harbinger," he answered.

"Hi, sheriff."

"Hi, judge. How's your day going?"

"Okay, but I need to get out for awhile. Can you do lunch?"

"Sure. Denny's?"

"I'm thinking O'Malley's."

"You buying?"

"Sheriff, what kind of girl do you think I am? Old fashioned girls don't buy lunch for guys."

"Old-fashioned girls don't drive seven series BMWs."

"Twenty minutes?"

"See you there."

The judge was Jan Harbinger, Dave's wife of just over a year. They met when Jan was the attorney representing Dave's ex in the divorce. After the divorce was final, they began dating and learned that they were meant to be together, and were soon married. She had been elected judge when her predecessor died in office. She had been a judge for one-year, next month. Unlike Dave, she was not up for reelection this year.

"I'm going to lunch," Dave said to Cheryl as he walked out of his office.

"Say hello to the Judge," she responded.

"How'd you know. I...a..?" Dave was confused.

"It's my job to keep track of you," she said off handedly.

"I keep forgetting."

He headed for the door.

It was a brisk February day. The temperature was mild for this time of year, in the mid-forties. There was no wind at all. It was a slightly overcast day, but no feeling of rain.

When he pulled into the parking lot next door to O'Malley's, he noted that Jan's blue BMW was not in the lot. But that didn't mean she wasn't there since the court house was only a few blocks away and she would most likely have walked on such a pleasant day. This was confirmed when he walked inside. He saw her in the back of the room. He waved to the hostess and headed toward the lovely late-thirties judge that he still couldn't believe was his wife. As she saw him approach, she smiled with a hint of seduction that always made him lose his train of thought.

She was wearing a beige blouse with the top two buttons undone, showing no cleavage, but hinting as she leaned on the tabletop. Her makeup was not evident, but her striking features and beautiful eyes could not have been natural. Her blond hair was perfect as if she had just come from a salon. Dave, as always, just wanted to look at her and take in the radiant beauty that almost made his heart stop.

"You're looking well today, Sheriff," she said as he sat across from her.

"And you may dear, are downright fabulous."

The waitress appeared. She took their order and went her way to produce the meals, have someone else do it, pop something in the microwave, or whatever else happens in that room behind the swinging doors.

"So, why did you need to get away for awhile?" he asked. "Something going on that's bothering you?"

"Well," she started slowly. "Yes. I'm beginning to sense that I may be experiencing some inappropriate behavior by the chief judge."

Dave's eyes opened a bit wider as he inhaled.

"No, down tiger, not that kind," she smiled at his reaction. "I don't think I'm being given the same type of caseload as the other judges. It seems that I only get the divorce, child custody, and family type cases. Don't get me wrong, I really don't mind helping to solve those problems. But, on the other hand, I don't want it to be because someone thinks that's all I can handle. I know the law and I can apply it in all cases."

"You're thinking maybe Judge Johnson is discriminating against the woman?"

"I wouldn't say discriminating," she said thoughtfully, "I'm just not sure he thinks I can handle all aspects of the job."

"Because you're a woman?"

She sat quietly for a minute looking down at the table. He waited. She slowly looked up at him, he could see her eyes were wet.

"Yes, I guess that is it. And, I don't like it."

"Could it possibly be because you're younger, or that you have only been a judge for a year, and not that you're a woman?"

Still looking in his eyes, her focus changed. She tilted her head slightly and stuck out her chin.

"You think I'm being overly sensitive?"

"I don't know, but I know that if it bothers you, I'm concerned and am on your side. I just don't know that there is anything I can do. Except maybe keep your mind on other less important things, like how many of those buttons will have to be undone before the show really starts."

"Pervert."

She wiped her eyes with a napkin. Took a deep breath and said, "You're right. It probably has nothing to do with gender or age, it's just the way he does it. I am getting all worked up over nothing, and my pervert husband is the only one that can settle me down. I love you."

"I love you, too."

"I can't believe how much just being with you helps. I'll settle down and do my job. Thanks, Sheriff."

"No problem. I just want you to be happy, all the time."

"So, what's new this morning?"

"Well, some excitement. D called. He says the Cub's scout called and asked him to come to spring training tryouts. It seems they have a need for a utility infielder that can hit from both sides of the plate. He spent the last year working on his batting, his averages got their attention. He may be able to skip the farm system and go right into the big leagues. He's thinking about skipping the rest of the semester and going to camp to see if he can make the team. He wanted to know what I thought."

D, is Dave Junior, the oldest son. He is a senior at ASU on a full baseball scholarship. He threw his hat into the major league draft last year at the end of his junior year. He was picked in the fourteenth round by the Chicago Cubs as a short stop. They asked him to report to the Cubs triple A team in Des Moines, Iowa. But D opted to turn down the offer and finish school.

"So, what did you tell him, dad?"

"I told him it was entirely up to him. But I sure wouldn't pass up the chance."

"So, he's going to do it?"

"I think he had already decided to do it. I think he just wanted to give me the feeling that he valued my input."

"Sounds like I should book some time off to go watch baseball in Arizona next month?"

"My thoughts exactly."

After lunch Dave had a meeting with a vendor who was interested in selling his department on a new crime system tracking software package. He had the command staff sit in on the meeting as well to get their input on the need. After the vendor left, they decided that the system they currently use would meet their needs for a few more years.

Dave was on his way home at about five twenty, deep in thought about D playing professional baseball, when radio dispatch broke his train of thought. A silent alarm call at a convenience store on the west side of Springfield. The radio communication was set up so that the individual units only heard the dispatcher. This one-way communication assured that there would never be cross talk that may interfere during emergencies.

As Dave listened to the radio, he only heard the dispatcher side of the communication. Dispatch asked units 14 and 27 to respond with supervisor back up from unit 12. Dave knew unit 12 to be the day shift sergeant, Roger Hardin. He knew Roger well since he had taken the handoff from him for years when Dave was night shift sergeant.

Dispatch confirmed the responses from 14, 27 and supervisor 12.

Dispatch also acknowledged two other responders near the scene, unit 38 and Command two. Car 38 was Sergeant Brian Rodriquez and Command two was Major Bob Cooper. Brian was Dave's best friend in high school and they were still very close. Bob was on Dave's command team as head of the patrol division of the Lincoln County Sheriff's department and Brian's immediate supervisor. Dave also herd dispatch inform them that a Springfield City Police unit was on the scene.

Within seconds, dispatch acknowledged Car 38 on the scene at the rear of the store.

After a couple of minutes, the radio barked again, "Shots fired, officer down, Westside Commons shopping center."

Dave hit the switches for the lights and siren as he threw the steering wheel hard to the left and hit the accelerator.

"Command One in route," he shouted into the mic.

The Dodge Charger spun around almost in place with tires smoking. He noted three cars that were behind him a few seconds ago, now heading for the shoulder in front of him. He didn't look at the speedometer, it didn't matter, he was going to get there as fast as he could.

Dave lived about eight miles north of the county seat of Springfield and was about half-way home when the call came in. He took a right onto the state route to the west which acted as somewhat of a bypass around the city. He

had made about four miles of the seven or so to the scene
when the radio barked again.

"Command One, Command Two requests you at the rear of
the Commons."

"10-4, eta 3."

Dave glanced at the speedometer, it was well over 100 as
he wheeled along the four-lane state highway. He went
under the interstate overpass and approached the Commons
from the east. He saw two sets of flashing lights about a
half mile to the west heading toward him which he assumed
to be the other units responding. He turned on the cross
street that bordered the east side of the Commons and
headed to the rear of the shopping center. He quickly
traversed the block to the rear of the buildings and as he
came around the southeast corner, he saw the county sheriff
squad at the far end of the center, a distance of about two
hundred yards.

As he got closer, Dave could see the squad was facing him
with the driver's door standing open. There were a couple
of people down on the ground in front of it and a bit closer
to the building. As his car came to a stop, he noted that
there were actually four people, two lying on the ground, an
SPD officer and Major Bob Cooper. Bob was down on the
ground next to the one farther away, ...the one in the
Lincoln County Sheriff's uniform with the Sergeants stripes
on the sleeve. Dave's heart raced as he realized Brian had
been shot.

Dave noted the other person on the ground was face down,
facing the west, closer to the back door of the last unit in
the shopping center. He was not moving. There was a gun

on the ground about two feet away and closer to the building. The Springfield Police officer was searching the subject.

Bob was on the ground with Brian's head in his lap. There was a bloody mass on the left side of Brian's head. Bob was holding a handkerchief against the wound in an attempt to control the bleeding. Bob was covered in the blood of his patrol Sergeant. Dave kneeled down next to them and checked for a pulse. It was there, but faint.

The siren of the approaching ambulance made conversaticn impossible, so Dave just took Brian's hand and waited. The ambulance crew consisted of two men and a woman. One of the men came running with a fiberglass case in his hand while the other two opened the rear doors, grabbed some more equipment and headed over. Dave stepped back out of the way. The first crewman started checking Brian's vitals. Once the other two were there, they motioned for Bob to move away. They got to work to stabilize his condition and prepare for transport.

Bob pulled out his cell and placed a call.

"Tom, this is Bob Cooper. Brian has been shot by a robbery suspect. It looks bad, but he's alive. He's being transported to Springfield General. How close are you to his house?" There was a pause and then Bob continued. "Good, 10-39 to there, pick up Marie and take her to the hospital 10-39. There may not be much time. I'm calling her now."

As Dave watched, Bob pulled up another number on his phone speed dial and pushed send.

"Marie, this is Bob Cooper," he said into the phone after a few seconds and a huge inhale. "Brian's alive, but he's been shot by a robbery suspect. He's on the way to the hospital now."

Bob hesitated and his expression told Dave that on the end of the conversation Marie was losing control.

"Now, Marie, calm down, no, just stay there. Tom Harrison is on his way there to pick you up and take you to the hospital."

Another pause.

"Yes, the siren you hear would be him. He'll get you there a lot faster and safer than you could drive. Don't worry, Tom will stay with you as long as you need him to. Okay, go, I'll see you there in a little while."

Bob hung up the phone. He and Dave just looked at each other for a few seconds. Emotion building up in them both. Dave broke the silence.

"I assume everything is secure here."

"I guess, let me bring you up to speed with what I know before we go inside."

"Okay."

"When the silent was reported, I was sitting at a light about six blocks east of here on my way home. I responded as in the area and then approached the shopping center with lights on but no siren. As I was coming into the lot, I saw two SPD officers approaching the door of the store on foot from the east. Their squad was parked at an angle in front of the store next door. I pulled up on the end of the lot just to the west side of the store. As I was getting out of my car, I heard the first gun shot from behind the building, I cautiously looked around the corner into the window. One of the SPD officers had a suspect in custody at gun point with hands behind his head. I went in. There was a man behind the counter that I assumed to be the clerk. The officer told me his partner was pursuing a second suspect out the back as I heard the second shot. I went to the back door, cautiously looked out the door and saw the second suspect and Brian, both down. I placed the "officer down" call. The other SPD officer was Sergeant Wilson. He was checking vitals on the suspect and indicated he was deceased. I attended to Brian. Once I assessed that he was alive, I called you and waited. That's what I know."

Brian was loaded into the ambulance.

One of the ambulance crew looked at Dave and said quietly, "I don't know." The ambulance was already moving when he closed the back door from the inside.

Chapter 2

Sirens had been coming from all directions ever since Dave arrived. The other three sheriff squads had come to the back of the building as well as another ambulance, a fire truck and two SPD units.

"Dispatch, Command One," Dave said into the hand held he had just unclipped from his belt.

"Go ahead, Sheriff," came the reply.

"10-25 Command Three to my location."

"He's already on the way, should be there within two."

"10-4, thanks."

Bob was talking with the three deputies over by Brian's car, just out of ear shot from Dave. He assumed Bob was giving them their assignments to assist with securing the crime scene and managing traffic control.

An SPD officer was in the process of running yellow "crime scene" tape around the area. Dave and Bob were within the cordoned off area already. An ambulance crew was with the suspect on the ground but were doing nothing. They appeared to be waiting on the coroner, or maybe permission to move the body. Bob approached Dave, having completed the discussion with his patrol officers.

"Let's go talk with Sergeant Wilson," Dave said to Bob.

Bob's uniform was covered in blood from just above the belt line to the knees. Dave handed him a handkerchief. Bob began wiping his hands as they moved toward the rear door of the store.

They entered into a small storage area about twenty feet wide and maybe ten feet across. There were shelves around the walls that went all the way to the ceiling, mostly filled with boxes of product. Directly across from them was a thick aluminum door that lead into the main store area. Dave used his elbow to push on the door.

In the store area there were about ten people consisting of Springfield police, firemen and a couple of guys in suits. One of the suits was an old friend of Dave's, Assistant Chief Walter Regan, Chief Investigator for SPD. When he saw Dave come in, Walt moved to greet him with an out stretched hand.

"Hi, Walt," Dave said as they shook hands. Walt Regan was a big guy, about six foot three and two seventy. He was in his mid-fifties and appeared to be in decent shape. He was always neatly dressed and seemed to care about his appearance. His gray streaked dark hair was always neatly trimmed.

"What say, Dave. How's your guy?"

"Don't know. He's alive but took one in the head. Looks bad."

"Sorry," Walt looked somber. "We lost our Chief."

He nodded to Dave's right along the back aisle. A row of coolers ran the length of the aisle, turned the corner and continued on the east wall of the store. In the far corner, cn the floor was the body of a man lying face down and facing away from them. There was blood on the floor. The blood seemed to be coming from the upper part of the body, maybe the head. A gallon jug of milk was on the floor near the cooler, leaking its contents through a small break in the plastic container.

Dave, Walt and Bob were about fifteen feet away.

"It's Chief Taylor, ' Walt said softly. "Apparently stopped in for milk on his way home and became the victim of a robbery."

"I only heard the two shots out back," Bob said thoughtfully. "He must have got it before I got here."

"Bob was on the scene right after your patrolmen," Dave offered.

"We're still piecing it together," Walt said. "But from what I'm hearing, the Chief came in right before the two perps. One held a gun on the clerk while the other checked the store. When he saw the Chief, he shot him. About that time, our guys came in the front door, got he drop on perp one while perp two ran out the back. Patrolman Jones took perp one into custody while Sergeant Wilson gave chase out the back. When perp two got out back, he shot your guy, and Sergeant Wilson shot him."

Dave nodded. "Sound right to you, Bob?"

"I guess it makes sense. Seems both the chief and Brian were at the wrong place at the wrong time."

"It's still very preliminary," Walt continued. "We've got a lot of statements to take. I'll be sure to keep you up to speed, Dave."

"Please do. And, thanks Walt. You need anything else from us right now? I'd like to get over to the hospital. Dan Muscovy, will be here any second to take over from our end."

Major Dan Muscovy was the chief investigator for the Lincoln County Sheriff's Department. Dan was the third member of Dave's command staff along with Bob and Craig Jackson.

"Sure, Dave, we can handle things here. I'll bring Dan up to speed, you go check on your guy."

"I'll be there as soon as I make sure the shift is handled," Bob said to Dave as he headed for the door.

The hospital was only a couple miles back into town. Dave used a very liberal interpretation of the traffic laws to get there. It only took him about four minutes. He parked the unmarked Charger in a spot designated for police and emergency vehicles just outside the emergency room ambulance entrance. He ran inside.

A fifties-something nurse saw him coming in the door, she waved him down the hallway to the left, mouthed the word "room" and held up four fingers.

He stopped in the doorway to room four. Brian was on a table in the middle of the room. There were eight people in the room, five men and three women. All were moving around frantically, checking monitors, taking measurements, and talking about what they were seeing. He felt it best to not interfere.

After only a few seconds observing what was going on, he heard one of the men say, "Okay, everyone, are we stable enough to move to ops?"

All responses were affirmative.

A flurry of activity began. Dave moved back out into the hallway as the entire group moved out of the room and turned up the hallway with Brian in the middle of them on a gurney.

They were hardly out of his sight when he heard steps behind him. He turned to see Brian's wife Marie and Officer Tom Harrison approaching from the emergency entrance. Marie was a small woman, only about five-foot-tall and not much over a hundred pounds. She had long dark hair and a pleasant face. She wore jeans and a light blue top and spotless white tennis shoes.

Dave hugged Marie briefly, "they've just taken him into the operating room. He has a gun shot wound to the head. That's all I know right now."

Marie looked at Dave with tears in her eyes, it was obvious that she had been crying for a long time.

"Is he going to be okay, Dave?"

"Let me see if I can find someone to give us some information."

There was a small waiting room off to the left side of the hallway. Dave took Marie over to a chair. He nodded at Tom who sat down in the chair on her left.

"I'll be right back."

Dave went to the nurses' station. There were two nurses there, one appeared to be in her late fifties and the other thirty-something. When she looked up and saw Dave, the older one said to the other, "Toni, would you please go get a status on the Deputy for the Sheriff?"

"Thank you, I'm in the waiting area with his wife."

She nodded as Dave turned back up the hall.

Dave returned to the waiting area and sat down on the right side of Marie.

"They're checking," he said softly. "Marie, would you like some coffee, a Coke or something? Maybe something to eat, a sandwich or even just a candy bar?"

Marie nodded, "I haven't eaten, maybe a diet drink and candy bar. Thanks."

Dave pulled a twenty-dollar bill from his pocket and handed it to Tom.

"Would you, please, Tom? I'll have a root beer and get whatever you want."

"Sure, be right back." Tom said and headed down the hallway.

"What happened, Dave? Brian's shift hadn't even started."

"There was a robbery at the convenience store in the Westside Commons. Brian was right there when the call came in, apparently on his way into the station. He responded to the call and approached the rear of the store. One of the robbers came out the back and shot him."

Marie looked at Dave with a puzzled expression.

"Did Brian shoot the guy?"

"No, an SPD officer did."

"Dave, Brian is really good at what he does. Don't you agree?"

"Yes, of course, he's one of the best."

"Then how could someone shoot him without him shooting them first?"

At that moment the nurse, Toni, motioned for Dave from up the hall. He excused himself and went to talk with her.

"Sheriff, your officer is in critical but stable condition. They have summoned Dr. Patel our best brain surgeon. He should be here soon."

As she was talking, Bob Cooper walked up and joined them. Bob had apparently stopped by home and changed into street clothes.

"They will be operating as soon as Dr. Patel arrives to remove the bullet and assess the damage," the nurse continued. "That's all I can tell you now. I'll bring the paperwork to his wife in a few minutes, if that's alright."

"Okay, thanks, and yes that will be fine."

Dave and Bob went to the waiting area to tell Marie what they had learned. They sat down on either side of her. When Dave finished, she nodded slightly and buried her face into his shoulder. The sobbing returned.

Tom returned with two diet cokes and a root beer. He also had several candy bars. Marie took a coke and candy bar, but didn't really attack either one. The food and drink seemed to be more something to do with her hands than to actually eat and drink. Dave opened the root beer and sipped it absentmindedly.

Over the next forty-five minutes to an hour, Dave, Bob and Tom took turns holding Marie as she continued to cry. The hospital admittance paperwork was completed, more by Dave and Bob than Marie, but it was accomplished to the satisfaction of the admitting staff. The hospital staff had suggested they all move down to the waiting room by surgery which they did.

Dave had broken away for a short time to call Jan and let her know what had happened. She was still in her chambers when he called and she told him she would be right over. Brian's mom and dad brought his kids. Brian and Marie had three, two boys and a girl: Brian Jr. age fourteen, Barry age nine and Mandy age twelve.

The waiting room was getting rather full. Tom had gone off duty, so Bob released him. Tom offered to stay, but Marie thanked him graciously and suggested he had done enough for today. Tom offered his help with anything she needed and left.

Along with everyone else in the room, Dave's stress level was over the top. He was struggling to keep composure and his emotions in check when Jan walked into the room She had a look of tension, stress and concern on her face, but still looked as fabulous as she had across the lunch table only a few hours ago.

Jan went straight to Marie and sat down on the coffee table just in front of her. They hugged briefly as Jan tried to console and give hope. Marie expressed her gratitude and attempted to smile. Jan talked briefly with Brian's parents and his kids before turning to Dave and motioning toward the hallway.

When they were in the hallway, they decided to grab a bite to eat in the cafeteria. They walked slowly down the hall, each dealing with the emotion of the possibility of pending disaster for the family of a close friend. Dave got a hamburger and a coke. Jan selected a fish sandwich with an iced tea. Neither felt much like talking as they ate. After they had finished eating Dave took out his cell phone and called his brother, Kent.

"Hey, little brother, what's up," Kent answered.

"Not good," Dave began. "You remember my buddy, Brian Rodriquez don't you?"

"Sure,"

"He was shot while responding to an attempted robbery. A small caliber bullet to the head. Thought I'd give a call to my favorite Chief Surgeon and see what he could tell me."

"Oh, I'm sorry. I assume he's alive, and my guess is he's in surgery."

"Right on both counts."

"Where was he struck, exactly?"

"Left side, fore head, maybe half way between the eye and the ear."

"Exit wound?"

"No, they told me they were going into surgery to remove the bullet and assess the damage. Dr. Patel is doing the operation."

"Naveen Patel?"

"Yes, I think that's right."

"Well, they don't get any better at brain and neurosurgery than Naveen Patel. He's in good hands. I've even heard of him being called up here to the Chicago area to assist with tough cases."

"So, can you tell me anything?"

"Well, if the bullet is still in there and it's on the outside of the brain, the chances are pretty good that the damage is minimal. The real issue is the angle of attack. If the bullet was going in on a glancing angle, it may have lodged between the brain and the skull. On the other hand, if the angle were more direct, it could mean more serious damage. They may need to induced a comma. If the entry angle was the former, at the very least, they will have to wait for the swelling to subside before any attempt at revival. If the angle was the latter, the diagnosis would not be as hopeful."

"How long would you expect the operation to take?"

"Hard to say, you say small caliber, what twenty-two?"

"Thirty-eight, I think. From maybe twenty to thirty feet."

"Again, it goes back to the angle. Was it straight on?"

"I'd say it pretty much had to be."

"Then you're probably looking at several hours of surgery. Maybe in the four to six range, but it could be more."

"I guess it's going to be a long night."

"Afraid so."

"Any chance of a full recovery?"

"From what you've told me, little. If he survives the surgery, there is a good chance he will recover to some degree but will probably never be the same. Do you remember Jim Brady being shot with President Reagan?"

"Yes."

"He recovered, but I don't think he ever walked after that. He also had speech issues and less than full mental capabilities. And, the recovery time was in years. Sorry little brother. What can I do? Would you like for me to check in down there and see if we can offer any resources or assistance?"

"No, I don't think we know enough yet. But thanks for the offer. I appreciate you giving it to me straight. I need to get back in there. I'll call you tomorrow. Thanks, Kent."

Dave signed off.

Jan took his hand. She had heard enough of the conversation to know it was not good. They sat together for several minutes before going back to the waiting room. Dave did not share any of his brother's comments with Marie.

Just before midnight, a nurse came to the waiting room door and motioned for Dave. He followed her out into the hallway...

"Sheriff," she said quietly, "your deputy will be coming out of surgery in the next few minutes. Dr. Patel would like to talk with his wife in conference room seven. He asked that one other person be with her. Do you have a suggestion?"

"Brian and I have been best friends all of our lives. I know Marie like a sister. I'll go with her."

Dave turned back into the room. Marie was looking at him.

"The doctor wants to talk with you."

"Will you go with me, Dave?"

He nodded and held out his hand. She took it and they walked down the hall.

Conference room seven was a room that Dave had been in many times. It was located near the main emergency room waiting area. Often times it was used to talk with family members of auto accident victims or other police business. It was a room about fifteen feet long by ten feet wide. There was a table in the middle of the room with eight padded chairs around it.

Dave and Marie walked into the room and sat down next to each other on the far side of the table. Dr. Patel was not yet there. Dave put an arm around Marie and she rested her head on his shoulder. They waited.

In about five minutes, a dark-skinned man wearing hospital scrubs came into the room. He closed the door and held out his hand to Marie.

"I'm Dr. Naveen Patel," he said softly as they shook hands. Dr. Patel was a small man, about five-foot three. He appeared to Dave to be in his fifties.

"This is Marie Rodriguez, the officer's wife," Dave offered as he stood and shook hands with the doctor. "I'm Sheriff Dave Harbinger, the officer's best friend."

They all sat and Dave put his arm around Marie's shoulders.

"The surgery went well, and although it is too early to say for certain, I'm optimistic," Dr. Patel began. His voice was clear with a sense of authority and experience.

Marie exhaled and Dave thought he felt her body relax although he could still feel a tremble.

"The bullet entered the skull on the left side of the frontal bone just ahead of the coronial suture." He pointed to the left side of his head about half way between the eye and the ear and little above both. "The bullet lodged against the parietal bone inside the brain cavity. The bullet was along the skull line enough to impede its progress. A couple of inches either way and the results would have been significantly different. Had the path of the bullet been a couple of inches to the right, it would have missed him entirely. Had it been a couple of inched to the left I don't think he would have survived."

Marie shook.

"When you say you're optimistic, does that mean full recovery?" Dave asked.

"Maybe, but far too soon to say. There did not seem to be very much actual brain damage, but any time there is an intrusion into the brain cavity there is cause for concern. We have induced a coma to allow the brain to rest and the swelling to subside. He will need to remain in intensive care for about seventy-two hours until the swelling has reduced. At that time, I can better tell what we are dealing with. Do you have any questions?"

"You say he is in a coma. How long before he wakes up?" Marie asked.

"We need to keep him in the coma for the seventy-two hours at least. If the swelling is down and we see no other problems then we can stop the drugs and close up the skull. It'll be a week to ten days, at least, after that before he wakes up. But it could be longer, everyone is different in how they recover from the treatment."

Marie looked worried again.

"So, we won't know if he is going to be okay until he wakes up?"

"Afraid so, but like I said, his brain didn't seem to be damaged and he seems to be in good physical condition. I think his chances are good."

Marie nodded slowly. She looked at Dave. He tried to offer a reassuring smile, but wasn't sure he accomplished it.

"If you need any other questions answered, here is my card." He handed each of them a card. "I'm sorry that I can't allow you to spend much time with your husband right now, Mrs. Rodriguez. We need to keep him in intensive care and can only allow you to visit for a few minutes. Once he is out of the care unit you will be able to stay with him."

"Thank you, Doctor."

"They should have him all set up in the ICU now. You can go in and see him, Mrs. Rodriguez, but only for about ten minutes."

"Thanks, Doc," Dave said as they all walked out of the room.

Chapter 3

It was almost ten when Dave got into his office the next morning. Not because he slept in, but because he went straight to the hospital from home and then to SPD headquarters. Brian's condition had not changed, the report was that he was stable but critical. SPD was in a state of total shock. Dave talked with several people that he knew. They all were deeply saddened by the loss of their chief. Rod Taylor was very highly respected and well liked, even though he had only been in the department for about a year. Dave had hoped to spend some time with Walt Regan, going over the details of last night, but when he got to his office his assistant said he was with the Mayor and would most likely be tied up all morning. Dave left his card and asked for a call as soon as Walt was free.

"Any change in Brian's condition this morning?" Cheryl asked as Dave approached her desk back in the office.

"No, same as last night. All we can do now is wait."

"Bob and Dan want to talk, should I tell them to come in?"

"Yes."

"I'll bring you some coffee."

"Thanks."

Bob and Dan came into Dave's office and sat down across from his desk. Right behind them came Cheryl with three cups of coffee on a plastic tray. One black and two with cream. She set the tray on the corner of Dave's desk and left closing the door behind her.

"I stopped by the hospital this morning. No change," Dave said as he picked up the cup with no cream.

"Cheryl said that's where you were," Bob said casually.

Dave started to ask how Cheryl would know, but moved on.

"Did you get anything of value from SPD, Dan?"

"Walt said you guys had just left when I got there. I watched as they processed the scene. Nothing came up that seemed irregular. I think they did a good job, took pictures of everywhere from every angle before anything was moved. As far as I can tell the scene was completely secure when they were going over it, except for Brian being moved and the surrounding area. Of course, that was disturbed to some degree by you guys and the ambulance crew. But other than that I think they got good evidence of the site. Although it looks like we all have a good handle on what happened."

"Yes, but it's good to have the evidence anyway. I stopped in to talk with Walt after the hospital but didn't catch him. What is your read-on timing of any reports?"

"It will surely be a high priority. I don't see them sitting on this, wouldn't surprise me to see some preliminary findings by next week."

"Okay, Cheryl said you wanted to talk. What's up?

"I think we need to talk about how we cover for Brian," Bob said slowly. "We're for sure looking at a considerable amount of time before he's back, if..." he trailed off, emotion getting to him.

"Oh," Dave said slowly. He had been so worried and caught up in the condition of his friend that it had been his sole focus. He was dumbfounded by the fact that he had not even thought about the impact on the department. This struck him as being close to a dereliction of duty. How could he allow his personnel feelings to overshadow the job he was elected to accomplish?

The room went quiet.

"I've asked Corporal Johnson to step up to acting Sergeant for the time being," Bob said after regaining his composure. "Tom Harrison is going to fill Joe's Corporal spot. But that leaves us down a patrolman."

"I don't think it should be a problem for the short term. What do you think? Can we work one short for a few weeks?" Dave asked.

"I guess we can, as you know, that is the lightest shift. And, we are in a low impact time of the year," Bob said thoughtfully. "Yes, we can make it work for a few weeks."

"Dan, do you agree?" Dave asked.

"Sure, no different than when we have someone call in sick at the last moment. Just more notice and longer term this time."

"Good, the Doctor says Brian should be waking up in a couple of weeks. We should know then how much damage has been done. Even a full recovery is going to take some time, but we'll have a better idea then what we're going to need to do."

Bob and Dan both nodded in agreement.

"Okay, moving on. I assume SPD will be asking for assistance to cover for them during the funeral for the chief. Get the word out that all on duty personnel can expect reassignments and off duty personnel are encouraged to volunteer for extra hours. We will pay standard OT."

"I'll touch base with them to get an idea what they are going to need," Bob said as he jotted in his note book. "Traffic control at the least, I'm sure, and most likely some response duties. And, of course, escort. I'm sure the staff will step up."

"Anything else?"

Before anyone could answer, the door opened. Cheryl stuck her head in. "Sorry, Sheriff, the hospital is on the phone."

No one else moved while Dave turned to pick up the phone.

"Sheriff Harbinger," he said into the receiver.

"Sheriff, this is the head emergency room nurse. We have your deputy's clothes and equipment locked up in my closet. Including his gun. I wonder if you could have someone pick it up. I'd like to get it out of here."

"Of course. Sorry, I should have thought of that. I will have someone stop by right away. Thanks for calling." As he hung up the phone he said, "They want us to pick up Brian's gun belt and stuff."

The others in the room all exhaled as one.

"I can do that," Dan offered. "I'm going right by there on my way to interview a home robbery victim. We picked up a dude last night that I'm thinking may be involved."

"Oh, you think we may have a serial burglar in custody?"

"Maybe. From the tracks on his arm, I'm thinking he's supporting a habit by ten fingering where he can."

"That's not very unicue, what ties it together?"

"Just that he lives in the same area. I'm curious to see if the victims know him, and if so, if he's been in that house."

"Oh, local knowledge thing. Ok, let me know what you find. Anyway, just check at the emergency room nurse station to get Brian's things."

"Will do."

"Thanks, Dan."

Dave spent the rest of the day, including working right through lunch, trying to focus on the work at hand. But, the nagging concern for Brian made concentration very difficult. When five finally came he was completely exhausted. The long day yesterday, little sleep last night, and the extra effort it took to stay focused had him feeling like he would fall asleep on the way home. As he was pulling his jacket on Dan came into his office carrying a gun belt and a large paper bag.

"What should I do with these?" Dan asked.

Dave pointed to the counter on top of a row of two drawer file cabinets that ran along the wall of his office. Dan put the gun belt and bag on the counter.
"Thanks, Dan," Dave said softly. Dan turned to leave.

"Wait!"

Dan stopped in his tracks. Dave went over to the counter and dumped the contents of the bag out on the counter. There was a bloody shirt, a pair of uniform trousers, a bullet proof vest, a tee shirt, boxer shorts, shoes and socks. The shirt still had Brian's name tag, his badge and other items just as if he had just taken it off.

"What?" Dan asked, puzzled.

Dave looked at the items.

"Something's wrong."

"What?" Dan asked, again.

Dave hesitated, "I...I.., don't know. But something's not right."

"Dave, this is just Brian's stuff. It's just as I thought it would be. What are you talking about?"

"Did you ever look at something you have seen a thousand times and sense that it's not the way it was, or that something is not right?"

"Well, I guess, but..."

"I just got that feeling. I don't know why, but it's something."

Dave and Dan stared at the pile of clothes and gear. Dave checked through the pockets of the shirt and trousers. He found things that would be expected, a pocket knife, a pen, a note book, a wallet, a hand full of change, a handkerchief, and a pack of gum. He checked the gun belt. He found two extra clips, handcuffs, keys, and all the other items a policeman carries in his belt. Nothing seemed out of place or missing.

"Maybe it's something missing that is in his squad?" Dan offered.

"No, it's something right here that's not right," Dave said sternly. "I don't know what, but something isn't right."

They went through the gear again. Nothing seemed wrong.

"Well," Dave shrugged after a few more minutes of looking, "I don't know. Maybe it will come to me."

They left it at that.

Before pulling out of the parking lot, Dave hit the speed dial to call Jan.

"Hi, are you on the way home?" she answered.

"Yep, how about you?"

"Already here, dinner will be ready when you get here."

"Okay, be there shortly."

Dinner was on the table when he walked in the door from the garage. Fried chicken, mashed potatoes with gravy, cold slaw and hot rolls.

"I suspect you had some help preparing this meal," Dave said with a smile.

"Never turn down an assist from a Colonel, I always say," Jan retorted. "My last case today ran longer than expected, so I punted. Hope you don't mind."

"Not at all. How about after we eat, we snuggle up on the couch in front of the tv. I could use some relax time."

"I was thinking that too."

About fifteen minutes into the couch time the phone rang. Dave picked up the wireless off the end table next to him.

"Hi, Dad, so sorry about Brian. How's he doing?"

"Thanks, Chris, he's doing as well as can be expected right now. It will be at least a couple of weeks before we know anything. They have him in a coma until the brain swelling goes down."

"Wow, that's tough. How are you?"

"I'm doing better today. Last night was pretty stressful."

"I can imagine."

"What's new with my favorite Purdue sophomore? How are classes going?"

"Everything is okay. Doctor Needler said to say hello."

"Really, do you have him for a class?"

"No, he's Chair of the EE department now. He pulled me out of my motors class. Asked if you and I are related. Said he saw my name and figured me to be about the right age to be your son."

"Well, tell him hello and next time we get up there, I'll make it a point to stop in and see him."

"Will do. How about D getting to go to spring training?"

"He told you, huh. Yeah, that's great. Hope he does well."

"Me too. I think it would be cool to see my brother at Wrigley. Do ya think he could get me a ticket?"

"I think you can count on that, but don't get your hopes up too high. It's still a long shot, I think."

"Why do you say that?"

"It's very rare for a player to go straight into the majors. Hardly ever happens. Most players spend several years in the farm system before getting up to the show. D is good, but so are a lot of other guys. And, a lot of the other guys that are good have been in the minors for years."

"But the Cubs drafted him last year. Must mean they want him."

"They drafted him for Des Moines. Not to go straight into the majors."

"But that was before he got to over five hundred on base percentage and a batting average of four-twenty."

"Yes, and that batting is why they want to take a look at him in camp. Remember, hitting in college is a lot different than hitting in the majors. I once heard an interview by a new big leaguer who said the difference between the majors and the minors was like night and day. He said that in the minors the pitchers didn't have the control that major league pitchers have. In the show, every pitch is either on the plate or just off. The pitchers have much greater control."

"So, you're saying that D may have trouble hitting a big-league pitcher."

"A lot different than college, I'd guess."

"Oh, I understand. Well, it's still a good thing to get to try out."

"Yes, it is. We can, and will, root for him where ever he plays."

"Of course."

"Jan and I are planning to go out to watch some of spring training. We may go out for a week to ten days toward the last of March. We're working on schedules right now."

"Would you pay my way to go too? Not sure I should take off that long, but I could certainly do three or four days."

"Sure, I'll spring for you. When we get our act together, I'll let you know when we're going to be there. Then you can decide when it fits for you. Just put it on your credit card."

"Great. That sounds like a lot of fun. Thanks, dad."

"I'm sure D will like us all being out there, too."

"I gotta run. Love you dad, tell Jan hi."

Dave hung up the phone and stretched back out on the couch. Jan resumed her favorite spot with her shoulder up under his arm pit and her head on his shoulder. He ran his hand down her side and rested it on her thigh.

"I love you," she sighed.

"I love you, too."

"Speaking of our little trip to Scottsdale, I can be off the eighteenth through the twenty-seventh, if that works."

"I think that will be fine. I'll ask D to get us a schedule of the games. I'll bet we can play some golf too."

"Baseball, golf and you, sounds like heaven to me."

"What a woman."

 The rest of the evening was spent resting and recuperating. They went to bed early. Dave slept soundly.

The next morning, Wednesday, the talk in the office was all about the upcoming funeral of Chief Rod Taylor. The wake was to be on Thursday evening at the Knox Funeral Home on East Main Street in Springfield. The funeral would be on Friday morning at eleven in the Eastside Christian Church. Burial was to be out of state in Chief Taylor's home town, where another service would also be held.

Dave stopped in Bob's office at about ten in the morning to check on things.

"How's it going?"

"Unbelievable," Bob responded. "Our entire patrol staff will be on duty for the funeral and Williams County is sending up 8 units. SPD had asked us to cover the city for them so that all of their officers can attend. I'm cutting our field patrols back to a corporal and two squads per quadrant. That gives us fifty-five squads to cover the city and the funeral. The city has eight patrol districts. We will put all six of our sergeants and twenty-four squads to cover the city. The rest will cover the funeral itself. I have coordinated with the city dispatch and will be sending them the unit numbers with assigned areas as soon as we have all of that put together."

"Good, let me know if you need anything from me."

"Thanks," Bob went back to his scheduling.

Chapter 4

Friday morning Dave and Jan stopped into the hospital to check on Brian's progress. The seventy-two-hour window had passed; the swelling had subsided. They had taken him back into surgery and closed his skull yesterday. The doctor was satisfied that the coma inducing drug could be stopped. So now they waited for him to wake up. Marie told them that the doctor was confident the internal damage was not as bad as it could have been. She was feeling excited for him to wake up and be fine. Although they were glad Marie was doing well, Dave and Jan were a bit concerned that her expectations may be too high. After the hospital visit they headed to the Eastside Christian Church for Chief Taylor's funeral.

Jan had on a plain black dress that certainly didn't look plain on her. Dave wore his dress uniform which consisted of a white shirt, black tie and a black jacket with insignia and shoulder boards with two stars on them. The jacket was loose fitting around the chest to allow room for the gun in the shoulder holster.

The church was a relatively new facility with a large octagonal sanctuary. The focal point was the stained-glass windows of various sizes in the front and down the sides. There were two main sections of seating in the middle with smaller ones on each side. The pews were padded with dark green cloth that complimented the green carpet on the platform and the aisles. When they entered the casket was already at the front of the church surrounded by flowers of about every kind. Even though it was about thirty minutes before the service was to begin, the room was already filled to near capacity. Dave and Jan found a place to sit on the far-left side about half-way back from the front. From this location they could look across the room and see most of the other attendees.

Seated around the room were dignitaries from not only the city and county but the state as well. Dave recognized several state police officials including Captain Josh Trubaldi and Colonel Paul Adams. Agent in Charge of the Drug Enforcement Agency (DEA) George Hoffman was seated with the State Lt. Governor. Sheriff Rob Alexander was there from Williams County as was the Mayor of Jackson in Williams County. Every Springfield City Council Member and senior staff member was also present. Most of the County Board Members were there along with Jan's fellow judges and state's attorneys. It was a who's who of Springfield and Lincoln County.

Springfield Mayor, the Honorable Herbert Wilson, opened the ceremony with a statement of appreciation for the Chief's service to the community and regrets to his family. He ending his remarks with: "Even though Rod had only served the city for about a year, he had proven to be a dedicated steadfast enforcer of the law who was unwavering in his commitment to the truth and what was right. He was well liked, trusted and could be counted on. He will be missed."

After the service, Dave fell in with his comrade officers as they formed up on either side of the walkway from the church as an honor guard. They all snapped to attention and saluted as the flag draped coffin rolled by.

As the black Cadillac moved slowly out from under the church canopy, Dave moved back into the crowd of mourners to find Jan. He found her in quiet conversation with an older gentleman that Dave knew to be the Chief Judge of Lincoln County.

"Good to see you, Judge Johnson," Dave said as he approached them.

"Good to see you, Sheriff, and let me tell you how wonderful it is to have your lovely wife serve in our courts. She is truly a wonderful person and a highly qualified jurist."

"Dave, Judge Johnson just asked if I would feel a conflict of interest if the case for the other robber in the Chief Taylor case were to land in my court."

"Yes, Sheriff, I know that you and Jan are close with the deputy who was also shot. I would not want to put Jan into a situation that would add to the stress, but I would like to give her the case."

"Oh, as a matter of curiosity, if you don't mind, why do you want to give her the case?" Dave asked. Jan's stare cut through him and looked more than a bit shocked.

"Well, no I don't mind," the judge began, "the Mayor asked me to take the case personally. He said he wanted to be sure the case gets resolved quickly and thought I could assure him that it would. I gave it serious consideration, but after looking at my schedule I just can't fit it in. Since the Mayor wants it done quickly, I decided to pass it on. Jan has the lightest case load right now. If anyone could get it done quickly it would be her. So that's why I want her to take the case."

"I don't think there should be any problem on my end," Jan interjected. "I'm sure I can work it in and get it done."

"Good, it will probably be a couple of months before it comes up, but try to keep your calendar flexible in that time frame."

They exchanged pleasantries and Judge Johnson moved on.

Jan looked at Dave with a bit of a frown and a wrinkled brow.

"I know what you're thinking, and I apologize. Yes, my question to the Judge was out of line. But it was an attempt to get information. My investigation senses are in full alert. I had a feeling the other day that something was not right, and I just got that feeling again."

"So, you feel that it's not right for me to get the case?"

"No, no, no. The feeling is that there is something that I'm missing about the case. I feel that you are the absolute best for every case that comes along. Forgive me?"

He smiled his best puppy dog smile.

She punched him in the ribs.

"Ok, apology accepted. Did you learn anything?"

"Maybe. Excuse me for a minute."

Dave left her standing and moved through the crowd toward the parking lot. He saw a group of people talking just off the end of the sidewalk. He approached them and reached out to shake the Mayor's hand.

"I'm really sorry, Mayor."

"Thanks, Dave. And thanks for all the support your guys are providing to SPD. We are in your debt."

"Think nothing of it. Rod will be missed, he was doing a great job, as far as I could tell."

"Yes, he was a rare bird. Honest as the day is long and a good officer. He will be missed."

"Well, I just wanted to offer my condolences and let you know that we are willing to help all that we can."

"Thanks, I've moved Walt Regan up to acting Chief. I'm sure he will be in contact with you if he needs anything."

"Walt's a good man."

"Yeah, he has a stubborn streak just like Rod, but at least he knows his place. Thanks again, Dave. I've got to go."

Mayor Wilson turned and moved away. Dave went, once again to find Jan.

"Well?" she said, when he got back to where she was standing, waiting on him.

"Well, what?"

"I saw you talking to the Mayor, what did you learn?"

"I don't know if I learned anything. I also don't know if there is anything to learn. I feel like I'm in the dark. You ever feel that way?"

"You mean other than right now?"

"Come on, I'll give you a ride in a police car, cutie."

On the way to drop her off at the court house, Dave and Jan stopped for lunch at a home style diner called Mary's Place. They took a booth along the windows. They had a view of the parking lot in front and the busy city street. A waitress introduced herself as Amy and took their order. Jan opted for the garden salad and Dave selected the corned beef and cabbage. Both also asked for the soup of the day which was beef vegetable.

"Ok," Jan said as they began on the soup. "Tell me what's bothering you."

Dave smashed up some crackers and dumped them into his soup. He sipped the soup. It was very hot.

"I can't say that I have anything concrete, but several times since Brian was shot, I've felt that something is really wrong."

"Tell me about each time."

"When I pulled up to the scene, as I was walking to where Bob was holding Brian, it hit me. A feeling that something was all wrong. The next time the feeling hit me was in the hospital while I was talking with Marie. Then again when Dan brought Brian's gear into my office and the last time was when you said Judge Johnson had asked you to take the case."

He took another spoonful of soup, this time it had cooled some and was very good. Jan was studying him closely as she listened and ate her soup. Dave could tell her mind was working on what he had just told her. He knew her to be one of the most intelligent people he had ever met. She had an unbelievable ability to understand a situation and predict an outcome. He thought it must be from years of close study of law cases and human nature.

"I see," she finally said slowly. "Yes, you were right to question Judge Johnson. Your subconscious has apparently picked up on something. You know what it is deep down, but the shock and stress of recent events has masked it from you. It will come to you, probably when you least expect it, but I don't think you will be able to force it. My advice is to just go about doing your job and wait. I know you well enough to know that if you have the feeling, it must be something important."

"You think I'm right?"

"No, I know you're right. Just give it time."

"But what if it never comes out?"

"Just relax, it will." She reached across the table and took his hand. "I have no doubt. And, when it does, you will kick yourself for not seeing it before. Give it time."

"Okay."

Lunch arrived before either of them had finished the soup. The food was excellent. Over the rest of the meal they talked about other things and enjoyed each other's company.

About an hour later, Dave walked into the station after dropping Jan off at the court house. Sitting in the lounge area by the reception desk was George Hoffman of the DEA.

"Hi, George," Dave said extending his hand.

"Hello, Sheriff. While I'm down here I wanted to take the opportunity to talk with you for a few minutes if you have time."

"Sure, let's go into the office."

Dave led the way back to his office. They talked about the funeral and some pleasantries for a few minutes. Cheryl brought in coffee and closed the door behind her as she left.

"The real reason for me being here is I wanted to talk with you about drug activity in the area. What have you seen since we shut down the drug farm in Williams County a couple of years ago?"

"Nothing significant. The typical dealing and using. I haven't been made aware of anything on the scale of the Williams County operation. Why?"

"Well, we know that the Martinez Cartel did not shut down after we closed up the Williams farm. They stopped shipments for a few months, but then started them up again. We've been able to trace some shipments across the border, but have yet to determine the final destination. We know that not all of the participants in the Williams operation were apprehended and are wondering if they have set up shop somewhere else in the area."

"That's a good question. To tell the truth, I haven't had any of that on my radar since we brought them down. I can look into it, turn some stones over so to speak and see if there are any critters crawling around."

"Please do. I asked Sheriff Alexander about it this morning after the funeral. He doesn't have any information either, but said he would check into it. I have no problem with you two sharing information about my request if it helps."

"Okay. I'll check it out. Before I get back with you, I'll talk with Rob to compare notes to see if anything doesn't add up. Maybe it would be good to set up a joint meeting after that to go over findings."

"Good idea. I'll wait to hear from you. Thanks, Dave."

Dave walked George out. On his way back to his office, he stopped in Dan's office.

"Got a minute?"

"Sure, Dave, what's up?"

"Well, Mister Chief of Investigations, what can you tell me about drug activity in the county since we brought down the Williams County drug farm gang a couple of years ago?"

"Not much to tell, mostly small stuff, and mostly working with SPD in the city. Nothing very significant, at least on the scale we dealt with that distribution facility a couple of years ago. Why?"

"DEA thinks the Martinez Cartel is still operating but they don't know where."

Dan looked thoughtful.

"The bad penny returns. I'll ask around, but I haven't heard of anything that points to that size operation."

Dave's cell phone buzzed in his pocket.

"Okay, thanks."

He headed for his office as he checked the caller I.D. "D" it told him.

"Hey, son, I was going to call you later."

"Hi, dad. Got a minute?"

"Sure."

"I just got off the phone with Joey Duran, the Cubs scout. He called to confirm that I plan to show up at spring training."

"That's a good sign, don't you think?"

"It's better than that, Dad. He says they need a utility infielder with a bat that can hit from both sides of the plate. As you may have heard, their lead-off hitter from last year went into free agency and left them. Joey says he wanted me to know that he thinks I may be their best bet at filling that hole, if I can hit like my stats from last season show."

"Wow, that's great, D."

"Yeah, I'm heading for the batting cage now, but wanted to call you first."

"Good idea, and thanks for the call. Jan and I are planning to come out the last of March for a week to ten days to watch the games. Maybe Chris too, if he can work out a few days away from school."

"Great. I'm getting pretty excited."

"I can imagine. But you really need to calm down and try to focus on what you need to do. Try to keep your mind in the batting cage. Work on those reflexes. Stay sharp."

"Got it, dad. I'm trying. See you next month. Bye."

As Dave was hanging up the phone, Bob leaned in the office door.

"Just stopped by the hospital, no change."

"Okay, thanks. Say, Bob, got a minute?" Dave motioned to the visitor chair. Bob came in and sat down.

"Have any of the guys reported any activity that could be related to an operation similar to the Williams County drug farm operation?"

"Nothing that has got to me, why?"

"DEA thinks they're back in operation somewhere. Ask your guys to be on the look out for anything that may be similar to what we saw before."

"Okay, are they thinking they set up another farm operation?"

"I don't think they know. They just know that the drugs are flowing back across the border again, but they don't know where they're heading. Based on the previous distribution network, it makes sense that they would set back up in the same general area."

"Maybe, but they would have to know we would be looking out for them. I don't think it would be likely that they would be back in our area, but I'll get the word out."

After work that evening Dave and Jan had plans to have dinner with Dave's sister and brother-in-law. Even though they lived in the same area, it had become evident that they would not see each other often if they didn't set up something on a regular basis. So, a regular dinner out together became the way to stay close. They tried to do it at least once a month, their "First Friday Feast," they called it.

Char and Jay were already at the restaurant when Dave and Jan arrived.

Chapter 5

Charlotte was named after Dave's grandmother on his mother's side. Everyone had always called her Char. She married Jay Miller shortly after she finished medical school and began practicing as a pediatrician in Springfield. The significant age difference between her and Dave, 19 years, caused their relationship to be less like sister-brother than the norm. She had always been more like a second mother to him than a sister. Dave's ex, Joyce, was still the head nurse in Char's office.

Jay, really Oliver but known as Jay, was a building contractor and developer. His business, Miller Contracting and Development. had grown to be one of the largest developers in a six-county area. Their two sons were now part of the business as well. The Miller Company, as it is often called, had built some of the largest commercial and residential projects in the area. No job too big or too small, Jay always said. Many years ago, Jay had had a falling out with the Mayor of Springfield and refused to do any projects in his city, but did about 75% of the work out in the county and the surrounding area.

As soon as they were seated at the table, Char turned to Dave, "Honey, I am so sorry about Brian. Are you ok?"

"Thanks, Char, it has been tough to keep my head straight, but I'll be all right."

"I stopped in to see him this morning when I was in the hospital," Char said. "Marie looked pretty beat up but she seemed to be in good spirits. Her mother was there and I think it may have been her sister. The nurse showed me Brian's chart. He is stable and they are just waiting for him to wake up."

"Dave, did I read it right that Brian was shot at the Westside Commons Quick Mart?" Jay asked.

"Yeah, at the rear of the store."

"Sorry to hear that, you know we built that building."

"No, I didn't know that. But it had nothing to do with the building, just the bad guys."

"So, other than that, how have you been?" Char continued with a pat on Dave's hand.

"We have been good. Living the dream. Oh, D has a try out for the major leagues," Dave beamed, just a little.

"Really?" Jay cut in, "that's great. Bet he is excited. When?"

"He is," Dave responded. "Next month with the Cubs in Phoenix, well actually it's in Mesa. We are planning to go out and catch a few games."

The waiter interrupted and they all realized at once that no one had opened the menus. They apologized to the waiter who accepted with a look that seemed to say it had happened to him before.

All through a nice dinner the topics of discussion were around the day to day activities of the families, grandkids, work and the like. As they were just cutting into the key lime dessert, Jay turned to Dave.

"So, what's new in the garage?"

"Not much, as a matter of fact, I've been thinking about culling the heard a bit," Dave said. He turned to Char. "Would you be okay with selling off some of dad's cars?"

"That's entirely up to you, Sweety. When Kent and I put you in charge of the farm and the collection, it gave you full responsibility to do whatever you felt best. At least that's the way I saw it," Char said.

"What got you thinking about that?" Jay asked.

"Well, with the boys both gone, I'm finding it really tough to keep up with the farm and the maintenance on all of the cars. If I can't maintain them properly, it's just a matter of time before they start to deteriorate. I don't want that to happen."

"Hey, there are a few cars the boys and I would be interested in, if you're going to let them go," Jay said. "Are there certain ones you plan to move out?"

"Of the 32 cars in the collection, I want to keep all 5 of the 1970 models, all of the Corvettes and the Shelby Convertible. All the others are fair game to go, I'm thinking."

"I sure would like to have that '56 Buick Convertible," Jay said. "And, I think the boys would be interested in those two old pickups."

"I'll need to run it by Kent, but unless he objects, they're yours," Dave offered.

"How far down in numbers to you plan to go?" Char asked.

"I think about 15 would be manageable, but it will be hard to let some of them go, that's for sure. Dad sure did love those cars."

"And, so do you," Char said quietly, looking at Jan.

Jan smiled and patted Dave on the knee under the table.

Saturday morning found Dave and Jan going over schedules and looking for hotel reservations in Scottsdale for late next month. They were getting excited about getting away for a few days. They really hadn't been anywhere other than family visits for a long time. As they searched, they found it difficult to find hotel availability since it was spring training. But eventually they were able to find a Marriott with two available rooms and booked them. They booked two rooms because they thought the boys may want to stay with them rather than at D's apartment with his roommates.

"Well, now that we have that accomplished, I'm thinking of going over to see how Brian is doing," Dave said to Jan. "You want to come along?"

"Yes, I would," she responded, "I have been thinking about Marie's comments yesterday. I want to stay close with her."

They took Jan's car into town. Dave was driving.

"You know the lease on this car is up next month," Jan said. "Winston, over at the dealership, called yesterday to remind me. He said he has a new one sitting in the showroom I might like. What do you think about running by there after lunch?"

"Sounds like fun to me. Do you want another Beamer, or something else?'

"I don't know. I really like this car, but did you have something else in mind?" she asked.

"I was reading about the Jaguar XJ the other day. Seem like the auto press likes it. Maybe worth a look."

"Okay, let's look."

As they walked into Brian's hospital room, they say that Marie was not there, as they expected. Sitting next to Brian's bed was Bobby, Brian's cousin. Bobby, actually Roberto, had been raised by Brian's parents after his own had been killed in a car crash in Mexico. Bobby was 14 when he came to live in the US. He looked up to Brian, who was 3 years older and became like a brother, but also wanted more than he thought working on a farm with Brian's dad could give him.

Bobby had been drawn into and became a part of the Williams County drug operation, but was not present when the State Police and the two county Sheriffs departments raided and shut them down. Of course, Dave and Brian knew of his involvement, but since neither had ever actually witnessed any criminal action on Bobby's part, they took no action against him. Bobby had always treated Brian and Dave with respect, as opposed to the attitude of the others in his gang.

When Dave and Jan walked in the room, Bobby jumped up and greeted them warmly.

"Hi, how you guys doin?" he said as he gave Jan a brief hug and shook Dave's hand.

"Fine," Jan said, "good to see you, Bobby, any change?"

"No, the doctor was in earlier and said all we can do now is wait. Everything is exactly as expected."

"So, you're taking over for Marie today?" Dave inquired.

"Right, Dad, Mom and I have been doing shifts with her. We want to make sure that one of us is here when he wakes up. I'm normally the midnight to morning, but she asked if I could hang around longer this morning so she and the kids could do some errands."

They continued with small talk for several minutes as friends who had not seen each other for a while will do.

"So, what're you doing now" Dave asked directly, "since your old business dried up?"

"I'm not sure dried up is the best way to say it," Bobby said with a smile, "more like crushed, I'd say. But, to tell the truth, Sheriff, I've been good, pretty much doing nothing."

"Are you living with the folks?"

"No, I stayed there for a few weeks, but now have an apartment in town. As you may've guessed, I have a nice savings, and other than working a little on the farm for dad, have done very little."

Brian's dad was the farm manager for one of the largest corporate owned farms in the area. They had several thousand-acres, and employed a large number of people.

"Why do you ask, you want me to come work for you?" Bobby inquired with a broad grin.

"Maybe," Dave responded.

Bobby looked shocked.

"You kidding, what you talkin about?"

"I'm wondering if you'd be interested in running my farm for me," Dave said rubbing his chin.

"What?" Bobby looked confused. Jan gave Dave a curious look.

"I hadn't thought of this until this very moment, but it strikes me that if you want to go straight, your farming knowledge and self sufficiency could make for a good fit. Look, I have a problem operating the farm since my sons have left home. I just don't have enough time to get everything done. If you don't need a regular pay check and could work for a share of the profit, it may make a lot of sense."

Bobby looked thoughtful. He glanced down at the floor and shifted his feet.

"I don't know, Dave. Some people may wonder about me working for the Sheriff, some people I used to work with. Ya know, it could...." Bobby trailed off in deep thought.

Dave waited. Jan gave an ever so slight nod, she would like it if Dave had more free time, she smiled.

"I've been advised that the renters in the farm house don't intend to renew their lease that runs out in June. I could allow you to live there as part of your compensation," Dave went on. "Of course, I will continue to help, but the operation could be yours on a day-to-day basis. I currently get fifty per cent of the profit from the operation, with my brother and sister getting the other fifty as part of our father's estate. I will talk with them to see if they are willing to give you some of their share, but that's up to them. For sure, I'll split mine with you. It has always been a money maker."

"Would my share be over fifty thou a year?" Bobby asked slowly.

"No guarantee, but historically it would have been well over that. Plus, free housing," Dave added.

 It was obvious to Dave that Bobby was interested.

"I'd have to learn equipment maintenance," Bobby said thoughtfully.

"That you would, but it really isn't rocket science, just paying attention to hour meters and keeping records. The hands-on stuff is more or less just oil, grease, drive belts and watching for wear. When it breaks, we fix it. And remember, I'll be around."

"I'm interested, let me think about it for a few days. I'll give you a call when I decide."

"And feel free to call with any questions," Dave concluded.

Later, over lunch at Denny's, Jan asked, "do you think Bobby will take your offer?"

"He seemed interested, but I don't know."

"I'm hoping he does. It would certainly take a lot of stress off you."

"And, give us more time to do things," Dave commented.

"You, my love, certainly had a great idea there. But, as I think about it, it just seems so obvious. Why didn't we think of him before?"

"Well, don't forget he has been a drug gang criminal, most people would see that as a big obstacle to gainful employment."

"So why don't you?"

"Because I've known him most of my life and know that his upbringing will come out and prove a strong sense of integrity. No, I'm willing to take a chance on him. I think I'm right, and to some extent, I think I owe it to his family."

When they walked into Delagoto Motors show room, a salesman greeted them and said that Mr. Delagoto had asked that he be informed when they came in. He then disappeared through a door plastered with a BMW logo at the rear of the showroom. Dave and Jan were drawn to a sparking green 760LI BMW sitting boldly in the middle of the showroom. It looked almost identical to the blue one they had arrived in, other than the color combination.

"For the money it costs me every month, if I'm going to get a new one, it seems it should look different than the old one. Don't you think?" Jan said.

"It is a lot like yours," Dave agreed as they continued to look it over.

Winston Delagoto approached, all smiles and hand extended.

"Judge, so glad you came in. Great to see you." Then
turning to Dave, "Sheriff, how have you been?"
Vigorously shaking their hands in secession. "So, are you
ready to drive this one home?"

"I'm just not sure, Winston," Jan directed, "it's just so
much like the one I've had for the last two years. I'm
thinking maybe something different. I really love the car,
but a change may be nice."

Winston looked down right deflated.

"But, it's the best car in the class. BMW is the world class
driving machine; you don't get better." Jan's look told
him, that ship had sailed. "Did you have something else in
mind?" he quickly pivoted.

"Jaguar." Dave said drily.

Winston turned toward a salesman standing near the door,
"Kerry, would you bring my demonstrator around, please."

"Wait, you drive a Jaguar? What about that "you don't get
better" stuff?" Dave questioned.

"Come on, Sheriff, I just go with what most people want
these days. You know how it is. Everybody wants the
status of BMW, but there are other makes."

As the dark green Jaguar XJL came into view outside the
showroom, Jan nodded approvingly, "Now, that's
different," she said.

They walked outside in the cool air with Winston in full sales mode.

"This car is very similar to yours in terms of options and features," he said to Jan. "However, you will find a significant increase in performance over your seven series. This car has a supercharged five-liter V8 with 470 horsepower. It has an eight speed automatic transmission with manual mode paddle shifters, and this one is all wheel drive. I'm told to expect 23 miles to the gallon on the highway, but since I just got it, I haven't had a chance to confirm that."

As they pulled away from the dealership on the test drive Jan noted to Dave that it only had 130 miles on it. She was grinning from ear to ear and Dave knew the sale was over. As they pulled up onto the interstate, she punched the accelerator to the floor. They were thrown back into their seats in much the same way as the big-block hemi cuda would do, or Jan's favorite in the collection, the Plymouth Superbird. If she wasn't sold on it from the grins before, Dave knew she was now.

When they pulled back into the dealership lot, Jan parked next to her Beamer.

"How many of these do you have in stock?" Dave asked.

"Oh, this is the only one. I would have to order one for you, take about six weeks."

"Can you have someone transfer the plates while we move our stuff from the other car, please," Jan casually asked Winston.

"Sorry, Judge, this is my car, I…" Jan's look stopped him. "I guess I can order another one for me. Yes, I'll get someone out here to transfer everything. We'll get the paper work ready and you can come back in and complete the process next week. Can you come in Monday, or when is best?"

"Can you be ready about one Monday afternoon?"

"We will be ready, and thanks for your business, Judge," Winston looked a bit depressed as Jan and Dave pulled out of the dealership, in the car he ordered especially for himself and waited almost four months to arrive from England.

Chapter 6

By the following Thursday, Dave had talked with Kent and Char about his offer to Bobby to help with the farming operation. Kent and Char both commented about how much they were in favor of Dave getting help to ease his stress and exhaustion levels. They both offered to share some of their profit from the farm with Bobby as well if he agreed to come on board. A new agreement was reached that Jan would draw up for signatures. Under the new contract, Dave would remain as the farm manager with full responsibility. Bobby would become operational foreman. The contract would provide for the first $50,000 profit after all farm expenses to go to Bobby. All profit over the initial $50,000 will be divided between the three owners and Bobby by 70% to Dave and 10% to each of the others. Dave offered that he was concerned that Kent and Char would not be receiving as much from the farm as in the past, but they both said they had never used any of the farm income. Char had said they always just put it away in an account for the kids, and the kids were in very good shape, so no worries. Kent said pretty much the same and insisted it was a fair deal for them.

Kent had also agreed with the idea of reducing the car collection to any amount Dave wanted. He also agreed that

Jay and his sons could have the Buick and the two pickups, if he could have the four Pontiacs.

So, it was decided that Dave now has seven less cars to worry about. The 1956 Buick Convertible was headed for Jay and Char's garage. The 1958 Chevy pickup was going to their oldest son and the 1934 Ford street rod pickup to their younger son. Kent would be shipping, the 1965 Pontiac 2+2 convertible, the 1964 Pontiac Gran Prix and the two GTOs, a 1964 and a 1967, to Naperville, Illinois to show off at cruise nights and car shows there.

Even with the reduction of the seven cars there was still a lot left. But there was another idea in Dave's head. If Bobby comes on board, maybe there will have time for the car collection. Dave was thinking about that in the storage barn as he prepared the Buick for delivery to Jay. He heard a car pull up the gravel drive. As he wiped his hands on a rag at the work bench, Bobby walked in the man door next to the closed garage door.

"What cha workin on, boss?" Bobby asked.

"Boss?" Dave waited.

"Yep, I'm in, if ya still want me."

"We do indeed," Dave reached out a grimy hand that Bobby took without hesitation.

"When do I start?"

"Any time you want. Jan is drawing up a contract that you probably should see first. My brother and sister are in full agreement so there are no issues. When did you have in mind?"

"I'm ready to get to work, but I still want to be there for Marie until Brian wakes up. Can we play it by ear for a couple of weeks?"

"I certainly understand that, and so, yes, whenever you're ready."

"Thanks, you need some help here now? I got nothing to do till I go to the hospital at 11."

"Sure, let's do an oil change on an old Buick."

Dave and Bobby got to work on the Buick. After that they pulled the '34 street rod pickup over to the rack and got it ready to go. Bobby was by no means a great mechanic, but he was willing to learn and seem to pick things up quickly.

After about an hour and a half of general chat, Dave asked, "Bobby, you don't have to tell me, but do you have any idea what the drug guys are doing these days?"

Bobby responded as if he knew the question was coming, "Dave, I got no problem with ya askin'. I expect it, and I'll let ya know what I can, but I only talk with a couple the guys, and they aint said much."

"Do you think they may be set up somewhere else now?"

"Don't know, haven't heard nothin." He got quite for a second, turned away from Dave and lay the oil filter wrench on the bench. When he turned back, Dave sensed high stress in his expression. He blurted out, "the guys who shot Brian…I know em."

Dave jolted upright. He tensed up. He could feel his adrenaline level rise.

"It ain't right, Dave," Bobby continued, "there ani't no reason they'd need to rob a store."

"Wait, how do you know them?"

"They was in the gang. They'd been in longer'n me. Rollin in dough. Why'd they need to rob?"

The alarm bells in Dave's head were not only going off, they sounded louder than a fire truck horn at an intersection. Is this what had been bothering him from the start? Was it the "why would they need to rob" that had caused him the unsettling, disturbing thoughts that something was not right? How could it have been, he didn't know who they were. How does what Bobby had just said play into the investigation. Dave had seen the names of the guys in the SPD report that landed on his desk about two weeks ago. But nothing indicated much about them, no priors other than a minor drug bust.

"When did you see them last?" Dave asked.

"Not since the bust, no idea what they been doin, or where."

"You in contact with any of the other gang guys?"

"A couple, guys like me, decided to cut the losses, try and stay clean."

"You think any of them may have had contact with the guys that did the robbery?"

"Don't know, could ask, see if anybody knows anythin."

"Would you, and let me know?"

"Sure," Bobby hesitated, "ya know takin Brian out don't set with me. I'll help ya."

Bobby squirted some Fast Orange on his hands, wiped them off on a rag, threw the rag down on the bench, nodded at Dave and walked out the door without saying another word.

When Dave walked into their family room a few minutes later, Jan was deep into the docket file for the next days proceedings. A legal pad was by her elbow on the end table half full of notes. When she saw Dave she straightened, dropped the pen into the file and closed it.

"What's happened?" she asked as she recognized his tormented expression.

"It's probably nothing, relax," he said, as he sat down next to her and took her hand. "Bobby came by the shop, by the way he's in, and when we were talking, he told me that he knows the guys that shot Brian. They were in the drug gang."

"So?" she asked, knowing there was more.

"He says they are rolling in money and would have had no reason to rob."

"Maybe they were just out for some kicks, wouldn't be the first criminal activity just for the fun of it."

"I don't know, I got that feeling again, like I'm missing something. I thought maybe that was it, but don't see how I would have been able to make that kind of connection without knowing more about the perps. There's something I'm missing, but I don't think that's it, but it may have something to do with it."

"So, what're you going to do, Sheriff?"

"Well, Judge, I think I'll take the rest of the night off to spend with my girl, and talk with some people about this tomorrow."

"Good plan, I'm on board with ya."

As Dave walked into the office the next morning he stopped at Cheryl's desk. She looked up at him and as he was about to speak, she held up her finger and asked, "Would you like for me to get Walt Regan on the phone?"

"A…yes, please, how..?"

"It's my job, Sheriff," she said turning toward her desk phone.

Dave slowly moved toward his office shaking his head slightly as he pondered the "how" of that exchange. He hung his jacket on the coat rack by the door and sat down at this desk. In the center of the desk was a copy of the overnight log and a hot cup of coffee, black. He glanced at the log as he started to sip the coffee. The light on his phone started blinking as he heard Cheryl say, "Walt's on one, Sheriff."

"Walt, how you doing, buddy?" he said into the phone.

"Okay, Dave, you?"

"I'm good. Have they started the search for Rod's replacement yet?"

"I think they are getting ready to go out with a nationwide post. My guess is it'll be just like the last one a couple of years ago before they found Rod."

"Are you going to get into the mix this time? As I recall you skipped it last time."

"Let's do lunch sometime and talk about that," Walt's message came through loud and clear that there were things he wanted to share away from his office.

"I'm good with that," Dave said, "early next week, maybe, I'd be good on Tuesday."

"Tuesday," Walt hesitated and Dave heard paper shuffling, "yeah, Tuesday works for me. Mary's at 11:30?"

"Putting it down now, good, see you there."

"So, what can I do for you today, Dave?"

"Walt, other than what I read in the report, what can you tell me about the perps who killed Rod?"

"Haven't heard much more, from down on the south edge of Williams County, no real records, not really much of a background on either, from what I've been told. As you read, both named Jose, a Flores and a Cruz. Cruz is the one in jail, hasn't said anything."

"Who was involved in the investigation? I see a detective Alberts signed off on the report. Did he do the complete investigation, or just sign the paper work?"

"I know what you are asking, Dave, we can talk about it more over lunch if you like, but his team did a complete and through job. The report speaks for itself."

"Okay, Walt. Thanks for the information, I appreciate your help. See you Tuesday," as they broke the connection Dave knew it would be Tuesday before he got the answers to his questions.

Dan Muscovy stuck his head around the office door, "Cheryl said you wanted to see me."

Dave motioned to the chair in front of his desk. Dan sat as Dave took a drink of coffee and collected his thoughts. "Have you talked with the investigators at SPD about Chief Taylor's case this week?"

"No, Dave, the case is closed."

"What, the report I saw was labeled preliminary findings. When did that change?"

"Last week, I got a final stamped closed on Friday. I went through it and found it to be exactly as the preliminary, same findings, same facts, the only difference was the final report from the coroner on both victims. Why, what's up?"

"Any indication from anywhere that the perps could had been part of the Williams County drug gang?"

"None, why."

"Because they were."

"How do you know that?" Dan was confused.

Dave ignored Dan's question, "Did SPD inform us before they decided to close the case?"

"No, why would they? It's their case."

"Yes, but our officer was shot. Do you think it strange that they would not ask if we had any concerns or wanted to follow up on anything before the case was closed? Wouldn't it be a matter of professional courtesy, especially with an agency that you work so closely with on a near daily basis?"

"You think something is being swept under the rug," Dan said purposefully. "So, what do we do?"

"I don't know, but why don't you nose around a bit over at SPD and see if you can get a sense if I'm all wet or not. I'm meeting with Walt next week at a neutral spot, I think he has something he wants to tell me."

"Got it Chief, I'll see if I can turn over a few rocks at SPD. I'll keep you informed."

Dave pulled into the parking lot at Mary's on Tuesday morning at eleven-twenty. He wasn't sure what Walt would be driving, but he didn't see anything in the lot that looked to him to be an SPD vehicle. However, when he walked in the door, he saw Walt already there, seated at a table in the back of the diner. Dave waved, motioned to the receptionist, walked across the room and sat down. Walt was dressed in a golf shirt and jeans.

"Didn't see a muni car outside," Dave said as they shook hands across the table.

"Yeah, I took the day off, I'm driving my personal car today. This meeting is completely off the record. Are you okay with that, Dave?"

"Of course," Dave waited.

But before Walt spoke, the waitress approached the table. They both ordered a burger and fries with an iced tea.

"When I was assigned as Acting Chief by the Mayor, he assigned Paul Jacoby as Acting Assistant Chief of Investigations. I was given no input, which I thought was odd. I would not have selected Paul for the temporary assignment to fill my old position, but since the Mayor had selected him, I let it go. This gave Paul complete control over the investigation into the shooting of Chief Taylor and your buddy Brian. As Chief, I am out of the direct loop and just review the final report, which I did. I have no issues with the report as filed, but the investigation was closed quicker than I expected. So, I thought I'd ask if you or your team had any input about the investigation based on your review."

"Well, I too was surprised that it was closed so quickly, and we have no foundation for any objections to the reports findings. However, I do have a subconscious feeling, that's been bothering me, that something isn't right," Dave offered.

"Me, too," Walt spoke softly, almost to himself. "Well, if you don't have anything, and my people haven't given me anything, I guess we need to ignore those subconscious feelings and move on," Walt took a deep breath and continued. "Can I share something with you in confidence, Dave?"

"Sure."

"I've been thinking of moving on. I liked Rod, and was fine with working for him, but others in the administration bother me. I would say even worry me. It may just be my imagination, I don't know, but I think SPD and I need to part ways. I've looked and sent out some resumes but nothing has really interested me much. So, I was wondering, is there any chance you'd have a spot for me?"

"I'm afraid there is no way I can match your current position or pay, but I could probably bring you on staff at a patrol sergeant level. How flexible are you?"

"Well, that is my permanent rate at the city, so if the new chief changes things up, I would revert back to that grade level here. Are you talking about Brian's position? What about when he comes back?" Walt sounded interested.

"It looks like that will be a long time, and there is a great deal of concern that he may never get back to full recovery. So, if you're interested, I'm willing to deal with that when it happens. Interested?"

"I am. Let me talk with Angela before we go any further, but I think she'll be okay with it. Thanks, Dave, you can't imagine the stress level I have been under. I'll let you know."

"No problem, Walt. It'll be great to have you on board, if that's what you decide. It will solve a problem with my staffing that I have not taken time to adequately address," Dave offered. "I must admit, though, I thought the reason for our meeting today was that you had information about the investigation to share."

"If I did, I would gladly let you know all I know. But, like I said, I have been out of the direct loop, and anything I have is just speculation. Sorry."

After lunch, Dave went by the hospital to check on Brian. There was no change in his condition. Marie was in good spirits and thanked Dave for stopping by.

"Dave, I've been wanting to thank you for what you are doing for Bobby," Marie said looking down at her hands. "Brian would thank you if he could. Brian has worried about Bobby for as long as I've known him. He wouldn't be worried any more. I can't wait for him to wake up so that I can tell him. It will mean so much to him."

She looked up at Dave with tears in her eyes.

"No thanks needed, Marie. I know Brian worried. Of course, I'm glad to relieve Brian's worries and help Bobby, but I was needing him to help me too. I'm not sure how long we could have kept the farm if it wasn't for Bobby. He'll do a great job for us and I have every confidence that it'll continue for the long haul. He's a good guy, I have no doubt. I think it's a win/win."

Back at the office, he shared with Dan Muscovy that Walt did not have additional information about the investigation as he had expected. He didn't say anything about the job offer. There would be a time and place for that later.

Dan said that he had been nosing around SPD but no one seemed willing to share any more information than was in the report. So maybe that's all there was.

Dave was still not convinced.

Chapter 7

"Hey, little brother, any chance you and Jan would mind a couple of old fogey house guests for a few days next week?" Dave heard Kent say through the phone.

"No minding here, bro, be glad to have you."

Dave and Jan had just finished dinner on Thursday evening and were clearing the dishes way went the phone had rang.

"Great, I've opened my schedule from Wednesday on through the weekend," Kent continued. "We thought we would drive down Wednesday morning, getting there early to mid-afternoon, if that works for you."

"Sure. You know that's the day after election day. I've been looking for a reason to cut out early that day. This is a great reason, thanks. Just give me a call when you're about an hour out and I'll meet you at home."

"Glad to help. We can celebrate your victory. Sounds good, I give you a call. Thanks."

"Not much to celebrate when I'm running unopposed. Looking forward to seeing you guys. I'll let Char know. We'll set up dinner on Wednesday or Thursday evening for the six of us. See ya then."

Jan had heard enough from the one side of the conversation that Dave didn't need to fill in too many details. He filled in those blanks while they finished up in the kitchen.

Dave spent the rest of the evening over in the maintenance shop at the farm getting the Pontiacs ready to hand over to Kent. If the weather was good when Kent and Duetta head back, Kent might want to take one with him.

The following Wednesday, Dave was glad to have won re-election. He and Jan had attended the election party, but had gone home well before the contested races were called.

Dave stopped by the hospital to check on Brian before getting into the office. He was excited about his brother coming for a visit as he walked into the office.

"Good morning, sheriff," Cheryl said with a bright smile as he approached her desk, "Congratulations on keeping your job. How's Brian?"

"Morning, Cheryl, thanks. Brian's pretty much the same. The doctor says there is an increase in brain activity which is a good sign."

"Walt Regan called, asked for you to call him when you have time."

"Thanks, I will. Oh, by the way, my brother is coming into town today. I plan to take off when they get here, early afternoon I'd guess. If I go missing, I'll be available on my cell."

"Sure thing."

Dave picked up the phone after sitting down at his desk. Walt answered on the second ring.

"Regan,"

"Harbinger, how's it going, Walt?"

"Good, Dave, thanks for the return call. I wanted to let you know that Angie is on board with what we talked about last week, so it's a go on my end. But, if you're okay with it, I'd like to hold on it for a bit. Can I let you know a date later? I'm thinking a month or so, but will keep you up to speed as things shake out."

"Great news, Walt, and sure no issues here with the timing. Do you have a problem if I let Bob and Dan in on the plan? I'd like to get their buy in. We will keep it confidential until you give the go ahead."

"Sure, I have no problem with that. And, thanks again, Dave."

About ten minutes later, Bob and Dan were in Dave's office for a closed door.

"Guys, I've got some news that we need to keep confidential for the time being. Agreed?"

"Sure," they both responded.

"Walt Regan is looking to leave SPD and has asked to join us. Based on what we hear from the doctors about his expected recovery time, I offered Walt Brian's position."

"Wow, Dave, that's a great idea," Bob exclaimed, "did he accept?"

"Yes, but he is still working out the timing, so we need to keep it quiet until he's ready."

"He'll be a great asset," Dan offered, "we couldn't ask for a better fit with our team. He knows the area, a lot of the people and is highly respected. I'm sure our guys will welcome him."

"Good, thanks for the input, Dan. Bob, I leave it up to you exactly where to put him. Of course, Brian's spot is the need, but if you want to shift people around and put him someplace you think he'd fit better, that's up to you."

"I'll give it some thought. That's a good point, someone with his experience could fit pretty much anywhere. I'll let you know what I come up with."

"Are the guys doing okay with covering for Brian's loss?"

"Oh, sure, I haven't heard a single complaint," Bob said. "They're doing what needs to be done. Stepping up, as they say."

"Okay, next subject, any information come to light on the drug dealer activity?" Dave asked.

Bob and Dan both shook their heads.

"No new dealers or increased supplies are evident to my guys," Bob offered.

"From all I hear, there doesn't seem to be any large-scale operation anywhere in the area. Speculation is that everything is coming in from farther away and in smaller quantities." Dan said. "Our informants say the dealers are looking for sources, which would indicate there is no operational wing nearby. Busts have actually been trending downward over the last few months."

"Okay, thanks, I'll pass that on to DEA." Dave looked at this watch, "I need to get some things done this morning, so how about we get together over lunch to talk about how Walt may best fit into our organization. Say 11:30, I'm buying."

There was no objection.

Lunch ran a bit longer than usual. When Dave got back to his office, Cheryl had a strange look on her face. She just stared at Dave as he approached. He stopped at her desk.

"What is it?" he asked, hesitantly.

She seemed to be listening to a far-off voice, held up her finger, looked down and said softly, "I think you should go see Brian."

"Did someone call?" Dave asked, his pulse quickening.

"No," was all she said as she made a "get out of here" gesture.

Dave made a mad dash to the hospital, even using the flashing red and blue lights at a couple of intersections. He parked in one of the spots for emergency vehicles by the emergency room and ran inside. As he walked slowly into Brian's room, he saw Marie sitting by the side of his bed reading a novel. She closed the book when she saw him.

"Hi, Dave," she said, "I didn't expect to see you again today."

"No, I didn't plan.." he began to say, but a nurse pushed by him in a hurry. She ran over to Brian and pick up his arm.

"His brain activity just picked up significantly," the nurse said. "The doctor is on his way."

Brian's eyes began to flutter, then squint and blink rapidly. Marie grabbed his hand. Dave could see Brian's hand squeeze Marie's hand. The electronic equipment which had been showing constant sine waves and little blips were now erupting in sawtooth and irregular patterns. As Marie leaned over him, Dave saw Brian's eyes focus on her. His lips parted, his tongue licked his lips.

"Baby, I'm here," Marie said, tears beginning to flow.

Dave was also tearing up as he watched his best friend regain consciousness after over a month. A doctor hurried into the room.

"BP and pulse?" the doctor asked.

"150 over 90, and 87," the nurse responded.

The doctor grabbed his stethoscope and began listening to Brian's chest. Another nurse came into the room. She began wiping Brian's lips with an ice cube. "Doctor Patel is on the way," she said to the doctor.

Dave saw Brian's chest expand as he took his first deep breath.

"We'll get you something to drink," the doctor said to Brian. "Can you understand me?"

Brian nodded, "Yes," he whispered softly.

The nurse put a cup of water up next to Brian's mouth and put the straw between his lips. He sucked down the cool water and Dave thought he detected a smile.

"Thanks, I needed that," he whispered.

Dave's cell phone rang. He stepped out into the hall.

"About an hour out," Kent said.

"Kent, I'm at the hospital, Brian just woke up."

"How is he?"

"Not sure, just happened. He seems to be okay."

"Okay, you stay there. I'll come there, see you soon."

Dave started to call his office, but decided to see what more he could find out about Brian's condition before he did. He went back into the room. In his absence, Marie and the doctor had explained to Brian what had happened to him.

"Hey, Buddy," he heard Brian say softly. Dave walked over to the side of the bed next to Marie. The doctor was still working on the other side of the bed.

"Good to see you awake," Dave said.

"How long have I been out?" Brian asked.

"About a month," Marie spoke.

"You were shot behind the Quick Mart," Dave offered.

"Don't remember that," Brian said, "I was on my way to work."

"Yeah," Dave continued, "you heard the 211 call at the Quick Mart on the westside. SPD was on the scene and you reported that you were approaching from the rear. Do you remember that?"

"Oh, yeah, I remember coming up behind the shopping center," Brian paused, wrinkled his forehead, was quite for a few seconds then continued, "that's all I remember.

Everything is dark after that. Just blank. Is that when I was shot?"

"No, it was sometime after that. You don't remember?"

Brian shook his head, and seemed to try more concentration.

Marie turned to Dave, "Would you call his folks?"

"Sure," Dave said and went out into the hall to make the call.

Brian's mom answered and upon hearing the new said they would be there as soon as possible. Dave then called his office and asked Cheryl to tell everyone that Brian is awake and seems to be doing fine, but no word yet on long term effects. He then called Jan, she said she would be there as soon as she could get away.

As Dave was turning to go back into the room, he saw doctor Patel coming at him from the far end of the hall. He waited and followed the doctor into Brian's room. Dr. Patel went right to work with just a nod at Marie. He began to assess Brian's mental and physical condition. He asked Brian questions as he moved his hands across various parts of Brian's body, pinching and pressing, working joints and asking Brian to move various body parts on his own. From Dave's perspective, he thought Brian was responding very well, maybe extremely well, for someone who had been in a coma for a month. As Dr Patel worked, the other doctor was writing on Brian's chart as if he was transcribing the events for future reference.

After about fifteen minutes, Dr Patel took Brian's left hand and said, "My boy, you are doing very well. I think you're going to be just fine. Here's where we are, we will begin to get you eating right away, just a little at first and gradually increase the amounts for a couple of days to get your system accustomed to solid food again. Later today we will begin to assess your mobility to see what motor skills may have been lost, if any. Once that assessment is complete, we will be able to set up any required therapy and get that going. Based on what I see right now, there's a good chance you can go home in the next four or five days. Any questions?"

As he was talking, Kent walked in from the hallway.

"Hey, Kent," Brian said.

"Who is that?" Dr. Patel asked Brian.

"Why that's Dave's big brother, he's a doctor too," Brian told the doctor.

"How long has it been since you've seen him, Brian?"

"It's been a long time," Brian thought, "maybe three years or so. He doesn't get back home very often anymore and a lot of the time when he does, I don't run into him."

Doctor Patel looked at Dave and Kent who both nodded their agreement with Brian in response to Dr. Patel's memory check.

Dave and Kent headed out into the hallway where they could talk while doctor Patel answered Marie and Brian's questions. Dave told Kent what he had learned from listening to Dr Patel.

A little while later, Dr. Patel came out. He extended his hand to Kent and said, "Dr. Harbinger very nice to meet you. I've heard a lot about you."

"And I you, Doctor," Kent responded.

"I'm aware that your bother is very close with this case, and if you have a few minutes, I'd be happy to go over it with you if you'd like."

"Why, yes, I'd like that."

"Let's go down to my office," Dr. Patel motioned for Kent to walk with him. They headed down the hallway.

As Dave turned back toward Brian's room, he saw Jan and Brian's parents coming up the hall together followed closely by Brian and Marie's kids. Dave stepped aside as they all went into Brian's room.

Dave waited in the doorway. Jan said hello to Brian and Marie, wished them well, then excused herself. She joined Dave in the doorway.

"It's about to get busy in there," Dave whispered in Jan's ear. "Kent said Duetta is in the cafeteria, let's go have a snack."

Jan nodded and they went off to find their sister-in-law.

Chapter 8

About thirty minutes later, Kent came into the hospital cafeteria. He got an iced tea and sat down at the table with Jan, Dave and Duetta. The three of them just looked at him, waiting for the information he was about to share as he got comfortable in the plastic chair.

"It looks good," he finally said after taking a long drink. "The bullet entered on the left side and tracked almost exactly along the skull line. All skull fragments were discharged externally and there is no brain damage evident from the bullet entering the cavity. He was extremely lucky that the path of the bullet was on a straight line with the left side of his skull. Also, it appears they were able to relieve the pressure in time to avoid any damage from swelling. Dr. Patel's preliminary checks show no significant loss of feeling in any extremities and his motor skills seem acceptable to this stage in recovery. Lung functioning and other internals seem fine at this point as well."

"Kent," Dave interrupted," are you saying full recovery back to his normal self?"

"Too soon to say for sure, but yes, it looks very possible at this point. From my experience, and Dr. Patel made a similar statement, as traumatic as the injury was, it appears to be relatively minor as brain injuries go. But, the next couple of days will tell the tale."

Dave and Jan relaxed visibly. Jan squeezed Dave's hand.

"I asked him what he remembered about what happened," Dave said. "He recalled getting to the scene, but didn't seem to remember any details after he got there. What about that?"

"Well," Kent responded, "adrenaline comes into play in high stress events. It can cause the brain to react differently as the adrenaline level increases. It's the old "fight or flight" responsive. Brian's brain may have generated so much adrenaline that it's total energy was spent on the events unfolding in front of him to the extent that the memory area of the brain became non-functional."

"You're saying he may never remember what happened."

"Maybe, or his brain may just be blocking it out and it may come to him at some later date. It's hard to say."

"Well, it seems clear what happened, but I was hoping Brian could confirm it for us."

"You were hoping he would put your mind to rest," Jan observed.

Kent and Duetta looked first at Jan and then at Dave.

"It's a long story," Dave said. "I'll tell you about it later. Let's head out to the house and get freshened up. We're meeting Char and Jay for dinner at The Firehouse tonight, if that's okay with you."

"Sounds great to me," Kent said.

"You guys go on. I want to run back upstairs for a few minutes and then I'll be along," Dave directed. "Dinner reservations are for seven, so we have plenty of time."

When Dave got back to Brian's room there were people everywhere. His parents were there, the three kids and Bobby. Marie's mother and sister were also there. Brian was sitting more upright in the bed with the head raised. Barry, the nine-year old, was sitting on the bed with his dad. Everyone was all smiles.

"Hey, buddy," Brian smiled as Dave walked in.

"I'm going to be heading out, but wanted to let you know I'll be back tomorrow," Dave offered. "You still feeling okay?"

"To tell the truth, I'm a bit stiff. It's like I've been sleeping for a month," Brian laughed. "But I can feel all of my fingers and toes and am ready to get up and run around as soon as the doctor will let me."

Dave said his goodbyes to everyone and headed for home. Bob Cooper and Dan Muscovy were walking toward the building from their cars as Dave walked out into the parking lot.

"He's doing much better than we could have hoped for," Dave told them as they approached.

"So, we hear," Dan said.

"It's amazing. My brother went over everything with Brian's surgeon and it looks really good. They think he may have a chance at full recovery. Said we will know more in a couple of day."

"That's great news," Bob said.

"I'm taking the rest of the day off," Dave told them. "See you guys in the morning."

The steaks were fabulous, as was the rest of dinner. It was great to have dinner with both his brother and sister, it happened so rarely anymore. But add to that the news about Brian, and Dave wasn't sure he could feel any better.

On the way back from dinner, Dave was driving Jan's new car with Kent next to him. Jan and Duetta were chatting in the back seat.

"If Brian does regain memory about the shooting," Dave asked thoughtfully, "how long would you guess it would be?"

"Hard to say," Kent replied. "It might take some sort of trigger to cause it to happen. Or, it may just hit him out of the blue. No real way of knowing. Why? Do you think there is something more to learn?"

"Just a feeling. Something has been bugging me since the day it happened, but I can't put my finger on it. You know?"

"No, I don't know, Dave," Kent said. "I'm just the surgeon, you're the super snoop. But if something is bothering you, don't you think it could be tied to how close you are to Brian? You know, emotional involvement clouding investigative judgement type thing."

"I don't know, maybe. I just can't seem to shake it."

"Maybe you should spend some time talking with Brian. It may bring his memory back, or maybe help you shake what's bothering you."

"Good idea. I'll go over tomorrow and see if it works into his rehab schedule."

About midmorning the next day Bob and Dan came up to Dave's open office door.

"Got a few minutes, Boss?" Bob asked.

"Sure, come on in."

Dan closed the door behind them and he and Bob sat down.

"Got a call from SPD this morning asking about Brian," Dan started off. "They said they heard he had come around and were asked if he had talked about the shooting. When I told them he apparently doesn't remember anything they thanked me and hung up. I thought it a bit strange."

"I would agree," Dave said. "Who called?"

"Paul Jacobs. But that's not why we wanted to talk with you," Dan continued. He turned to Bob, "Go ahead, Bob, bring him up to speed."

"Dan and I have been talking about where Walt fits in," Bob began. "We had pretty much agreed that the patrol supervisor position was the best fit until Brian comes back. But after seeing how well Brian was doing yesterday, our thinking has changed. We assumed that Brian would be off for an extended period at the very least, and at the worst would not be able to rejoin at all. Walt's experience and expertise would allow him to fill that slot temporarily, but he would fit much better elsewhere on a permanent basis. Since the timing of Brian coming back may not be as long as we were expecting, we're now thinking of just going along as we are. We can revisit this when we get more information on Brian's expected return, but for now we're thinking Walt to be a better fit on the investigations side. Dan's had a Lieutenant slot open from a couple of years back."

"I can sure use the help," Dan added. "We could finally get going on that interagency cooperation agreement we've been talking about for the past 5 years. He'd be the ideal person to head up that initiative. Our case load continues to grow and the backlog is getting out of hand."

"Okay," Dave agreed. "Sounds like a good plan to me. But as you say, Bob, we should leave it in limbo until we get a better handle on Brian's expected recovery. Also, Walt has not given us a start date yet, so we have that flexibility as well."

After lunch Dave went by the hospital. Brian was sitting up in bed watching the Price is Right on TV, a lunch tray was pushed to the side with what had been his lunch. Marie was sitting by his bed, reading a book. He smiled and waved as Dave walked in.

"Hey, Boss, what's up?" Brian said cheerfully.

"You're looking good, how ya feeling?"

"Doing well, thanks. Getting the kinks worked out. Found out last night that my sea legs still work but are in need of some exercise. Started on a rehab procedure this morning. They think I'll be back to walking fine in a few days. For now, they require me to use a walker." He pointed to the chrome wheeled devise sitting near the bed.

"Here, Dave, have a seat," Marie said getting up from the chair. "I'm going to take a walk down to the cafeteria while you guys talk."

Dave gave Marie a brief hug as she walked by and out the door. He sat next to Brian.

"I'd like to talk about what happened," Dave began, "if you don't mind? I have a gut feeling that we're missing something in all this. No idea what it might be, and it may be nothing, but I'll feel better if I keep trying to figure out what's bothering me. Kent suggested that if I ask you direct questions it may stimulate some trigger and bring your memory back. Are you up to some questioning?"

"Sure, no problem. Like I said, I don't remember but sure would like to know what happened. So, fire away and let's see if something comes back."

"Let's talk about what you do remember first. You said you remember approaching the back of the shopping center, right?"

"Yeah," Brian replied as he switched the TV off. "I heard the radio call just as I was turning onto the state road about a mile west of there. I responded as "in the area and responding," switched on the lights and was there in less than a minute. I remember hearing that SPD was on the scene, and that Bob was approaching, so I judged that they would be in the front. I radioed that I was approaching the rear and turned to the back of the shops."

"Exactly where were you when you made the decision to go to the back?"

"Just before I got to the cross street on the west side of the shopping center that goes into the subdivision behind."

"Did you see the SPD unit or the officers?"

"No, the out-lot building on the west end blocked my view of the store. I didn't see Bob either, but there was considerable traffic."

"What were you planning to do?"

"I was going to observe the rear of the store."

"What's the last thing you remember?"

Brian thought for a moment and then said, "I remember making the left turn off the cross street, but nothing more."

"Do you remember pulling up behind the store?"

"No."

"Do you remember getting out of the car?"

"No."

"How about pulling your weapon, do you remember that?"

"No. After turning off the cross street, I woke up here. That's all I remember."

"Did you hear any shots fired?"

"No."

"As you approached the back of the store, do you remember if the car window was down?"

"That would be procedure, but I don't recall."

"You don't remember the suspect coming out the back door of the store?"

"No, Bob told me what happened, but I have no recollection of any of it. It is just one big blank in my mind."

"Okay, can you remember what you had in your pockets?"

"I think I had my pocket knife, a pack of gum and some loose change in my front pants pockets. Wallet and handkerchief in the rear. Shirt pockets would have been my little notebook and a pen. I think that's about it."

"Well, I guess that's enough for now. I may want to talk about it more later on, especially if you remember more," Dave told Brian.

The rest of his visit they talked about all of the things that had been going on it the department while Brian was sleeping. Marie came back after awhile and joined in. Dave also shared with them about D's opportunity with the Cubs and the plans he and Jan had to go to spring training the following week. It was a great time of sharing and it struck Dave that he appreciated this time spent with his old friend much more than in the past.

As he was leaving, Brian said, "Have a great time at the ball games. Tell D that we are pulling for him. And, don't worry about me. I'll be fine and waiting for the travel stories when you get back."

Travel plans were all set and they were ready to go. As had become the custom since she resigned her law firm partnership and bankrolled a small fortune, Jan lined up the private jet to take them to the Phoenix area. They would actually be flying into Chandler Municipal Airport which is about 10 miles south of Mesa. They would fly out on the last Thursday afternoon in February, with the return flight 10 days later on Sunday afternoon. They expected to see 7 or 8 games, and get in a couple rounds of golf during the trip. Chris was able to arrange his schedule to allow him to travel out on Saturday and back on the following Wednesday. It was looking to be a great time in the sun.

Chapter 9

The Cessna Citation business jet was parked on the tarmac when Jan and Dave arrived. The fight crew, a husband and wife team named George and Loura, was standing by the plane. Dave didn't catch their last name.

"Welcome," Loura said with a big smile, "thanks for booking with us again."

"We're glad you were available," Jan said.

George took their bags, including the two sets of golf clubs, and headed around the wing of the plane to put them in the rear storage compartment.

"So, it's a family business?" Dave asked Loura.

"Sort of," Loura nodded, "George learned to fly in the Navy and got into commercial aviation after he got out. As our kids got older, I decided to get my commercial ticket so that we could fly together. It's been great and we really enjoy it."

"A naval aviator, was he a top gunner?"

"No, he wasn't a fighter pilot. He flew transport planes. But he is one of the best pilots in the sky. What's interesting about George is that he suffers from acrophobia and aerophobia. When he joined the Navy, he requested aviation to help him overcome his fears."

"A pilot who is afraid of heights and of flying. Now that's something," Dave said as George walked up to them.

"Yep, still am," George joined in, "I'm okay when I'm in the cockpit, but on a commercial airline flight I'm white knuckles all the way. I guess I just want to be in control."

A short time later the plane propelled Jan, Dave and the two pilots into the air with a woosh and a whine from the two jet engines mounted on either side of the fuselage just in front of the tail section. Flight time was expected to be approximately three hours and twenty minutes. Loura had told them that the weather looked to be clear and smooth all the way, so they could expect a nice flight.

About fifteen minutes after takeoff, they had reached their cruising altitude of thirty-five thousand feet. The Citation was fitted to carry six passengers and the two crew members. The passenger compartment was structured with three seats on either side of the plane, two facing rearward and four facing forward. Since Jan and Dave were the only passengers, they selected the first two front facing seats. The seats were high quality leather and had all of the features one would expect in a high-end aircraft. Jan had comfortably reclined her seat about halfway back and was reading. Dave kicked off his shoes, put his feet up on the seat in front of him and reclined his seat to a comfortable napping position. The noise level from the engines just behind them was louder than being in a car, but the plane was well insulated so that conversation was not difficult over the constant droning sound.

"Not a bad way to get from A to B, huh?" he said.

"That's for sure," Jan answered.

They had flown on this very same plane before on a trip to the Florida Keys. Dave thought about that trip and the particular time on a beach when Jan agreed to marry him.

"Yep, and this very plane took us to the spot where you agreed to marry me. So, this plane was part of our beginning."

"I remember that very well," she said. "I was trying to make a decision about what to do with the rest of my life. I asked you to help me decide and you said, "Jan, you should marry me," or something like that."

"It didn't take you long to decide, as I recall."

"Nope, I had already decided. I was just waiting on you."

She smiled at him seductively and went back to her reading. Dave felt an overwhelming sense of satisfaction as he turned to look out the window. He had to be the luckiest guy in the world. His life could not have been any better, or at least he certainly had no idea how it could.

The earth sped by below them. He wasn't sure where they were, maybe over Missouri or Arkansas. He wasn't sure what their route would be, but it really didn't matter much.

When you're thirty-five thousand feet up in the air it's hard to see much detail. All he could make out were different colors and shades of green and brown that indicated forests or farm fields or cities and towns. He closed his eyes briefly but realized that his mind was not going to allow him to nap. He was just too excited about all that was going on.

There was a copy of the Springfield Journal in the pocket by the seat. He pulled it out and began reading the morning news. On page two there was an article about Brian waking up from the coma, with background information about what had happened at the Quick Mart almost two months ago. As Dave read, his mind flashed back to the death of Sheriff Will and all that transpired in the days, weeks and months after.

He remembered how he felt when he and Dan Muscovy got to the cabin where Will was found dead of a shot gun blast. The feeling he had that something was not right, even though everything seemed to be obvious. It looked like a cut and dried suicide. Nothing pointed to foul play. There was no indication that further investigation would lead to any other conclusion. But Dave had a feeling.

The fact that all of the specific details of the crime scene were not released to the public became the deciding factor in proving Dave's feeling had merit. It also identified the murderer without doubt and protected others who were implicated. Could there be some parallel in Brian's case?

What parallel could there possibly be? Brian was obviously shot by the robber who had just killed Chief

Taylor and was not about to be caught and tried for that. If it were a simple robbery, he would probably have given up and allowed Brian to arrest him. But the murder rap gave him the added incentive to do whatever necessary to get away. He would probably have been successful in his escape if SPD hadn't been on the scene as well.

The robbers didn't expect to find the police chief in the store. When they did, they killed him. They didn't expect the SPD team to get there so fast, so one of them ran out the back. He didn't expect to find Brian waiting in the back, so he shot him. And the SPD officer giving chase to the fleeing robber shot him after Brian was shot. It all makes sense and the investigation proves it. So, what is Dave's feeling all about, and why can't he shake it off.

In Sheriff Will's case Dave asked questions and followed up. He listened to what everyone said, put all the pieces together and followed where they led. What is different now? Well, for one thing the case is being handled by SPD since it is in their jurisdiction, and their Chief was killed. They have a more vested interest and have done a complete investigation.

Another difference is that Brian was not killed, even though it was very close. It appears that he will recover so the direct impact on Dave and his team is very different than in Sheriff Will's case. By all accounts at this juncture, it seems everything will be back to normal soon.

"So, I can let it all go and relax," Dave thought. "Or can I?"

"What could possibly be different than it seems in this case?"

He closed his eyes to ponder the answer to that and drifted off into nap land.

Sometime later the most terrifying thing you could hear on an airplane, he heard.

Quiet.

No noise what so ever. No high-pitched whine and no droning. The engines had stopped.

Dave looked across at Jan across the aisle. Complete and utter terror covered her face. She grabbed his arm. He could feel her tremble through the death grip she had on him. He had never seen Jan's eyes opened so wide, or so full of fear. He tried to take a deep breath to calm himself, but his lungs would not inflate, he could only pant. His mind was going a mile a minute but the fear wouldn't allow it to keep a rational thought. They felt the nose of the aircraft drop.

Although they were only about eight feet away, Dave had not heard a word the flight crew had said on the entire flight. Now he could hear them clearly, but was sure it wasn't a good thing.

"Do both fuel filters show bypassed?" George asked in a raised voice.

"Yes, but there is no fuel flow," was Loura's hurried answer.

"How can that be? I could understand one blocked fuel filter, or if the fuel is somehow contaminated both filters clogged, but the bypass should allow flow. There must be an obstruction," George puzzled.

"What would obstruct both tanks and lines?" Loura asked.

"No time to try and figure that out, I'm turning the auto pilot off, would you confirm fuel levels?" George said. "I'm going to try and keep a reasonable glide slope you try switching from tank to tank to see if that will jar something loose so we can get them going."

"St Louis center 7 Gulf Tango declaring an emergency," George shouted.

"Tank switching doesn't seem to change anything. One restart negative," Loura said.

"Both engines out, descending," George shouted apparently into the radio.

"Number two restart, negative," Loura said.

"Got my hands full, give me altitudes," George said, "try to find a spot to put down."

"Fifteen thousand," Loura said, "I think I see a highway off to the right."

Dave and Jan sat stiff, grasping each other. Neither could speak due to the terror they felt at what was unfolding in front of them. It struck Dave that even if the engines started, he wasn't sure he could hear them over the pounding of his heart. The throbbing inside his head was that loud. He had never been so completely terrified.

But at the same time, he felt strangely disassociated with it what was happening. It was like he was watching it happen to someone else. Through his terror and inability to hold a thought in is head, he realized, his mind was paying attention to what was going on in the cockpit. Was it a defense mechanism? Was the feeling of admiration for the professionalism of the flight crew a way to disassociate himself from what was about to happen? A means to control the terror? George and Loura had to be as frightened as he was but still performed. Why could he remember their names at a time like this?

"Nine thousand," Loura said, "it's an interstate."

"I see it," George responded, "dump fuel. Air speed?"

"Fuel dumping, 340 knots."

"We need to scrub some speed, watch the stall for me."

The nose of the plane started to come up as George pulled back on the wheel. Dave could see George's forearms tighten against the strain, as his mind shouted inside his head that dumping fuel meant they had no choice but to go down. The terror level started to go back up.

"300," Loura said.

"Give me a click of flaps."

Dave felt the plane shutter as the nose came up more.

"Flaps one click," Loura said, paused and then, "Four thousand and 270."

"7 Gulf Tango at 4000, lined up on an interstate. Let's try another click of flaps."

"Flaps to one half "

"I'm thinking gear down when we get below 200 knots, I need the drag."

"2500 and 210 knots, gear down that fast could rip them off," Loura said.

"Well if so, it would certainly increase the drag."

Jan now had both hands gripping Dave's arm. It was hurting him, and cutting off his circulation to his hand. But it didn't matter. Even if it had mattered, he had no ability to speak, let alone say anything to her without shouting in terror.

"Are we going to be okay?" Jan asked in a trembling elevated voice that seemed far louder than necessary in the near silent aircraft.

Dave swallowed and tried to speak in a normal voice, but what came out seemed anything but normal. It sounded more like a trembling shout inside his head, "I don't know. They're doing what they can."

"1500 and 190, gear coming down," Loura said.

"There's a lot of traffic on that road. 7 Gulf Tango at 1500, over highway going in."

Dave had heard of people saying that your life flashes through your mind just before you die. He wasn't seeing anything, but as his mind wrestled with what was going on, he became reflective on what life is all about. He was convinced that it all boils down to a single factor, kids. He was proud of his two sons, but even if they had never accomplished anything, they were his offspring and that is what life is all about. Bringing other life into the world.

If there's one thing I would like to yet live for, he thought, it would be for Jan to be a mother. She seems happy, but I'm sorry she has missed out on motherhood. She would have been a wonderful mother to a child. That's really all he was sorry for.

Well, it would have been nice to see grandkids too, he thought. Or even meet the wives of my boys. To see them happy with someone like Jan would have been great.

"500 and 110 knots," Loura said. "Are you going for the oncoming lanes?"

Dave's mind snapped back to terror mode.

"Yeah, at this speed the traffic going with us wouldn't have a chance, we'd kill everyone. At least this way they see us coming and have a chance to get out of the way. 7 Gulf Tango going down on the east bound lanes."

The next few seconds felt like an hour. Dave was unbelievably aware of all things around him. He saw a blue Corvette out the window beside the plane. The driver was staring at him with his mouth wide open as if yelling at him. There was a large green highway sign that went by so fast that he couldn't read it. A semi broadcast in large letters on its side about having a delivery of Pella Windows.

Jan looked over at him and smiled peacefully. She had released the grip on his arm, and now was just holding his hand. There was no fright or terror in her face anymore. She just looked calm, satisfied and loving. Wow, he loved her. The last two things he remembered was the astonished look on the truck drivers face he saw out through the plane windshield, and that he hadn't put his shoes back on.

Chapter 10

"Are you okay?" Jan asked with a worried look.

Dave thought his chest was about to explode from the pressure of his beating heart. He was sweating and felt out of breath.

"Yeah," he said, "just had a bad dream. How long have I been sleeping?"

"Maybe forty minutes," she unbuckled her seat belt so that she could move closer to him. "You're burning up," she stroked his forehead and cheeks. "And you're all flushed. Tell me about it."

"I dreamed I was about to die," he said, giving no more details. "I realized how much I'd miss seeing how the boy's lives turn out, you know, wives and grandkids. But most of all, how much I would miss spending the rest of my life with you."

She leaned over and kissed him. Then she moved back into her seat, leaned toward him, and said, "It's been stressful the last few weeks. You've held up well, but it hasn't been easy. But now we have ten days to spend in the sun watching baseball, playing golf and, most of all relaxing."

The sound of the engines suddenly decreased.

Dave gasped.

"What is it?" Jan asked.

"Guess we're going to be landing soon," Dave said shakily.

When the plane stopped on the tarmac, a red Cadillac Escalade pulled up. One of the perks of traveling in private planes is that rental cars could be delivered right up to the plane. Bags and golf clubs were unloaded and placed in the rental car. Dave and Jan thanked George and Loura for the smooth flight.

"We'll see you in ten days," George offered. "Have fun."

"Thanks, we're going to try," Dave responded, still shaky from his nightmare. "You guys be careful up there."

As they pulled away from the airport, Dave commented on how nice the rental car was that Jan had ordered for them. Jan told him it was this or a mini-van. He agreed with her choice, a Cadillac always tops a mini-van.

As Jan drove, Dave called D to let him know they were in town. He had been waiting for the call and said he would meet them at the hotel. When they pulled into the hotel parking lot D was there waiting for them. Chris would be coming in on Saturday and he and D would share a room so that the four of them could spend time together. They checked into the two rooms on Dave's credit card, and the three of them went to dinner at a nearby steak house.

Conversation over dinner was mostly about what D had experienced in his first week at Cubs camp. He and Dave had talked almost every night on the phone, but D was anxious to make sure he filled Dave and Jan in on everything. His excitement level was obviously very high.

"Even if I never make it, this is an experience I'll never forget," D explained. "Just being around these guys is unbelievable. I even enjoy the way they pick on me, making a big deal out of everything I do wrong or that could be better. I see it all from the aspect that they are paying attention to me, and helping me to learn."

"Good attitude," Dave offered. "The seasoned players may be seeing themselves when they were in your shoes. Learning is good, getting down on yourself will get you nowhere, and may destroy any chance you have. Keep it up, and most of all, have fun."

Later on, back in the hotel room, Dave had trouble getting to sleep. What he had learned about D's experience so far excited him. The team had already played six games with D playing at least a couple of innings in each. His batting average was 0.438 and his on base percentage was 0.375. Not bad considering the normal averages in the big leagues is around 0.250 for batting and 0.320 for on base. As a matter of fact, these numbers were very good. D was on his way to something big, maybe.

The next morning Jan and Dave made their way to Sloan Field. They got there at ten fifteen to watch the workout before the game against the Padres at 1:05. D had told them that he expected that he would be taking batting practice around eleven, or so.

When they got into the bleachers, the Cubs were spread around different parts of the field working in small groups. Pitchers and catchers were down the third base line throwing on a rotational basis as directed by the pitching coach. Outfielders were in a group in right field snagging flies hit by a coach from left field. Infielders were fielding grounders hit by a coach located to the left of home plate. D was in a group of four guys rotating in and out near the second base position. As D stepped in at one point the coach yelled, first and third get two.

"What does that mean?" Jan asked.

"It's a play simulation," Dave answered. "It means there is a man on first base and a man on third base and the fielder is to try to get two outs.

He then hit a hard ground ball to D's right, D snagged the ball just above the ground while moving toward the base. He planted his right foot on second base, looked at third base then threw hard to first.

"Did you see that D looked at third base before he threw to first? That meant he was making sure the man on third was not attempting to score before he threw to first." Dave explained to Jan. "If the third base runner was going for home, he would have thrown to home. That look is called holding the runner at third."

"Oh, so the two outs he got were at second and first, but could have been at second and home based on what the guy on third was planning to do," Jan concluded.

"Right. See baseball's not complicated."

A similar process continued as players rotated the positions and were given different play situations. All of this going on under the watchful eye of the manager who took it all in and made comments while an assistant jotted everything down on a clipboard. Jan also quizzed Dave and learned a lot about the game as she watched her stepson in a Chicago Cubs uniform.

Shortly before eleven, the ground crew moved the batting cage around home plate and a protective net was set up in front of the mound. As this was happening everyone was called in from the field and a meeting was held near the dugout. People were given assignments and players took the field for batting practice. About eight or ten players went into the dugout, D was one of those.

The net in front of the mound was L shaped so that a pitcher could throw the ball toward the plate but be protected from a ball hit back at him. The L was reversable so that it would work for either right or left-handed pitchers. It was set up for a left-handed pitcher as they began batting practice. A coach stood next to the batting cage and gave batters instructions as they hit. He was apparently telling the player where he wanted them to hit the ball, as was obvious by each player hitting balls down the third base line, then up the middle then over first base. D was the fourth player to come out of the dugout.

As he stepped up to the plate, he nodded in the direction of the coach, and sent the first pitch screaming over third base and out of the ball park just clearing the fence to the right of the foul pole. The next ball went just over the third baseman's glove as he jumped and landed thirty feet in front of the charging left fielder. He then hit one directly at the short stop who caught the ball without moving.

The coach said something to D and he nodded again. The next pitch was sent right back at the pitcher who flinched and ducked as the ball hit the net in front of him. The force of the ball hitting the net caused it to jump as it withstood the impact. Dave's heart skipped a beat.

"That's it," Dave said out loud. "That's what I've been missing."

"What?" Jan asked. "What are you talking about?"

"That's where Brian was, that's what was wrong," Dave exclaimed.

Jan was looking at him just as she had on the plane, the "are you all right" look.

"Sorry, I'll explain later, I have to make a call." Dave said as he pulled out his cell phone and punched the speed-dial. "Cheryl," he said into the phone, "are Bob and Dan in the office?"

"Yes, they are in their offices, I think," she said.

"Ask them to get together at a speaker phone, and call me. I need to talk with them right away."

"Okay, Sheriff, are you having a good time?" Cheryl asked.

"We certainly are, and it just got better. I'll fill you in when I get back. But I'm on to something right now that I need to get Bob and Dan's input."

"Okay, I'll get them to call you right away."

"I'm going up to where it's quieter," he said to Jan, "Can I get you anything while I'm up there?"

"Hot dog," Jan said hesitantly, as he vaulted up the steps.

Just as he was getting to the top of the stands, his phone rang. The caller ID said it was Bob.

"Is Dan there, too?" he asked as he put the phone to his ear.

"I'm here," Dan said.

"What's up, boss?" Bob asked. "Did D hit a homer?"

"Not yet," Dave said. "Listen, when I was talking with Brian the other day, I asked him if he had his car window down as he approached the back of the store. He said he didn't remember, but that it was procedure so he assumed he did. So, from that, we can assume he was following standard procedure when in a high-risk situation. Procedure would dictate that he be prepared for an armed robber to exit the back of the store. Where would he be?"

"Oh, ...My God, Dave," Bob's voice was elevated. "We're dummies, he would have been behind the door of his squad watching the back of the store. You're right, why would we have not thought of that before? There is no way he would have come out from behind the car door until he was sure any threat was neutralized."

"Right, exactly what I was just thinking." Dave responded.

"Then, with that in mind, why was he where he was when he was shot?" Dan asked thoughtfully.

"As Bob said, he would not have been there unless he was sure the threat had been neutralized." Dave said confidently. "Dan, we need the investigation reopened. Get on the horn to SPD and tell them we have reason to suspect that more investigation is warranted."

"Wait, Dave," Bob interjected, "Let's think this through. What could cause Brian to believe there was no longer a threat? Do we want others to be thinking what we're thinking before we get a handle on what we're dealing with? In particular SPD?"

"That's right, Dave," Dan stepped in, "Sergeant Wilson confirmed the report and he was there. Anything different would implicate him. We may not want anyone at SPD knowing we have concerns, let alone what they are."

"That's a good point, Dan. Maybe it's best to keep it under our hats. As I think about it, this points directly at Sergeant Wilson. He either took part in what happened or knows about it, whatever it was. And, Mayor's son or not, this doesn't look good for him. You guys think about this.

We'll get together when I get back and try to work out a plan."

"You know, Dave, I've heard of bad blood between Brian and Wilson," Bob said. "Do you think he could have taken the opportunity to even the score?"

"It goes back to high school when Brian and Roger were sweet on the same girl. Turns out she had no interest in either of them, but they didn't know that at the time and really went at each other. She thought it was fun to watch them go at each other so she kept fanning the flames so to speak. Brian was more upset with the girl when all was said and done, but Roger was different, and never seemed to get over it." Dave concluded. "We'll talk when I get back."

Dave got hot dogs, cokes and nachos and headed back down to Jan. She told him that D had hit every pitch that was in the strike zone as far as she could tell. He seemed to be able to hit it exactly where the coach asked. As he was walking back to the bench the coaches were talking with a lot of nodding going on. Then she just looked at him, which he knew was the "okay what's so important that you can't watch your son" look.

He filled her in on what had transpired and the phone call with Bob and Dan. As he was talking, he became more and more concerned that if in fact Roger Wilson had taken revenge on Brian, there must be involvement of others in SPD to cover it up.

"So, you're thinking there may have been two separate crimes," Jan said thoughtfully, "the robbery, and that Roger Wilson saw a chance at revenge and took it. I don't know, sheriff, sounds weak to me."

"You may be right, Judge, but I'm going to find out."

The rest of the day was down right fabulous. The Cubs won in a blow out of the Padres, seven to one. D played second base for six innings. He had four at bats with two singles and a near home run double down the third base line that hit the fence about a foot below being gone. He got an RBI on one of the singles and scored from second on a long single after his double. His other at bat was a well hit line drive straight up the middle that the center fielder dived for and just barely caught. In the field he played error free ball with a nice double play where he leapt to catch a line drive and threw out the runner before he could get back to first base.

That evening over dinner they were all excited about how well D had played.

"That double play was a thing of beauty," Dave offered.

"Like Joe Morgan, Dad?" D joked.

"Yeah, just like Joe Morgan," Dave laughed. Then he added, "Maybe better."

"You guys want to let me in on the joke?" Jan asked.

"Joe Morgan was a second baseman for the Cincinnati Reds when dad was growing up," D said. "He always told me about how Joe would make double plays and how fluid he was making the turn and throw from second to first base. He was one of dad's favorite ball players along with Tony Perez, Johnny Bench and Pete Rose."

"So now your son is better than your hero?" Jan asked Dave.

"No, not better than my hero," Dave replied, beaming, "Now my son is my hero. He's the best major league ball player ever."

"I'm not in the majors yet," D said, "but as long as you think that, that's all that really matters to me. Thanks dad."

"Well, don't give up," Jan said, "I don't know a lot about baseball, but you certainly looked to me like you belonged out there on that field. Makes me proud too."

D had morning work-outs the next day, Saturday. Dave and Jan planned to visit Jan's cousin who lived in Scottsdale in the morning and then pick up Chris. His flight was expected to get into Phoenix International airport at 1:30 that afternoon. After they picked up Chris, they planned to go straight to Sloan Park for the 6:40 p.m. game against the Milwaukee Brewers.

Chapter 11

The next ten days were a blur of baseball games, golf and family time with D and Chris. They saw a total of seven ball games in which D played at least some in every game. His batting average after the ten days was 0.493 and he had an on base percentage of 0.427. It was looking like the numbers were moving in a direction that could get him a call into the minors at the very least, or go straight into the majors at best.

Over dinner the night before they left, Dave asked, "what do you think you have learned so far, D?"

"The most important thing is about major league pitching." D responded. "I've learned that what you told me is in fact true. It is night and day different from college. The pitches are always on the plate or just off. And the speed is always much faster than what I had been used to in college. There is also much more movement of the ball, mostly down and away from right handers and down and in from lefties. But I have been able to learn from it and adjust."

"Adjust," Dave asked, "how?"

"Well, the biggest thing is what the pitching coach told me. He said that if I move closer to the plate, I can hit pretty much any pitch." D offered. "Since everything is going to be near the plate, by moving in closer to the plate it assures me that I can make contact with any pitch. All I have to concentrate on is the altitude, so to speak. And it has worked for me so far. I just step up close and try to make sure that the bat comes through at the same level as the ball. I hit more foul balls, but I haven't seemed to miss as much, which equates to fewer strike outs. My timing at getting the bat and ball to meet over the plate has always been my strong suit, so with that, I'm having some success."

The time spent together was like a fastball. As Dave and Jan climbed aboard George and Loura's plane to head back they were both drained and relaxed. They were drained from the repeated excitement and exhilaration of the ball games. And they were relaxed from the quiet times with D and Chris, the warm sunny rounds of golf and lying around the hotel pool in the sun.

"Was it a pleasant ten days?" George asked as they boarded the plane.

"It certainly was," Jan answered quickly, "we had a great time, thanks for asking."

"Well it looks like a bit of a bumpy ride home," Loura said. "It would be a good idea to keep your seat belts fastened."

"I hate bumpy," Jan said with a frown.

"We'll do all we can to find smooth air, but it's best to be prepared," Loura cautioned. "The good news is we were fighting a strong headwind all the way out here, which is unusual, but means a tail wind on the way back. We're estimating it will only be about two-hours and thirty minutes flight home, if the winds hold as strong."

"Bumpy two and a half or smooth three and a half, is that what my choices are?" Jan asked.

"Nope, sorry, no choices," Loura smiled, "but don't you think bumpy two and half beats the bumpy three and a half that we had coming out to get you?"

"Touché," Jan laughed.

The flight home was really not very bad at all. There were a few bumps as they descended to land but not bad. They threw all of the suit cases, bags and golf clubs into the back seat of the crew cab pickup that they had left parked at the airport and headed home. It was just getting dark as they got everything unloaded and collapsed on the couch in the family room.

"Boy that was a great time," Jan said, "but I'm beat."

"Yeah, me too," Dave sighed. "But tomorrow it's back to reality and what I need to do about it."

"Me too. My docket will not have gotten any lighter while I was gone. And, based on what the Sheriff has shared with me, one of my upcoming cases may have an unexpected twist."

"I'm sure he will let you know if anything comes of that, Judge."

"So, tell me about D in the big leagues," Cheryl instructed as Dave got into the office the next morning. "Was it fun?"

"Fun in the sun," Dave answered. "We had a great time and D is doing very well. It still remains to be seen if it will get him anywhere, but it's a great experience for him. He seems to be handling it well, no out of sight expectations or unrealistic hopes that I could see."

"That's great. Glad you had a good time. Welcome back."

Dave noticed Dan and Bob were heading in his direction. He waved them into his office, "Did Walt Regan call while I was gone?"

"No," Cheryl answered, "should I get him on the phone for you?"

"Not just yet, but if he calls put him through, please."

"Will do. You want coffee?"

"That would be great, thanks."

Dave closed the door behind him as he walked into his office. Bob and Dan were already seated in the chairs in front of his desk.

"How was the trip?" Bob asked.

"Great. D is looking like a major leaguer, but we'll see."

"Did he get to play a lot?" Dan asked.

"Yeah, he was in every game we saw for at least a couple of innings. He had an almost 500 batting average and just over 400 on base percentage. So, the hitting is doing well. In the field he played well, with only a couple of errors in all of the games. I think he has a shot, but who knows."

"Was he playing short stop?" Bob asked.

"Most of the time they had him at second base. He did play some short stop and even a couple of innings at third. He thinks they are in the market for a utility infielder who can get on base. He thinks they're fine at short stop so second may be his spot on the team."

"Well we're all pulling for him," Dan added.

There was a brief knock on the door and it opened. Chery brought in three cups of coffee, two with cream and one black. She set them down in front of each of the guys and left.

"Thanks, Chery," Dave said as she walked out and closed the door behind her. "Where are we?"

"I snooped around at SPD a bit more," Dan began, "in particular I was trying to get a handle on who was involved in the decision to close the case. As best as I can tell, the investigators were just as surprised as we were. It appears that Paul Jacoby took his acting chief investigator title seriously and closed it without consultation. John Alberts says he thought it was still preliminary when he signed off on it."

"Did anyone seem curious as to why you were asking?" Dave inquired.

"No, just the opposite, they all seem to have the same question. No interest at all in why I was asking. Seemed like they were expecting us to ask."

"Any feeling that they might reopen it?"

"Alberts said he requested it be reopened on the grounds that all the ballistics have not been reviewed, but was told in no uncertain terms to not bring it up again."

"Can we open our own investigation, since Brian was shot?" Bob asked.

"Inside the city limits is not our jurisdiction," Dave replied, "Unless the city asks us, and that sure doesn't look likely."

As he was speaking a thought flashed through Dave's mind. "Wait, we may have missed something. Let's continue this discussion in a few minutes. I need to make a call." Dave waved the guys out of his office.

After they had left and the closed the door behind them, Dave flipped through his rolodex, found the number he wanted and dialed.

"Miller Construction and Development, may I help you?" the voice on the other end of the line said.

"This is Dave Harbinger, is Jay available?"

"One moment Sheriff," the voice said.

After a few seconds, "Hey, Dave, what's up?" he heard his brother-in-law say.

"A quick question for you, Jay. Over dinner the other night you said you built the Quick Mart building. I didn't think you built anything in the city."

"I don't," Jay responded. "The property that strip mall sits on is half in the city and half out. Remember it was built in sections. The east half was built three years or so before the west. The reason was that the city limits ran right through the middle of it. The owner was trying to get the city to annex the rest of the partial, but couldn't get it done in the time frame he wanted so he gave up and built the west half in the county. That's when I bid on it."

"But the city limit sign is west of the property?"

"Yeah, that was another fiasco. The city wanted him to put the sign in the middle of his parking lot. He went round and round with them and finally agreed to deed one sixteenth of an acre of property to the city on the west end so that they could put the sign there. It's what they call a flag lot. Funny, the city didn't have any problem annexing that sign parcel in."

"So, the Quick Mart is in my jurisdiction, not the city's," Dave stated thoughtfully.

"The last I knew, yes, I thought you knew that?"

"I didn't, but I'm going to check with the assessor to confirm that. Thanks, Jay, you've been a big help."

Dave called the assessor's office and they soon confirmed that what Jay had told him was, in fact, true. The building property that housed the Quick Mart was not in the city. Dave asked Dan and Bob to return to his office.

"I have learned something that changes everything," the sheriff told his two staff members after they were seated in the closed-door office. "The Quick Mart building is not in the city. It is our jurisdiction."

Dave then brought them up to speed on his phone conversations.

"Does that mean we can do our own separate investigation?" Bob asked.

"No, I don't think we want to do that," Dan said thoughtfully. "We don't have the crime scene photos, measurements and data, and certainly can't collect our own now. We may have grounds to request a review of SPD's investigation on the grounds of jurisdiction, a reopening of the case in essence. But, since we were provided the reports, I'm not sure SPD would see that as warranted just on jurisdictional grounds. They would probably need some new evidence or the like for reopening."

"So, we really need the entire case file transferred over," Dave concluded.

"Yep, I don't see any other way to get everything we would need to do a thorough review, and based on our thinking right now, that's what we need. If SPD is hiding something, they would not want to give us the evidence." Dan finalized.

"Kind of the old rock and hard place position, huh?" Dave thought out loud. "Well let's keep it in here just between us at this point. If the SPD investigation is dirty, and there is any suspicion on their part that we think it may be, the information could be compromised. The chances of us getting anything from it would be slim. We need to get exactly what was collected from the scene with no alterations."

"Dave, who knows you've been asking these questions?" Dan asked.

Dave and Bob both looked at Dan as they realized he was asking the question to determine if there could be an avenue for their suspicions to get back to SPD.

"My brother in law, Jay Miller, who built the building and the clerk at the assessor's office that looked it up for me."

"Maybe you should call Jay back to make sure he keeps it under his hat. What was the clerk's name, I think I'll go pay the assessor's office a visit," said Dan.

"Good idea, I'll call Jay back, and her name was Ivy," Dave offered.

"I know Ivy," Dan said, "Ivy Artica. She's a friend of my daughter. I'm sure she would not be a problem, but I'll talk with her anyway."

"Okay, guys, that's it for now."

As they headed for the door, Dave added, "By the way, Dan, good catch on the who knows issue. Good investigators are always thinking ahead, right?"

"It's my job, Sheriff, thanks."

That evening, after a quiet dinner with just the two of them, Dave and Jan sat together on the sofa in the family room. They were both exhausted from the first day back on the job after a vacation. The tv was on, but they were not paying much attention to it. Jan was lying on the sofa with her head on Dave's chest. His arm around her. Dave had his feet up on the coffee table. One of their most comfortable positions.

The home phone rang. Dave picked up the extension on the end table beside him.

"Harbinger's."

"It's Walt, Dave, did I get you at a bad time?"

"No, Walt, it's fine. Jan and I were just relaxing on the couch. What's news?"

"Sorry to call you at home, but I didn't want to call from the office. I still haven't decided on a time to make the switch, are you okay with waiting a bit longer?"

"No problem on our end. Brian will be coming back soon, so we've been talking about bringing you on in the investigations side. Working directly for Dan."

"That sounds great. I'm sure it will work out. Let me just give you a bit of insight into the reason for my hold up. I have become aware of some things that people are keeping from me in my current position. I find it troubling. I can see no obvious reason why I would not be in the loop in certain matters, but since I'm not it makes me wonder, why not. The investigator in me won't let me walk away without an answer to the why. It may be nothing but I need to spend some more time to find out."

"Does it have anything to do with Rod's death?" Dave inquired.

"I don't think so, but…" Walt trailed off as if thinking of something. "Anyway, I just wanted to touch base to let you know what's going on."

"Let me ask you something else, Walt. Do you think the Quick Mart case should be reopened?"

"I have no concrete basis to recommend that. But if evidence presented itself, I would certainly be in favor."

"Okay, message understood. Thanks for the call."

After hanging up the phone, Dave was convinced that he had to find a way to reopen and investigate the case. Walt's answer gave him the idea that there was something else to be learned.

But, enough of work stuff, there are far more important matters at hand. He turned to Jan and kissed her on the forehead.

"How old are you, my sweet?" Dave asked.

"Sixteen," she answered. They had often played the too young for me game, or pretending to be teenagers in love. Maybe hiding from their parents or being afraid of getting caught doing something they shouldn't.

"Too, bad," he said back at her, "I'm thinking you would need to be at least eighteen, twenty or maybe even twenty-two."

"For what?"

"To have my baby."

She jolted upright. She starred into his eyes. A tear began to form as she whispered, "are you serious?"

He nodded and smiled. She jumped up and threw both arms around his neck. She kissed him passionately.

"How did you know? I've been wanting to ask you but was afraid you wouldn't want to." Tears streamed down her face. "It would make me so happy. I want to have a baby so bad. Did you know?"

"No, I didn't. Remember my dream on the plane. One of the things I regretted when I thought I was going to die was not having a baby with you. I want to make sure I don't regret that any longer."

There wasn't much talking the rest of the night.

Chapter 12

As the end of March approached, Brian had gotten home from the hospital. Dave and Jan went by on a Saturday morning to check on how he was doing.

Brian and Marie lived in a small neighborhood out in the county about six miles southwest of Springfield. The subdivision was about thirty homes on three-quarter acre lots on two streets running off the county highway. Their house was on the backside of the subdivision. They had a sloping backyard that allowed for a walkout basement that was mostly unfinished except for a rec room that Brian had insisted on finishing so that he had a place for a pool table. Behind their property were farm fields and wooded areas in the distance.

Marie showed Dave and Jan into the family room where Brian was sitting in a recliner.

"Looking good, buddy." Dave greeted his friend.

"Thanks, I'm coming along," Brian smiled broadly.

"Now that you've been home awhile is it better than the hospital," Jan asked as she bent over and gave him a kiss on the cheek.

"I have to admit the meals here are better, but the nursing, not so much," he smiled at Marie's flinch and stare.

"He has to work on being a better patient," she said, "but I'm not about to send him back. Can I get you guys a coke or something?"

"No thanks," Dave said, "we just wanted to stop by to see if he is doing okay, and to see if there's anything we can do for you guys."

"We're fine," Marie said, "I can't even tell you how good it is to be back to a more normal routine. He is doing so much better than we ever thought he would be. It is really such a blessing. I just can't say how good it feels."

"Now for the bad news," Brian interjected. "The doctors are saying I may have to go back to work in about a month. I was hoping this would last a long time, seeing who I work for."

"Didn't Marie tell you that we filled your position with a sixth grader and he's doing a better job? We're looking forward to him getting a driver's license, but other than that we aren't missing you at all," Dave joked.

They all heard the front door open and Bobby's voice call out, "Yo, anybody home?"

"Come on in, Bobby," Marie called out.

Bobby came into view over in the kitchen carrying two shopping bags. "Brought you some food to cook for me,

Marie. I guess you can share it with the kids, too. But not that lazy bum over there till he starts pulling some weight around here."

"No trash talking in front of company, Weasel," Brian retorted.

Bobby sat the bags on the counter and began to unpack.

"Hey, boss, how ya doin?" Bobby said to Dave. "They ain't company, they're family," he threw back at Brian.

"Well, we're going to take off, lots to do," Dave said taking Brian's hand and shaking. "Glad to see you doing well."

"Thanks, and thanks for stopping by."

"Hey, they's a problem with the 6430. I be in shop later, can ya come by?" Bobby said as Dave walked toward the door.

"Sure, about three?"

"That works," Bobby answered.

"What's a 6430?" Jan asked as they walked to the car.

"That's one of the four-wheel-drive tractors," Dave answered. "My guess is he can't get the oil filter off. I had problems with that before."

Then they went to the grocery store. Absolutely one of Dave's most dreaded experiences. But, since Jan worked, he felt it his duty to go along, at least some of the time. Dave knew that Jan, on the other hand, did not mind shopping of any kind. She wouldn't have complained if he made up a reason that he couldn't go, but it needed to be done so there he was. He pushed the shopping cart while she made purchase decisions that followed her meal planning for the next week or so. There were also times that he couldn't help but drop a box of Ho Ho's, a bag of chips or maybe even some cashews into the cart on his own. She may give him a look, but seldom objected to his cravings.

After the groceries were put away back at the homestead, Dave excused himself to go over to the farm and meet with Bobby in the workshop.

"Oil filter stuck?" he asked as he walked into the shop to find Bobby by the work bench filling a grease gun.

"How'd ya know?" was the response.

"Been there, done that."

Dave walked over to the tool box and pulled out a breaker bar. "I've used this in the past. If you put an extension on the filter wrench this will give you the extra leverage to break it lose. Not the way it's supposed to be done, but it works for me."

The tractor had the covers open, so Dave showed Bobby how to position the filter wrench and the extension. Bobby put the breaker bar on the extension and broke the filter lose easily.

"Got it," he said. "This the only one that needs that?"

"Yeah, no idea why, but this one seems to tighten filters as it runs. What else you working on?"

"Lubin' on the planter, right now. Got all the oil changed after this one and the stake bed truck. Be ready to go get seed next week. Ya get the order in?"

"Yep, there're ready. I told them to expect pick up on Tuesday."

"Ok, I'll go then. Great to have Brian back, huh?"

"Sure is."

"I put the word out I'd like ta know what Jose' and Lefty was into. One a the dudes say they had a hustle goin'. Weren't sure what it was, but somethin' that didn't smell like robbin to him. Said it was bringin' in big bread."

"You think it was drugs?"

"Nope, he didn't think they was sellin' stuff."

"Any ideas?"

"Na, but ya don't get big bread from jackin a Quick Mart."

"That's for sure."

When Dave got back from the farm, he decided he would call D to see how he was doing. The final stats for D's spring training were a batting average of .561 and an on base percentage of .496. He had the second highest on base percentage on the team.

As the team packed up and got ready for the season opener, he didn't get the news he had hoped for. He was told that he was on his way to Des Moines. The assistant coach that gave him the news said that he could expect to spend a few weeks there while the brass evaluated the long-term plan for the season. The plan could be for him to remain in the minors getting experience and being evaluated or it could be a quick call up and into the show. He was not given any indication which was the most likely.

"I feel like I have to give it a shot, dad," D said on the phone. "But the minor leagues sure don't pay much, only about fifteen grand a year. I'm not sure how long I want to do that. I need to finish college after dropping out of my last semester to go to camp. If I'm not going to get to the show, I need that degree. I'm not interested in living in poverty my whole life because I didn't finish the degree. If it only paid better, I might be able to do both. I'm not sure I can live on that."

"Yeah, fifteen grand a year is not really enough to live on." Dave said as Jan waved at him to hand her the phone. "Wait, Jan wants to talk with you."

"D," Jan said into the phone, "I just heard one side of the conversation, but are you only going to make fifteen thousand dollars a year to play baseball?"

Jan listened to the response through the phone.

"Okay, well look, I've been looking for a place to invest some money. If you're interested, I'd like to invest in your baseball career. I'll send you a check for thirty thousand so that you can live comfortably while in the minors. After a year, we'll revisit the arrangement. If you make it to the majors and get a big contract, you owe me one hundred thousand after your first million."

She listened.

"If you don't make it, we'll talk about what the pay-back would look like. It's an investment. I don't think I'm risking much at all. You will do well, and I'll make money off our deal. I think it's fair for both of us."

Again, a pause.

"Glad to do it, here's dad." She handed the phone back to Dave, smiling.

"I guess I'm in for the long play, dad. You heard, right?"

"Yep, sounds like she intends to take advantage of you to me," Dave said.

"I don't care if she does. Thanks to you both. I'm feeling much better. Got to get packing, I'll leave for Iowa in the morning. Let you know when I get there. See ya." He hung up.

Dave looked at Jan with a quizzical expression.

"Well, maybe I should have discussed it with you first, but that money is not a marital asset, I had it before we were married, and I can spend it how I please." She made a pouting face as if he had just scolded her.

"But what if he doesn't make it, he may not be able to pay it back."

"Well, then I'll take the money out of marital assets and pay me back so he won't have to."

"I'm okay with that as long as half of the hundred grand goes into marital assets when you get that."

"Agreed," she smiled and poked him in the shoulder.

"So, what's going on at the courthouse next week?" he changed the subject. "Are you going to be missing me while I'm out of town on business?'

"My docket is full to the brim, so I'll be staying busy while you're off on your exotic trip to KC."

"I didn't find much exotic about the last Sheriff's Convention," he observed. "Not really the group of people that would be expected to be all out party types, if you know what I mean."

"Can't fool me," she said with a grin, "it's a let the gray hair down group, for sure."

"I'm sure Kansas City is bracing for the chaos."

"What are you driving to the airport tomorrow?"

"Actually, Rob Alexander is driving me. I talked with him when I was deciding to go and we agreed to travel together. He's picking me up at my office and I'm leaving my squad there so maintenance can do their thing on it while I'm gone."

"The Lincoln County Sheriff and the Williams County Sheriff travel together for the chaos in Kansas City," Jan gestured in a big deal manner, "I can see the headlines now. You better hope that never gets out."

"Well, I'm confident an unnamed local judge will come to my rescue and bail me out." Dave patted her on the cheek and headed upstairs to pack.

The annual sheriff's convention was an opportunity for Dave to learn from his peers who had been running departments much long than he. He found some of the presentations boring, but got a lot out of others. It was all about the presenter and their particular ability to make it interesting and beneficial.

Dave and Rob got into the conference hotel just before 4 in the afternoon. They checked in and headed for the conference registration area off the main lobby. After picking up their registration packets they headed for their respective rooms.

When he got to his room, Dave sat at the desk and looked through the materials he had been given. The general format was a series of presentations on a wide range of topics. The program brochure gave the time and place of each presentation and a brief description of the subject matter. He quickly picked out a few programs he found interesting and circled them in his program. The big kick off for the convention was the cocktail party on Sunday evening beginning at five in the ballroom. He glanced at his watch and headed down for the party.

When Dave walked into the massive ballroom there were bars set up in each corner of the room and four large tables in the center with various hors d'oeuvres. There were many small round tables about chest high located all over the room. The room was already quite full. He walked up to one of the bars and got a beer. Not seeing anyone he recognized, he walked over to one of the small round tables with a guy about his age leaning on it with beer in hand.

"Hi, Dave Harbinger," he said without stretched hand.

"Nice to meet you. I'm Dan Weatherford," was the response as they shook hands.

"Where you from, Dan?"

"Wapiti County Arizona, this is my first trip here as sheriff."

"It's only my second," Dave replied. "I'm from the mid-west. Did you beat out the incumbent?"

"No, he died in office. Kind of left me the job, so to speak, I'm not sure anyone else wanted it."

"The same thing happened to me, sort of," Dave said. "Our former sheriff was in his eighties. He had been sheriff forever. After he was killed, I was asked to run based on name recognition in the county. I still don't think I'm qualified, but here I am."

"Me too," Dan reflected.

"Do you know anyone here, Dan?"

"Not a soul, except for you, Dave," Dan smiled.

"Okay, buddy, well I know one other guy. Rob Alexander is sheriff of Williams County just south of me. How about you, Rob and I hang together for the conference?"

"I'd appreciate that, thanks."

Just at that time, Rob came into the ballroom. Dave waved him over and introduced him to Dan.

"Unlike us, Rob has been to many of these chaotic events," Dave said.

"Stick with me, whipper snappers, I'll show you the ropes," Rob retorted.

They had a few beers and split out to find dinner. There was a very nice sea food place about three blocks from the hotel the bellman told them. Two hours later, after a T-bone and baked potato meal, they agreed the bellman knew his stuff.

After getting back to the hotel, they agreed to meet for the opening breakfast meeting the following morning. Dave got back to his room, called Jan to say good night and then went right to sleep.

Chapter 13

After the breakfast meeting the next morning, the three guys split to go to separate sessions. Dave had selected a session on how to establish go no go criteria for high speed pursuits. When the session was over, Dave's take-away was that it wasn't an easy decision.

As Dave was walking toward the dining room to get lunch, he saw Dan Weatherford approaching from the other direction.

"Want to have lunch, Dan?" he asked as they met at the door of the dining room.

"Just what I had in mind," Dan replied.

They were shown to a table by the receptionist. As they sat down Dave placed his notebook on the table next to him. The notebook had been given to him as a present by his sons. They had sent pictures of the car collection to a printer who printed them on the cover.

"That's a neat notebook," Dan said. "Are you into classic cars?"

"I am," Dave smiled, "those are part of our collection. My sons had this book printed for me as a Christmas present a few years ago."

"Really, may I?" Dan picked up the book for a closer look. "I've always been into cars, but never had the extra money to get anything. So, these are all yours?"

"My dad started collecting years ago. Since he passed, I share it with my brother and sister. But they really aren't into it as much as I am so it's pretty much just me."

"I have a friend who has a Shelby like that one, except his is a fastback," Dan said pointing to the '67 convertible.

"We had a fastback as well, but it was stolen several years ago."

"Really? You never got it back?"

"No, and it's not the only car stolen from the collection. Before I was born, dad had a '57 Chevy stolen. I guess it was really nice. The state police found one just like it a couple of years later, but all the serial numbers had been changed so it couldn't be proven to be the one dad lost."

"So, you've lost two cars to theft. That stinks."

"Yeah, but after the '57 couldn't be proven, dad started stamping numbers in the cars in case it happened again. He had a stamp made with 4748 on it and stamped in places that would not normally be seen. So, if the Shelby ever does turn up, I can tell if it's ours or not."

"That's interesting," Dan said thoughtful, "where would he stamp?"

"Depends," Dave offered, "if he had a car apart, he would stamp on top of the frame rail. If he removed a component, like the rear end, he would stamp on top of the diff housing. The top of the transmission and bell housing were also favorite spots for him."

"Sounds like good planning to me. Does that effect the value of a restoration?" Dan asked.

"Probably, if it's a hundred pointer, but for the most part it just adds peace of mind and is worth any loss of value."

"Speaking of value, the one my fiend has is the car that was once owned by Jim Morrison of the Doors," Dan said. "He believes it to be one of the most valuable Shelby's out there."

"Really?" Dave looked puzzled. "I didn't think that car still existed. It was supposed to have been wrecked by Morrison and abandoned in LA. Most believe it was towed away and scraped."

"He says he found it in a wrecking yard out in the desert east of LA. Says the restoration cost him a ton and took two years," Dan offered.

"The one we had was very similar to Morrison car called the Blue Lady. It was an early production car, signified by the close together driving lights in the grill. It also was the same color with the stripe delete, which was rare. But ours had a black interior which was more common than the parchment interior Morrison's had."

"Tell you what," Dan offered, "when I get a chance, I'll take a few pictures and send them to you."

"That would be great," Dave smiled. "I'd like to see it. But make sure your buddy doesn't mind. He may not want it to be known that he has that car."

"Good point. I'll ask before I send anything."

The afternoon session was just about over when Dave's phone vibrated. He checked the caller ID which told him Cheryl. He closed his notebook, collected his things and headed for the exit. When he was out in the hall way he called up his office number and pushed the send button.

"Hold on," Cheryl said, "Dan needs to talk with you."

There was a brief pause and Dan said, "Dave, something has happened, we're not sure what, Bob is just getting to the scene. Brian is okay, but it appears he may have been shot at."

"What?" Dave's heart jumped away from the starting blocks in a hundred-yard dash.

"Marie was taking him to the doctor and a bullet went through the car. It just missed Brian, in through the passenger side window and out the windshield. She hit the gas as Brian called it in. Bob is meeting them now."

"Where were they?"

"Wait, Bob's calling," Dan picked up another phone. Dave could not make out anything but he could hear talking.

Dan came back on the line, "Bob says they were going through the wooded area off the state highway about four miles from home headed into town. He's with them now at a gas station about two miles out of town. Brian says it could be hunters "

"Could be, but not likely," Dave said, "tell Bob to stay with them until they get back home. And have him put a squad at their house 24/7. I want an escort anywhere they go, got it."

"Loud and clear, sheriff."

"I'll be back tomorrow afternoon but keep me posted till then. Do me a favor, Dan, make sure nothing happens to them."

"Bob and I will babysit if that's what's needed, Dave. Don't worry, we've got this."

"What's going on?" Dave asked out loud as he hung up the phone. He thought for a moment to collect his thoughts. Then flipped through the numbers in his speed dial to Walt Regan and pushed send.

"Regan," Walt answered.

"Walt, it's Dave, I wonder if you could do some checking and find out where Roger Wilson has been this afternoon?

My guess is it would be best to not be obvious while you're checking."

"What's going on, Dave?" Walt sounded worried. "Something I should know about?"

"Hopefully it's nothing, but if it is you may want to be careful," Dave cautioned. "That's about all I can say right now."

"Okay, I'll be discrete. I can check the assignment logs and call sheets without any questions. I'll let you know what I find out."

"Thanks, Walt."

When Rob dropped Dave off in his office parking lot the next afternoon, he was surprised to see both Dan and Bob's squads sitting in their usual parking slots. Based on his instruction that Brian be protected, he expected one of them to be with him. He put his travel bag in his squad and headed inside.

As he walked through the office it became evident that they had followed his order because Brian was sitting in Bob's office.

"Hey, Boss," Bob said when he saw Dave. "I'll get Dan and we'll be right into your office."

"Walt Regan called about an hour ago," Cheryl said as Dave approached. "He asked you to call. George Hoffman of DEA called yesterday and asked you to call him. Nothing else you haven't heard, coffee?"

"Okay, and no thanks to the coffee." Dave put his jacket on the coat tree and sat down at his desk. Cheryl had all of the correspondence, reports and other paper work neatly stacked in piles according to his priority ratings, A, B and C. A was the get on it pile. B was look at it tomorrow and recategorize it, and C was file it away in case it comes up again. Dave was constantly amazed at how Cheryl seemed to always know which pile he would put something.

"Welcome back," Dan said as he walked in with Bob and Brian close behind him. "How was the party? Oh, I mean convention?"

Dan pulled another chair over from the conference table on the other side of his office and the three of them sat down in front of Dave's desk.

"The party was fine. Got some good information and tips and met some good people. We'll get into that more later. Brian, you look to be okay, but what happened?"

"I'm fine," Brian answered. "Marie thinks we were doing about sixty. A single bullet, came in through the passenger side window nine and a half inches in front of the B pillar and eleven inches above the door sill. Exited out the windshield below the rearview mirror four inches above the dash. Trajectory indicates it was fired from the right, slightly to the rear and a bit elevated."

Bob and Dan nodded agreement.

"I've got a team in the woods looking for brass or any signs," Dan said.

"Caliber?" asked Dave.

"From the entry, my guess is a 30-06 or similar rifle," Dan offered. "The guys are also looking to see if they can find the bullet, but that's a tall order. From the angle and the terrain along there, it most likely buried itself deep in the ground."

"Look, Dave," Brian injected, "I know you're thinking someone tried to take me out, but it doesn't make sense. If that was the case, they would have come at me more from the front. There's no time to get a good shot from the side of a moving car. They would have set up in an elevated position with a good head on shot."

"Unless they wanted to make it look like a hunting accident," Dave responded. "Then they would have to take the shot from the woods."

"Dave, there aren't many guys that could begin to make that shot from the side. I'm not sure I know of any," Dan offered.

"Well, maybe he set up for a frontal shot but wasn't ready and was forced to try the side shot."

"So, we're dealing with a hunter who didn't realize how close they were to the road, an amateur who didn't realize he had no chance of making the shot, or a professional that barely missed," Bob concluded.

"If it had been anyone else, I would lean toward the first," Dave said thoughtfully. "But based on what Brian may know, I'm leaning toward number three."

"Wait, what do I know, Dave?" Brian looked puzzled.

"That's what we've been trying to figure out, buddy," Dave answered. "Something is not right, we're convinced of it, but we don't know for sure what is going on."

Dave, Bob and Dan filled Brian in on the details of what they had been attempting to figure out since he was shot. He agreed that it seemed like something was not in order, but like them, he had no idea what. He pledged to try hard to stimulate his memory in hopes of shedding light on the case.

"If your memory comes back, it may give us answers. But until then, it looks like you're going to have a lot of company," Dave ordered.

"Come on, Dave, I can take care of myself," Brian complained.

"No doubt about that," Dave confirmed, "but an extra pair of eyes around can't hurt. Also, the presence of a squad and a uniform sends a signal that we're on guard. Besides, it's not for your sense of security, it's for Marie's."

"We've also set up a regular check of the long-range perimeter," Bob said. "Any place in rifle range of your house will be checked on a rotating basis."

"Okay, guys, I guess that's it for now," Dave concluded the meeting. "Are you taking Brian home, Bob?"

"No, Tom Harrison is swinging by. We've got a rotation all set up. It's covered."

After they left, Dave dialed Walt's number.

"Hey, Dave," Walt answered.

"Got anything for me?"

"Nothing out of the ordinary. Let's do lunch tomorrow and I'll give you what I have."

"Okay, Mary's at 11:30?"

"See you then," Walt signed off.

When Dave pulled into Mary's parking lot next morning, he saw a dark blue Impala with muni plates. He found Walt sitting in the same general area of their last meeting there.

"This is a copy of the dailies," Walt said handing Dave a sheet of paper. "Roger and his partner were in the 7 northeast and responded to six calls, made four traffic stops and assisted fire on one of their calls. Pretty routine, nothing out of the ordinary. Can you tell me why you asked?"

"Not just yet, but thanks. I guess it was nothing."

The waitress took their orders and brought their drinks.

"Let me fill you in a bit on what's bothering me," Walt offered.

"I'm all ears."

"Since I moved into the corner office, I've been under close scrutiny. My secretary, Paula, has been keeping close watch on me. She asks questions about what I am doing and thinking all the time. It's not a surprise, because I heard from Rod and former Chief Moorie about her."

"Isn't she the wife of Hal Beck, the councilman?"

"She is. Councilman Beck is the best bud of the mayor. I guess they were in high school together. One of the reasons that I didn't want to be Chief when Moorie retired, was what he had told me about the close watch he had from the political side."

"I wondered at the time why you didn't get the job."

"Didn't put my name in the ring. I just didn't want to work that close with the mayor and council. Don Moorie had a way to let things just slide off his back. I really liked that about him, but I'm not sure he should have been that way."

"You know," Dave offered, "I've always been friends with former Chief Moorie. I still see him often. He is quite the car guy as you know. He has a couple of nice Corvettes. A blue '58 with yellow coves and a gray '64 hardtop. He's also really big into motorcycles, Harleys anyway."

"I knew about his cars and motorcycles, but didn't know you and he are friends. I still see him from time to time."

"Anyway, getting back to what you were talking about, you think Paula is a direct link to the mayor's office."

"Yes, I'm sure of it," Walt continued. "I have no interest in being spied upon that closely. But what I've been wondering is the why. It's one thing to have a job to do, but another to be watched that closely while you do it. So, that's the reason I've got you on hold. I'm attempting to determine if it's just the way it is, or is there something nefarious going on."

"I see," Dave said. "Well, no worries on our end right now. We're ready when you are."

Chapter 14

When Dave got back into the office after lunch, he took the opportunity to stop and chat for a few minutes with Angela the front desk receptionist.

Angie had been working for the sheriff's office since high school. Now in her early-twenties she had just recently gotten married. Her new husband, Neal, was a tech school graduate and working as a welder for the boiler manufacturing plant in town.

Angie was filling Dave in on the wedding trip to the St. Thomas when Cheryl interrupted.

"Sorry sheriff, caller says it's urgent."

"Okay, I'll take it in my office," Dave responded, "hold that thought, Angie, we'll continue later."

When he got into his office line one was flashing on his desk phone. He picked it up and pushed the button.

"Sheriff Harbinger."

"Sorry, Boss," he heard Bobby say, "got some news, won't wait."

"What's up, Bobby?"

"Somebody took out one a ma old buds. Ya remember me talkin bout other guys who're goin straight? One em got run off the road and wasted."

"What are you talking about? There hasn't been a fatal crash in the county in over a month."

"Down Williams county, yesterday. Word is people ain't happy we walked. Gonna get us and our kin. Another dude says he being followed."

"Give me a name of the deceased."

"Pete Gonzalez, think his real name may be Pedro, don't know for sure."

"Let me check it out."

"Hey, boss, they knew Brian and me was close," Bobby added. "They may be after him, cause I don't think they know where I'm at."

"Okay, good to know, stay low."

Dave punched the phone button to an open line and dialed Rob Alexander's number.

"Sheriff Alexander," came the voice through the phone.

"Rob, Dave, what can you tell me about a crash fatality yesterday named Gonzalez."

"On Route 17, swerved to miss a deer we think. Lost control at high speed, took out a power pole and into a culvert. DOA on the scene. Why?"

"We believe he was a member of the drug farm gang. Anything look suspicious or out of the ordinary?"

"Not really," Rob answered, seeming to be in deep thought. "What are you suggesting, Dave?"

"I'm wondering if there is any evidence that it could have been a hit? My source tells me that the old gang may be out to get the former members that decided to go straight after the bust."

"Really? That's interesting. Let me talk to my people and see if there could be something to that. I'll get back with you. How many of these guys do you think there are, that went straight?"

"At least three that I know of, counting Gonzalez. I'm not sure if there are more."

"Okay, we'll be in touch."

Next, Dave dialed the number for the State Police Drug Task Force in the capital city.

"Trubaldi," the voice said.

"Josh, it's Dave Harbinger, any update on the new location of the Williams County gang?"

"Not really, Dave, some rumors over in Walker county but nothing concrete. Why, have you got something?"

"Just some speculation that there may be some retaliation against former members that walked away after our bust."

"Hum, any evidence?"

"There was a vehicle crash yesterday, down in Williams County, that killed a guy we suspect was one of them. Cause of the crash is unknown, suspect that he may have swerved to miss a deer."

"You're thinking that maybe someone caused the crash with intent?" Josh quizzed.

"Maybe worth checking out. I talked with Alexander about it. He's following up down there. I just wanted to see if you had anything or maybe a lead to follow."

"Let me see what we've got going. I'll let you know if anything shakes out."

"Thanks, Josh."

The next call was to the DEA. Dave talked with George Hoffman to see if they had any information, with the same results. Everyone was looking into it.

Later in the afternoon when they were both in the building, Dave asked Bob and Dan to meet in his office.

"We have information that suggests there were several members of the drug gang who walked away after our bust and are attempting to go straight. Those guys may now be targets for their former buddies. I'm also led to believe that members of their families may be targets as well. One of those guys was killed in a car crash yesterday in Williams county."

"I heard about that crash," Bob offered. "What I saw was that they suspected the cause of the crash to be a deer."

"Yep, that's the one."

"So, he was one that got away?" Dan asked.

"Yes," Dave answered. "He wasn't at the farm when we raided."

"Dave," Bob looked very serious, "are you thinking the deer was one of his former buddies?"

"Why else would it want him dead?" Dave said dead panned.

After a period of laughter and other slightly insensitive cracks, Dave brought the meeting back to seriousness.

"I need to share some information that I'd like for you guys to keep confidential."

Dan and Bob both nodded their agreement.

"You both know Brian's cousin, Bobby," Dave began. "Well what you don't know is that Bobby was one of the drug gang."

The surprise was evident on the faces of both senior staff members.

"Brian and I've been aware of this for many years, but have not shared it. Neither of us has ever been witness to any illegal activity by Bobby, but we were aware of his ties to the drug gang. He was one of the guys that wasn't at the farm when the raid took place. Had he been there, we would have taken him down with the rest of them. I have to admit that I was glad he wasn't there when the bust went down."

Bob and Dan continued to listen intently with no comments.

"Anyway, in the years since the drug bust, Bobby has kept clean. He's been working some for Brian's dad but mostly just hanging around. After Brian was shot, he and I were talking and I offered him a job on my farm. He has been working for me since. He tells me that he has had no contact with the drug guys except for a couple that went straight like he did. One of those guys was the guy killed in Williams county yesterday."

"And he thinks it may have been a hit?" Dan offered.

"Right, he has heard that another of the guys suspects that he's being followed."

"What about Bobby, is he feeling heat?" Bob asked.

"No, but he doesn't think they know where he is. He's living on my farm and has no idea how anyone would know that. Which bring me to my other point. Bobby says that they may go after family members if they can't find him. He says they know how close he is with Brian."

Dan's eyes opened wide, "Are you thinking they may have tried to hit Brian?"

Dave nodded slowly.

"Dave," Bob said cautiously, "this morning our guys that were checking on the perimeter saw a car coming up the farm road on the property behind Brian's house. It turned and made a fast retreat when it got in sight of were their squad was parked. They got a license number with the binoculars. By the time they got back to the squad and gave chase it was in the wind. There was no other unit in the area and even though they got the description out, no joy. Here's the thing, the car was on the hot sheet. Reported stolen in the capital two days ago."

"Now that is interesting," Dave said rubbing his chin.

"I'll get on the horn and see what the capital cops have on the theft," Dan offered. "Did your guys put the description out to the state boys, Bob?"

"Yeah," Bob answered absentmindedly, obviously in deep thought. "Sounds like we might be dealing with someone from outside the county. Which would make the attempt on Brian something unrelated to the robbery. Don't you think?"

Dave and Bob nodded their agreement.

"So, two separate cases," Dan concluded.

"Maybe so," Dave continued nodding, "unrelated but both involving Brian."

"Doesn't seem likely," Dan scratched behind his left ear. "But that seems to be where it's leading us. And, I always say, go where the case leads."

Dave was pondering the case, which was now cases, on his way home from work in deep thought. As he was sitting at the traffic light at the bypass his attention was drawn to a woman in a Jaguar next to him at the light. He looked at her and she stuck her tongue out at him. He blew a kiss back at her as the light turned green and she took off and left him in the dust. He followed Jan home at speeds that should have caused him to get out a ticket book.

She was in the garage leaning on the rear fender of her sleek new car when he walked in from of his squad. He had just parked it in the normal spot at the end of the driveway past the garage.

"You know you could get a ticket driving like that," he said.

"A girl has ways to handle big bruiser cops, if need be," she said batting her eye lashes.

"You think that would work with me?"

"Yes, I do," she smiled, "and if it doesn't, I know the judge."

"No one is above the law, including…."

She kissed him hard on the lips as he was speaking. One kiss led to a second and then a third.

"Maybe we should go inside," he said trying to catch his breath.

"Nope, later, get in the car, Sheriff. You're taking me out to dinner."

As they waited for their fajitas with extra flour tortillas they talked about the activities of day.

"The states attorney tells me they're getting ready to go to trial on the Jose Cruz case. He asked about scheduling a meeting to discuss timing," Jan said.

"Really, that means the city has turned everything over to him, doesn't it?"

"Yes, why?"

"I think that's what I've been looking for. All of the investigation information is now in the states attorney's hands, no longer in the control of the city. So, if we want to reopen the case, it would be his decision."

"I guess so, but you would have to have new evidence or some other reason to reopen."

"Right," Dave said thoughtfully, "can you tell me who has the case in his office?"

"Bob is doing it himself."

"Tiernan is doing it, that's a bit unexpected isn't it?"

"It is, he normally has his hands full keeping the office running, but apparently the mayor requested he handle it personally. The word I get through the grapevine is the mayor wants it done quickly and is afraid the rest of Bob's staff may be too tied up with other things."

"And Bob agreed?"

"I don't know if he agreed with the reasoning, but he's taking the case."

"Okay, I think I'll give him a call," Dave said as the food was placed on the table in front of them.

The next morning Dave placed the call to the States Attorney's office.

"This is Bob," the state's attorney stated as he came on the line.

"Dave Harbinger," Dave answered, "how are you today, Bob?"

"Doing great, Sheriff, thanks, how about you?"

"I'm good. Say Bob I hear you have the Jose Cruz case or am I misinformed."

"That's right, your information is correct. And, I can't begin to guess who that informant might be," the sarcasm was thick. "Do you want to talk about it?"

"As a matter of fact, we would. Would you have time to talk with my chief investigator, Dan Muscovy, and me in your office later today?"

"Sure, how about three?"

"That's good for us. see you then."

At just before three that afternoon, Dave and Dan walked up to a door in the county office building with the words "Robert Tiernan, Lincoln County State's Attorney" in large gold letters. As they were shown into the corner office, Bob got up from his desk and motioned to a large conference table on the left side of the office.

"Bob this is Dan Muscovy," Dave said.

"Nice to finally meet you, Dan, I have seen your name on many reports."

They each took a chair around the table. On the table was a stack of file folders and several storage boxes.

"Here it is," Bob said, "the case against Jose Cruz. Not much they can argue against as far as I can tell."

"Is this the entire file?" Dave asked.

"Yep, every piece of evidence and report filed by the city as part of their investigation. I believe you've seen most of it."

"We have a bit of an issue, Bob," Dave began, "it seems that the city ran the investigation on a crime that was committed in our jurisdiction. The location of the crime was not within the city limits."

"Really?" Bob looked at Dave.

"Yes, the Westside Commons is generally thought to be in the city because the "Welcome to Springfield" sign is on the west end of the center. But in fact, the city limits cut through the middle of the center. As you know there are two separate buildings, each housing several units. The easterly building is within the city limits but the westerly building is not. The Quick Mart where Chief Taylor was killed is on the west end of the west building."

"Wait," Bob held up his hand, "you are not about to suggest we throw all of this out and begin a new investigation due to a jurisdictional blunder, are you? Because if you are, I think we may have a real problem and I don't want this guy to walk."

"No, no, no, not at all," Dave consoled. "But what we would like is our own thorough review of the case files, and all field notes, based on it being in our jurisdiction."

"I'm about ready to set a trial date, Dave."

"We understand that, but wouldn't it be better to recognize the jurisdictional issue now, and resolve it, than to have the defense bring it up during the trial?"

Bob leaned back in his chair, deep in thought. He took a deep breath and rubbed his temples.

"You make a very good point Sheriff. I guess you are right. How long do you expect this review to take?"

"It shouldn't take us too long," Dan spoke, "my guess is that we can get through all of this in a couple of weeks."

"So, you're saying I'll have everything back in my hands and moving forward in two weeks?"

"Not necessarily," Dan continued. "That will happen only if we find nothing that we feel needs further study or investigation. For example, when I last saw the report the ballistics weren't included. If they still aren't in there we would want to know why."

"Are you talking about reopening the case?" Bob's frustration level was rising.

"We have no additional evidence at this point that would require us to reopen, but we also haven't reviewed the entire case file, yet."

Bob leaned forward and dropped his elbows on the table and clapped his hands together. He looked first at Dan then at Dave, and finally at the piles of files and boxes.

"Okay, I guess you guys are right. Take it. But, please let me know what's going on and put a rush on it."

Dave and Dan stared to pick up files and boxes and head for the door.

"Wait," Bob said, "let me help you."

Chapter 15

When Dave and Dan got back to the office they recruited help to unload the boxes of information that the states attorney had allowed them to review. It was taken into the conference room and placed on the large table.

"I'll need to check up on where my people are on current assignments to see who can work on this," Dan commented. "I think we will need at least two others besides me to get through all of this in a timely manner."

"I guess I can put some time in on it," Dave offered.

"Thanks, Dave, but I will need complete control of this process. Although you would be a great asset, your time is often not your own, if you know what I mean."

"What would you think about bringing Brian in to help? It may be a good way to get him back without putting him back out on the street right away."

"I'll give that some thought. Let me talk with Bob. Has he been released by the doctors?"

"I don't know, but last I heard they were talking like he would be expected to be on desk duty for a few weeks when he returns."

"Sheriff," Cheryl stuck her head in the conference room door, "D is on the phone, asked me to see if you could talk."

"Ok, I can talk, check with you later, Dan."

Dave hurried back to his office to take the call.

"Dad!" There was excitement in the voice, "I just got out of the coach's office, they called me up!"

D had spent the last couple of weeks playing class AAA ball with the Iowa Cubs.

"What, already?"

"Yeah, I'm flying out in the morning. They want me to meet the team tomorrow night when they arrive in Houston for a three-game series."

"Three games in Houston?"

"Night game on Friday and afternoon games on Saturday and Sunday."

"Let me call you back, I need to see if Jan would like to spend a weekend in Houston."

"Really? But, Dad, I may not even play."

"I don't care, I want to be there."

"Okay," D hesitated, "Dad, if you and Jan use the plane, any chance that you could bring Mom? I'd like for her to see it too."

"Not a problem, D. I'll see if she can come too. Let me get on it. Do you know the hotel?"

"No, I'm on my way to the office now to get my travel arrangements. I'll let you know."

"Okay, I'll call you back."

"Dad, thanks."

Dave could barely make his fingers punch the speed dial for Jan's office. He couldn't remember when he had been so excited. Wait, yes, he could, on the beach in Key West when Jan had said yes.

"Judge Harbinger." Man, he loved that voice.

"You want to watch the Cubs play ball in Houston this weekend?"

"What? You're kidding. Already?"

"Yep, looks like you're going to get your investment back in a hurry."

"Of course. I wouldn't miss it. Let me call the airport and see when we can get the plane. Wow, this is great. You must be so excited."

"I am. Hey, D asked if we would bring Joyce."

"Of course. That's an understandable request and I'm glad to do it. Let me get on it. Down and back when?"

"It's a night game tomorrow and afternoon games on Saturday and Sunday. So, let's figure to be in Houston by about three and return from there around nine or ten Sunday night."

"Okay, I'm on it."

Dave called his sister's pediatrician office. Joyce was the head nurse for his sister.

"This is Joyce."

"It's Dave, the Cubs have called D up."

"I know, he called me. Isn't that great. I'm so excited for him."

"Look, Jan and I are working on going down to Houston to watch. Would you like to go along?"

"What do you mean?"

"We would take a private plane down tomorrow afternoon and come back Sunday night. We will try to stay in the same hotel as D and get tickets for all three games."

"Well, I appreciate the offer, but I'm not sure I can get off. When would I need to leave?"

"I'll tell you what, ask your boss if she and that cranky old husband of hers want to go along too. That should get you off."

"Are you serious?"

"Sure, why not? It's a six-place plane."

"Let me call you back."

Dave called Jan back to let her know that he had invited Char and Jay to go along too. She told him that the plane was available and they could be ready to go anytime after ten in the morning. She booked the plane and told them she would call back to confirm the departure time.

Friday morning Dave parked his pickup near the man door entrance to the hanger. They were a little earlier than planned because they had picked up Joyce on the way and were not sure how much time to allot for that. Char and Jay had not arrived yet. The plane was out of the hanger and George was just completing his preflight inspection as they carried the bags out.

"Five of you this time, huh?" George said to Dave.

"Yes, we're going to watch my son break into the majors. He got called up by the Cubs against the Astros."

"Wow, that's great. What a great event. You must be really proud."

"I am," Dave motioned toward Joyce. "We're also taking his mother and my sister and her husband with us. They should be here shortly."

"No hurry, my flight plan is good anytime between noon and two."

As George was loading the bags into the plane the doors to the hanger next door opened and a mechanic drove a small tug out. Dave noticed the plane parked in the hanger. It was painted red, white and blue in a very distinctive pattern. The plane itself was a twin-engine jet and appeared to be similar to the one they would be flying in except maybe a bit larger.

"I haven't noticed that plane before," Dave said to George, "that's an interesting paint job."

"Yeah, it is. You don't see that hanger open very often. That's a very nice plane but it isn't used very often. It's the mayor's plane."

"Wait, the mayor has an airplane?"

"Well, it's not really his plane. I think it's owned by some big corporation or something, but he's the one that seems to use it the most, as far as I can tell. I have seen one of the councilmen use it some, and some other folks, but mostly the mayor or his family."

Dave pulled out his pocket notebook and jotted down the tail number of that plane. He punched a speed dial button on his cell phone.

"Dan Muscovy."

"Dan, can you write something down?"

"Just a second, Sheriff, I'll need to pull over."

Dave waited.

"Okay, pen in hand, what ya got?"

Dave read back the tail number of the airplane.

"That's a plane in a hanger at the Springfield airport. I'd like for you to run a trace on it and see if you can determine ownership. Also, see if you can track destinations for say the last year."

"Okay, I'll get on it when I get back into the office. What's the interest?"

"Maybe nothing, just curiosity as much as anything."

"Okay, have a good time at the games. Hope D does well."

They touched down at Houston Hobby airport at six minutes after three. This time the car that came out to meet the plane was a minivan. Dave looked at Jan as they loaded the bags into it.

"All they had," she frowned.

The team was staying at the Hilton but there weren't three rooms available. However, Jan was able to find and book three rooms at the Westin which was right across the street from Minute Maid park, home of the Houston Astros. It was only about ten miles from the airport to the hotel so they had plenty of time to check in and get to game. The start time was 6:05, but Dave wanted to get to the park early to try and catch D in batting practice. Ball park hot dogs sounded like dinner tonight.

D was able to get tickets for everyone and they were waiting for them when they checked at the will call booth. Their seats were on the first base side a little less than half way up the first section right behind the visitor's dugout.

As they walked up out of the tunnel to the stands, Dave saw the batting screen was around the pitcher's mound and the Cubs were on the field. He quickly scanned the infield and his heart skipped a beat when he recognized the player in Cubs jersey number ten standing behind second base. As much as he would hate to admit it to anyone, tears welled up in his eyes as the emotion grabbed him. He couldn't speak. He touched Jan's arm and pointed.

"Wow," she said softly. She squeezed Dave's arm, leaned over and whispered, "It's okay, Dad. Nothing wrong with getting emotional at a time like this."

She kissed him on the cheek.

"Is that him out there?" Char said behind them.

"Yes, number ten," Jan answered.

Dave looked at Joyce, there were tears streaming down her cheeks. She didn't speak either.

"He sure looks like a ball player to me," Jay said.

Dave felt like he was floating, as they found their seats. More accurately, as Jan found their seats. Dave was not prepared for the emotional rush that had overtaken him. It had not really sunk in until right now. D actually had a chance to play major league ball. So much time and effort could be about to pay off, and his dad was just now realizing that.

Wait, about to pay off? No, has paid off. This is a regular season professional baseball game and D is in uniform on the field. Game On!

"I have no idea why I hadn't thought about how I would feel," Dave said to Jan. "It hit me like a ton of bricks."

"You?" Jan said. "Look at Joyce."

The five seats were in a row. Dave, Jan, Jay, Char and Joyce in order from the aisle. Dave leaned over to where he could see Joyce who was bawling like a baby. Char had her arm around her.

"There're coming in," Jan said.

Dave turned his attention back to the field. The players were all heading for the dugout. As he trotted toward them, D was looking up into the stands in their direction. Dave made eye contact with him just as he was crossing the baseline. Dave stood up. D waved.

D slowed his pace to a walk and he made eye contact with each of them and waved. He stopped at the top of the steps leading down into the dugout and waved. He took a little extra time waving toward Joyce.

The Astros took the field to warm up.

"Dave, I think it's time you and I get these lovely ladies their supper," Jay said with a grin.

"I'm in," Dave agreed. "How many dogs do each of you want?"

"Oh no," Jay continued, "it's the works, not just dogs, but chips and drinks too."

Off they went to procure the meals.

About an hour later as they continued to enjoy the atmosphere of the ballpark the voice of the PA announcer came through the speakers.

"Welcome to tonight's game between the Chicago Cubs and your Houston Astros. Here's the starting lineups for tonight's game. First for the Chicago Cubs. Batting first and playing second base is number 10 David Harbinger Junior, Harbinger."

Dave gasped. Jan grabbed his arm again. The emotion returned. He didn't hear another thing the announcer said though entire lineup of both teams. As a matter of fact, he was pretty much in a daze. Jan talked and he nodded agreement not really sure what she was saying. She didn't seem to mind. She seemed to know what was going on inside him.

Someone came out onto the field and threw the first pitch to the Astro's catcher. The teams came out to the baselines for the "Star Spangled Banner" as everyone stood. Dave removed his Cubs cap and saluted. Everyone sat down and the Astros took the field. As the pitcher threw some warm up pitches, D came out of the dugout, bat in hand and swung in the on-deck circle. The pitcher nodded to the catcher who threw the next pitch to second base. The umpire yelled play ball and the game was on.

D stepped up to the right side of the plate.

"Right-hand pitching means left-hand batting," Jan said with authority.

"You learn so well."

D took a couple of practice swings while the catcher showed the pitcher a sign. The pitcher nodded, stood up, twisted putting his right shoulder behind him, and sent a rocket velocity hard ball right at D.

From their position to the right of the plate, Dave could not tell if the pitch was over the plate, but he could see that it was coming in just above belt high. Dave saw D's right leg extend as his weight shifted to his left. Dave could not see the bat strike the ball but he heard it. The crack of a wood bat against a baseball is a sound like no other, and this time it was his son in the major leagues making that sound.

Dave could not pick up the ball as it left the bat, but he did see it as it flew just over ten feet high between first and second base. Neither in-fielder had a chance at it. It skipped onto the ground about fifteen feet in front of the charging right fielder. By the time the ball was in a glove on the first bounce, D was almost to first base. By the time the ball hit the first baseman mitt, D was making his turn into foul territory in right field.

The first pitch in his major league career was a line shot single to right off of right-handed pitching.

Dave, Jan, Joyce, Char and Jay all jumped up cheering at the same time. Other cheers besides theirs were not very plentiful. The Houston Astros fans did not greet D's first at bat accomplishment with the same degree of appreciation.

The next batter hit a line shot right at the short stop for the first out. D had taken a lead off of first but had no problem getting back on the bag before the throw from short thumped into the first baseman's mitt.

D was taking a big lead off of first. Being a right-hand pitcher, he had a better chance of recognizing a play on him than if the pitcher had been a lefty. The pitcher attempted a pick off play between the second and third pitches to the next batter but D saw his foot slip off the rubber and lunged back to the bag just in time.

"Dave, you're hurting me," Jan said.

He looked down and realized that he was squeezing Jan's hand so hard that his knuckles were white.

"Oh, baby, I'm sorry."

"It's okay," she offered, patting him on the shoulder. "But, please, try to remember to take a breath every once in a while."

Two more pitches made the count three balls and one strike. The first base coach stepped over and whispered in D's ear as the catcher was throwing the ball back to the mound. D nodded.

"Any idea what he said to him?" Jan asked.

"Not really, but it's a good bet they wouldn't be relying on D to know the signs in his first game. They're probably telling him what's going on. You know, new guy thing. But with a three and one count, the odds are good for it to be a good pitch, so maybe it's a hit and run."

As Dave was talking the pitcher let go off the ball and D took off for second base. The batter hit a ground ball to third. The third baseman made the play, looked at second and saw that D was already sliding in, so his only play was to first. D was in scoring position with two outs. He should be able to score on a base hit.

Chapter 16

"I guess you called that one," Jan said. "Good job."

"Thanks, now if they can get a base hit he can score. Wouldn't it be great if he could score on his very first at bat in the major leagues? Now that would be something."

But it wasn't to be. The next batter struck out in five pitches. D was left stranded on second base as the side was retired.

As the Cubs took the field for the bottom half of the first, D took his spot to the left side of second base. The inning had no action for him and the Astros went down one, two, three. He did not come up to bat in the second inning. In the field in the second inning he caught a line shot hit just to his right for the last out.

D was up second in the third inning. He walked in six pitches with one long foul ball into the left field stands. The next batter hit a hard grounder to short and D was thrown out at second on the front end of a double play, to end the inning. There was still no score by either team.

The Astros scored in the bottom of the third on a home run to right center. The fourth inning was scoreless but the Cubs left two on base on a pair of well-hit singles.

In the top of the fifth D came to the plate with a man on first and two outs. The Astros had changed to a left-handed pitcher so D was now batting right. He hit three long foul balls down the left base line and was facing a full count of three balls and two strikes. The pitcher delivered pitch number seven and D pounded the ball right down the left baseline just out of reach of the diving third baseman. By the time the left fielder got to the ball, D was standing on second base and the runner from first had scored. D had tied the game at one to one.

The next batter took a walk. Now there were two on with two outs. The following batter entered into a duel with the pitcher to see who would give up first. Every pitch was in the strike zone and every pitch was hit hard. Eight pitches came in and eight pitches ended up in the left field stands or out of the ball park to the left of the left field fowl pole. Naturally the left fielder and the third baseman were playing toward the line by the ninth pitch. When the ninth pitch came, with a count of no strikes and two balls, the batter sent it straight toward left center field into the gap created by the line hugging left fielder. D scored easily from second and when the dust had settled there were men on second and third and the score was two to one, Cubs.

In the bottom of the fifth, with one out and a man on first, D grabbed a hard-hit grounder on the first bounce while moving to his left. He flipped the ball under handed behind him, while still moving left, to the short stop on second base. The short stop bare-handed D's throw and threw the batter out at first for a double play to end the inning.

As the third batter in the Cubs' half of the sixth walked up to the plate, Dave's cell phone vibrated in his pocket. He looked at the caller ID but did not recognize the number.

"Hello," he said hesitantly.

"Hey, dad, what ya think," D's voice said.

"You're doing great. Better than I had hoped."

"Well, I'm out for the rest of the game. They want another guy to get some playing time. I told the batting coach that you are here and he gave me his phone and said I should call you. He said to tell you that he thinks I'm in with this team. Of course, he says it's not his decision. But he says he has little doubt."

"That's great D."

"Hey, you all come down beside the dugout after the game. I'll come out for a few minutes. Okay."

"Sure."

"Gotta go," D hung up.

"That was D on the phone," Dave said leaning over so Jay, Char and Joyce could hear. "He's out for the rest of the game to give another guy some playing time."

They nodded. Dave noted that Joyce still looked as excited as when they arrived. Bet I do too, he thought.

"Does that mean you can take a breath now?" Jan asked.

"Okay, I'll settle down. But, man, has this been something or what?"

"It certainly has. I'm so glad we got to do this. It would have been tragic to miss it." She squeezed his hand and smiled.

He took a deep breath and for the first time in hours exhaled deeply and relaxed. He inhaled again, held it, and felt his body use the oxygen to calm him. After a few seconds he exhaled. He was feeling much more relaxed now and felt ready to enjoy the rest of the game.

"You look like you're much more relaxed now," Jan said close to his ear.

"Yes, I am."

"Good, because I want to let you know that I'm pregnant."

"What? Really?"

"The doctor called this morning with confirmation. Looks like you're going to be a daddy again."

Dave laughed, "Wow, I don't see how any day could be as great as this one. I'm overwhelmed."

"Me too. I wanted to tell you earlier, but you were so excited about D that I didn't want to spoil that. Also, I didn't want to upset Joyce. I don't think we should tell anyone else just yet. Are you okay with that?"

"Oh, that is good thinking. Yes, you're right. We can tell everyone anytime we want to. But for now, it's just you and me. I love you."

They talked together in low voice for the rest of the game, hardly noticing what was going on out on the field.

Their conversation was interrupted when Jay asked, "Hey, you two want to just sit here, you know the game's over, right?"

"Right, yeah," Dave came back into the present. "D wants us to go down by the dugout. He says he'll come out for a minute. We were waiting for the people to go by."

"Un huh," Jay retorted. "Looked like some long-range planning for my nephew's baseball career going on there to me."

"Okay," Dave responded, "you're about right."

They followed the aisle down the steps to the right side of the visitor dugout. As they went Dave checked the scoreboard and saw that the Cubs had won two to one. Just as they all got down there, D walked up out of the dugout.

"Hi, mom," he said as he leaned over the fencing to hug Joyce. "I'm glad you could come."

"I have your dad and aunt Char to thank for that," she answered. "You looked really good out there. What did the team think?"

"I think everything went okay as far as they're concerned. But the only feedback I have so far is from the hitting coach who says I did well," he moved over and hugged Char. "Aunt Char, thanks for coming and letting mom off work."

"Oh, sweety, I'm just so glad we could be here. And it would have been terrible if your mom couldn't have been here to see this."

D shook his uncle Jay's hand while Char was talking.

"Great game, son," Jay said.

"Thanks Uncle Jay."

D hugged Jan, "This all wouldn't have happen without you. I'll never be able to repay you."

"You already have, whether you know it or not. I just watched your dad pop every button on every shirt he owns. Even the ones he isn't wearing. To see him like that is more than any wife could ever hope to see. You owe me nothing, that's for sure."

"Just the same, thanks."

Dave and D hugged.

"It was great fun, Dad, glad you could make it."

"Are we going to see you later?"

"Not tonight, and early workout in the morning. We can do dinner after the game tomorrow. I have to run, now. My teammates want to throw me into the shower with all my clothes on or something. I don't know, part of being a rookie. I love you guys. See you tomorrow." He headed back into the dugout.

"I'm buying steaks for everyone," Jay said pointedly. "Let's go find the best steak in Houston. How can we not celebrate at a time like this?"

"I can't let you buy for everyone. This is my party," Dave objected.

"No, I'm buying dinner. You paid for the plane and made all the arrangements. Food is on me, no argument."

"No, Jay, the plane was on Jan, not me. She's the one that sold the law partnership, that's what pays for planes."

"That's bull, Dave. She's your wife, so that money is yours as well as hers. You can't pull that on me. Here's the deal. You and Jan have paid your share, now Char and I will pay our share by picking up all the meals. And through all of this Joyce is our guest because she's the one, out of all of us, that is the most deserving as mother of the ball player. If not for her none of us would be here. End of discussion."

"But, Jay," Char interrupted, "it's ten at night."

"Okay," Jay looked deflated, "how about White Castle?"

The next afternoon, D batted in the lead-off spot and got a base hit in the first inning. He chalked up his first major league at bat without getting on base in the third inning when he hit a shot directly to the short stop for the final out of the inning. He played four innings at second base. The Cubs lost that game four to two.

That evening they all met with D for dinner at a nice steak house near D's hotel. As could be expected, D went on and on about the experience of being on a big-league ball team. He shared his impressions of the other players, at some length. After only two games he had already determined a lot about the guys, some good, some not so much. Dave and the others took it all in realizing the unique opportunity to share in an adventure of which most could only dream.

Sunday evening found them climbing on board the plane for the return flight to Springfield. The weekend had been a blur. They had seen the Cubs win 2 of 3 ball games. D played in each game. He played second base in the first two games. In the third game he entered in the sixth inning at third base. For the weekend he was five for seven at the plate with one walk. He played error free ball in the field. All in all, it was an excellent start for his career with the Cubs.

D had shared with Dave and Jan that he had signed an initial contract for one year at $567,000, with incentive bonuses of $1 million each for batting average (over .300) and on base percentage (over .350). They also gave him a

$200,000 signing bonus. It seemed like a good bet that Jan would get a return on her investment in D, at least for the time being.

"I bet you're going to have a tough time getting back in the work grove tomorrow," Jan said after they dropped Joyce off and headed for home. "I know I will."

"I think you're right. But that's okay, I wouldn't trade this weekend for anything, and I mean that."

"Me too. I even think Joyce had a great time, although I think she did feel like a fifth wheel."

"Well, just the same, I'm glad she came along. She deserves some good times," Dave added.

"Anything exciting expected this week at work?"

"Not that I know about right now, how about you?"

"Nope, and now that you grabbed the Cruz case away from Tiernan my schedule may be opening up some."

"Don't get to sure of that, we haven't found anything that would create any delay. At least that I'm aware of yet."

"Remember your feeling that something wasn't right? That still makes me think that you will find something. We'll see."

Sleep did not come easy for Dave. Even though he was worn out from the weekend, as he shifted his thoughts back to the business at hand in the Sheriff's office. He was troubled by what could be going on. The Cruz case was now in their hands, so they would be able to comb through all the data and investigative material to see if there is anything more there. He felt that issue could now resolve itself. But he was not nearly as confident about how they would be able to protect Brian, and Bobby, from the drug gang revenge. All the drug guys would need to do was wait until the current heat blows over. Brian and Bobby could be easy targets after that.

He needed a plan that would force their hand and flush them out. Or a way to find them without them knowing he is onto them. There must be a way, but how, he was thinking as he finally fell asleep at just before two.

Chapter 17

"Oh, brother, I'm not ready," Jan complained as the alarm went off. "Can I be sick today?"

"Now, judge, how would that look to the criminals?" Dave mumbled while he fumbled to find the alarm shut off.

"I tell you what, sheriff. If you don't catch any, I won't have to deal with 'em. So, you just stay right here in bed with me and neither of us will have to deal with it."

"And neither of us will have a job tomorrow," he countered.

"Wait, let's think this through. That may not be all bad," she remarked but got up anyway.

Their morning routine was a bit different this morning. More causal and less hurried, with considerable amounts of hugging and kissing. They were not eager to part company, and the result was that time got away and the next thing they knew they were both going to be late.

So, Dave finally walked into the office almost an hour after he normally did. When he walked pasted the reception desk into the main office area, he was shocked. There was a standing ovation and a considerable amount of cheering. As he looked around, almost everyone had on Cubs attire. There were Cubs jerseys, Cubs hats, Cubs jackets, Cubs coffee cups, you name it. Across the wall above his office door was a large banner that read, Go Harbinger, with the number ten and the Cubs logo repeated all over it.

"Whoa, I'm overwhelmed," Dave said. "Thanks everyone."

"So, tell us about how it feels to be the father of a star," Bob said standing in his office doorway, a Cubs hat on his head.

"I have to say I wasn't prepared for the emotional rush I felt when I saw him on the field in that uniform. It was unbelievable."

Questions came from every direction as Dave filled his people in on the trip to Houston. Everyone had watched at least some of the games. They wanted as much information as they could get about the inside of the major leagues. Dave sat down on the edge of desk and spent almost thirty minutes answering questions and providing information about what he had seen over the week end.

"Sheriff, call on one," Cheryl finally interrupted.

Dave went into his office, sat behind his desk and punched the flashing button.

"Harbinger," he said.

"Dave, it's Josh. You got a minute?"

"Sure, Josh, what can I do for the State Police Drug Task Force today?"

"Well first let tell you how great it was watching your son play ball. What a break out series. You must be proud."

"Thanks, Josh. Yes, we are very proud. Jan and I were able to go to Houston for the games. It was great."

"I'll bet that was a good time. Good for you."

"It was, thanks again."

"Hey, the reason for my call was that I got some intel on that stolen car you asked about. There was another car boosted from that same location at about the same time. We think that second car was used in a contract hit of a drug dealer over on the west side of town. At least it matches the description of a vehicle seen nearby just prior to the hit. The car was later abandoned in a shady area on the south side. It was recovered but had been wiped clean."

"That's interesting. How do you know it was a contract hit?"

"We don't really, but PD says it has all of the makings of being a pro, shot gun at close range, weapon left on the scene, wiped clean, no markings," Josh concluded.

"Okay, I appreciate the info. Anything new on the Williams County drug gang?"

"No, still nothing more that we had before. They'll pop up somewhere, I'm sure of it."

"Okay, Josh, thanks."

"See ya, Dave, and go Cubs."

As Dave hung up the phone, Cheryl said, "Dan asked for you to meet him in the conference room when you have time."

Dave headed down toward the conference room. As he walked in, he saw the table was covered in paper. There were several file folders, glossy photos, charts and graphs. The boxes they had carried out of the states attorney's office were sitting on the floor or on chairs, mostly empty.

Dan was at the far end of the table, his nose buried in a file folder. There were two other officers at the table, one in uniform and one in plain clothes. Both the officers had yellow legal pads and pen in hand.

"What have we got?" Dave asked, sitting down in a chair near at the table.

"What we don't have is a ballistics report on any of the weapons," Dan stated. "So, we have a reason to do a complete reopen of the case, if we decide we need to."

"Where is the report? State crime lab?"

"Yes, they say it is expected to clear there next week, but they have no authority to give it to us. SPD sent it in, so that's where it goes."

"Does SPD know we have the case?"

"Since no one has called me, my guess is no. I'm sure they would want to know what we're up to, if they knew."

"Have we found anything else that doesn't hold muster, besides the ballistics report?" Dave inquired.

"Maybe, the interview of the clerk seems to be lacking. Either it was not well documented or some obvious questions weren't asked."

"Give me a for-instance."

"They asked the clerk to tell his version of what happened. Which he did. But there's no record of him being asked what the perps said, either to him or to each other. He didn't offer any dialog in his statement."

"Did he offer what the SPD guys said when they came in?"

"No, no documented dialogue at all."

"Did the SPD guys offer dialogue in their statements?"

"Yes, quite detailed about what they said," Dan said.

"Well, sounds like the clerk didn't offer and no one asked. But is that a reason to open the case?" Dave scratched his chin. "Anything else? I think we need more."

"Still looking. But, oh, wait, one other thing, there seems to have been very little effort spent on the background of the perps. The info on Cruz came mainly from interviewing him, no real checks on that that we see. As far as Flores is concerned there is not really any back ground," Dan looked though some papers, "that we can find."

"Nothing?" Dave quizzed.

"Current address in Williams County," Dan read from a sheet of paper, "driver's license, green card, some cash. Sounds like they just went with what he had on his person."

"Did they search the residence?"

"No documentation of a search. They may have not thought it relevant."

"Do you have the address? Is it the same for both of them?"

"Yes, I do, and it is the same for both," Dan confirmed as he handed the sheet of paper to Dave.

"Let me see if Rob Alexander will check on ownership of that property for us." Dave got up to leave, "you guys keep digging, and thanks for the effort."

Rob agreed to check out the ownership of the Flores and Cruz residence. He told Dave he would get back with him.

Dave started to review the monthly financial report that had been waiting on his desk for approval. He realized as he started looking at the number that it was not going to work. His mind would not let him. He needed some time to think and maybe some fresh air. He dialed the phone.

"Hello."

"Marie, it's Dave, is Brian busy?"

"Hold on Dave, he's right here."

"Hey, pal, what a series. I about popped my skull back open," Brian joked.

"Yeah, it was great. Hey, are you busy, could I stop by for a few minutes?"

"Sure, that'd be great. Something up?"

"No, not really just want to run somethings by you. Leaving now."

"Cheryl, I'm going to be out for a while. Probably till after lunch."

"Sure, Sheriff, tell Brian I say hi."

As Dave drove toward Brian's he continued to mull over the various issues confronting him. He knew he needed to get his thoughts organized and hoped that by talking them through with Brian he could begin to put a viable plan together. He just felt like he was reacting rather than investigating or solving anything.

Deep in thought, he was about five miles from Brian's when the radio broke his trance.

"All units, gray late model Nissan last four 8847 wanted for questioning, last seen north bound on County 17, use caution may be armed."

Dave was coming up to County 17. A gray Nissan was making a right hand turn off 17 onto the state highway. As it passed going in the opposite direction Dave noted the last four of the license number, 8847.

"Command One, gray Nissan spotted going east on State 42 just east of County 17, in pursuit."

Dave hit the switch for all of the lights as he pulled over onto the right shoulder preparing for a u turn. There was an oncoming Cadillac that he let pass before jerking the wheel hard to the left, spinning the Charger around almost in its tracks. The Cadillac had made a dive toward the right shoulder giving him the road as he accelerated past it.

"Command One is in pursuit of Gray Nissan on State 42 east bound just east of County 17," his radio said.

He saw the Nissan pass a car a little less than one quarter mile ahead. He was accelerating but didn't seem to be gaining. He glanced at the speedometer. He was doing eighty. He hit the siren.

"Nissan is not stopping, high speed pursuit underway, east bound State 42 approaching Stark Road," he shouted into the mic.

"All units, Command One in high speed pursuit of gray Nissan, last four ending 8847 east bound State 42 approaching Stark Road," dispatch responded.

The speedometer read one hundred twelve. The gap
between them was closing now but not nearly as much as
Dave would have liked. On the good side, traffic was
relatively light and the motorists seemed to be paying
attention based on their movements to the respective
shoulders as he approached.

"Command One continuing pursuit east bound on State 42
approaching County 13," he reported.

"Command One, squad twenty-two approaching your
position from the south on 13, will join pursuit," dispatch
responded.

As he passed through the intersection with County 13, he
saw the marked county sheriff cruiser with all lights
flashing approaching from the south. Shortly after he
cleared the intersection squad twenty-two fell in behind
him.

"Command One, squad seventeen approaching your
position from the east, near Bunker Road," dispatch said.

Bunker Road was about one mile east of Dave's current
position.

Dave was catching up with the Nissan. He was about fifty
yards behind it when the brake lights came on and the car
made a quick left turn.

Dave also hit the brakes, and spun the wheel to the left at
the same time setting up a sliding turn to follow the Nissan.
He released the brake and pushed back down on the gas.

He was now heading north on Cedar Road behind the Nissan. His drifting high speed turn had cut the distance to the Nissan down to about twenty yards.

"Command One continuing pursuit, now north bound on Cedar Road, north of State 42," he told dispatch.

As the dispatcher was relaying the change in direction, Dave noted that the county road they were now on was straight and clear as far as he could see. The turn had reduced their speed to just under fifty. He stabbed the accelerator to the floor.

The 5.7liter hemi V8 in the Charger accelerated far quicker than the four cylinders in the Japanese car. In about 2 seconds Dave was right on the rear bumper of the Nissan. He jerked the wheel to the left and before the other driver could react, pulled along beside him.

Dave could now see that the driver was a dark-skinned man with jet black hair. The Nissan moved toward the center of the road, but Dave did not give. As the two cars came together Dave hit the brake and spun the wheel to the right. This caused the front bumper of the Charger to contact the Nissan just behind the rear wheel in the quarter panel. The smaller car began to spin to the right. The right rear tire dropped off the side of the asphalt and before the driver could correct for the skid, the car was off in the ditch. It began to roll violently.

Dave brought his squad to a halt about the same time that the Nissan quit rolling. It had completed four complete somersaults and ended up right. The top was crushed in and the glass was all broken. The car looked as if it had just come out of a crusher.

"Command One, pursuit terminated, ten seventeen on Cedar Road half mile north of State 42, request fire and ambulance, possible entrapment."

Squad twenty-two was stopping just behind Dave's car and as he got out, he could see the flashing lights of another squad less than a quarter mile away.

Dave's cell phone rang.

"Dave," Bob's voice said as Dave stood next to his squad listening, "that car was on the lane behind Brian's. Our guy put a scope on him and saw a long gun. Be careful."

Deputy Nelson approached the battered Nissan with weapon at the ready.

"Thanks, but he just took a hard roll. I don't think he's going to give anyone any trouble ever again, unless I miss my guess."

"That bad?"

"Afraid so, I put a pitman on him and it caused a rollover. The car is crushed," Dave said. "Deputy Nelson is checking on him now."

As Nelson returned his weapon to the holster, he shook his head. Several sirens could now be heard approaching their position. In a matter of a few short minutes the county road was clogged with emergency equipment. The fire department had to use the jaws of life to cut the top off the Nissan. Once that was done, they were able to pull the driver out of the wreckage. He had not been wearing his seat belt and had no chance of surviving the crash. There was a Nosler M48 long range rifle with a high-power scope in the front seat of the car.

The driver had no identification of any kind. He was wearing driving gloves. All that he had on him was nine thousand six hundred and sixty-two dollars in cash. No credit cards, no cell phone or even a watch, nothing.

When they ran the full plate number, it came back that the car had been reported stolen in the capital the day before. The rifle had no numbers on it. There was a box of hollow point bullets in the car. The box of bullets was full except for the same number that were in the gun.

Of course, they would check, but they didn't expect to find any finger prints on anything, except his hands.

Chapter 18

Dave called Brian to let him know that he would not be coming by after all and headed back to the office. Once there, he asked Bob and Dan to come to his office.

"I'm thinking we have just apprehended a professional hit man," Dave began. "What do you guys think?"

"Sure looks that way to me," Dan offered.

"How do we prove who he was and who he was working for?" Dave asked.

"Good question," Dan rubbed his forehead. "I'll get on the horn to the Capital PD and see what they have on the car theft. That seems to be the only real lead we have to follow."

"Maybe, but if we assume it's the drug gang going after Brian doesn't that give us a direction?" Bob suggested.

"Let's follow that train of thought," Dave said thoughtfully. "If that's the case, is it possible that they were the ones that set up the robbery as a means to get Brian?"

"Wait, you're suggesting that both the robbery and this hit guy was the same motive?" Dan questioned. "How would they have known that Brian would have been at the scene of the robbery?"

"Maybe they had him staked out and timed the robbery when they knew he would respond," offered Dave.

"If that was the case, Chief Taylor got in the way of a hit, disguised as a robbery," Bob said.

"Interesting theory, Dave," Dan said. "Let me dig into Cruz interrogation report to see if there is anything there. I don't recall anything like that, but I wasn't looking for it before."

"Good idea, Dan. I'll get with DEA to let them know what we're thinking and see if they have any recommendations. Thanks guys," Dave said as Bob and Dan got up.

"Oh, Dave," Dan said pulling a slip of paper out of his shirt pocket, "I got the info from the FAA on that plane you asked about. It's owned by a company in the Caymans, Integrity Developmental Consulting. They have an office in Memphis. Here's a list of the flight plans it filed for the last year."

"Thanks," Dave took the slip of paper.

Dave dialed George Hoffman at the DEA.

After catching up and talking about D and the Cubs, Dave shifted the conversation. "The reason I called, George, is to bring you up to speed on some developments we think may have to do with the remnants of the Williams County drug gang."

"Oh, what's up?"

"A couple of events, first, an auto crash two days ago killed one of the former members who was not arrested in our bust. Our information is that he had gone straight. The cause of the crash is not known, maybe caused by a deer but also could have been run off the road. The second event this morning is a suspected attempt on the life of a close family member of another drug guy gone straight. One of our deputies observed a guy with a long gun near the residence. We attempted to apprehend the suspect but he was killed in a crash during high speed pursuit. He appeared to be a professional hit man. We're wondering if the drug gang is attempting revenge on the guys that walked away, or their families."

"I see your point," George commented. "If they have set up shop somewhere in the area, they could very well be looking for the guys that were with them before. They wouldn't want anyone around with knowledge of who they are or how they operate. So, they would take them out. I don't think they would go after family members though, unless they can't find the guy they're after. Then they may try something like that to flush him out."

"Bingo, that particular guy is off their radar, we think."

"What do you have on the hit man?"

"Not much, he had no ID. Finger prints are being processed. We only know that the car was stolen in the Capital. We're checking on that."

"Okay, Dave, thanks for bringing me up to speed. You may very well be on to something. I'll start shaking the bushes a little harder to see what we can scare up. We'll be in touch."

As he put the phone back in its cradle, Dave picked up the slip of paper Dan had given him. He looked down the list of destinations for the plane George had called the Mayor's plane. There were four trips to Grand Cayman Island. There was a single trip to Los Angeles and to Seattle. It showed two trips to Washington D.C. There was a trip last winter to West Palm Beach, Florida. In all the plane had made nine trips in the last year. This seemed like a significant amount of money to tie up in a plane to be used so little.

Dave turned his attention to the ownership. He had never heard of Integrity Developmental Consulting. He turned to his computer and did a google search. He found several variations on Integrity Consulting, but no result for that exact name.

Dave pick up the phone and dialed information and asked for Memphis. His inquiry for Integrity Developmental Consulting produced a phone number. He wrote it down on the slip of paper next to the company name. He dialed the number.

He heard a machine answer with the standard, "Integrity Developmental Consulting, we're sorry we can't take your call, please leave a message." He didn't leave a message.

He picked up his national directory and found the number for the Sheriff's office in Shelby County, Tennessee where Memphis is located. When his call was answered he identified himself and asked for the investigations section. His request was simple, to see if they would assist him in a discreate check on the location of the company with that phone number and any other information that may be relevant. He was told they would be glad to assist and would return his call once information has been gathered.

He was curious about the plane, but based on where he believed the case was taking them, it was probably not part of the investigation.

That evening after dinner, Dave had filled Jan in on all of the events of the day. They were talking about baby names and cuddling on the couch waiting for the Cubs game to start on TV when the phone rang. Dave picked it up.

"Hey, Dad," Chris said.

"Hi, Chris, how are things?"

"Great, D called me this morning. He sounds like he is having the time of his life."

"Who wouldn't? We're waiting for the game to start, I suppose you're watching too."

"You bet. Hey, I'm going to be coming home this week end. Are you guys going to be around?"

"We are, no plans, other than the normal stuff."

"Good, I want to go car shopping. Can you go with me?"

"Sure, Chris, but what's wrong with your car?"

"Nothing, except it's old and not especially great."

"I'm sensing there's more."

"Okay, D says he is looking into leasing a car and thought he would just lease two. One for him and one for me. He asked me to pick one out and let him know what I want."

"Well, that's great, Chris. Any idea what you may want?"

"I'm thinking Corvette, but I'm open to other ideas."

"Did D say he would pick up the insurance too?"

"He did. He said he would pay for the lease, insurance, and all car expenses. He's going to give me a credit card to use for gas and stuff."

"Okay, sounds like your big brother wants to help you out. I've got no problem with that."

"All right, I'll be home late Friday night. I get out of class at two."

"We'll leave the light on."

"D's leasing Chris a car," Dave turned to Jan.

"So I gathered. Guess you're going car shopping."

"I guess so. Want to come?"

"Oh, I think you boys can handle it. I think I'll stay home and start planning for my little girl's room."

"Little girl? You know it could be a boy."

"Could be, but it's not. It's a little girl, I just know."

"Are you going to be disappointed if it's a boy?"

"Of course not, but it's not."

The game came on and they sat glued to the television as D and the Cubs played a close one against the Reds. D played second base and hit in the leadoff spot. He had three walks, a single and was hit by a pitch.

"The other teams are already pitching around him," Dave told Jan in the sixth inning. "he's already becoming an on base threat. It's going to be hard for him to get hits if they don't pitch to him."

After nine innings the game was tied at four. D scored off of one of his walks and got an RBI on his single. He had played the entire game.

In the tenth inning D came to the plate with the bases loaded and two out.

"They have to pitch to him now," Dave told Jan. "With the bases loaded there's nowhere to put him so they have to throw strikes to try to get him out."

The first pitch was down the middle and D hit a line shot along the third base line just foul. The second pitch was way outside for a ball. The third pitch was down the middle but low for the second ball. As D stared into his eyes, the pitcher stretched, paused to check the runners, then threw a fast ball right down the middle at belt level. D's bat met the ball right over the plate and sent it right back over the pitcher's head. It dropped into centerfield behind second base as runners scored from second and third. When the play was over, there was a man on third and D was on first with a two-run single. The score was six to four.

The next batter hit a line shot to the third baseman for the third out. In the Reds' half of the inning they went down in order and the Cubs won on D's tenth inning single.

On Saturday afternoon Dave and Chris went out car shopping. They stopped by the Chevy dealer to get a close look at the Corvette. Chris was sure it was exactly what he needed for good weather driving, but not so sure it would be best for winter in Lafayette, or hauling stuff back and forth to school. Dave suggested that they at least look at some other options. Chris agreed and they headed over to Delagoto Motors.

"Maybe an SUV would better meet your current need," Dave offered, "The Porsche Cayenne or a Range Rover, perhaps."

"You may be right, let's see what's out there."

As Chris was checking out the selection in the showroom, Dave was reminded that not only had Jan leased cars from here, but also the drug dealers. He asked to see Winston.

"Hi, sheriff, you're not here to take my newest car from me, are you?" Winston said with a smile.

"No, not this time. Chris is looking for a car. I wanted to take the opportunity to talk with you about the leases you had with the drug dealers a few years back. Did you get all of your cars back?"

"Mostly. We never found a couple of the cars, a Mercedes and a Porsche, as I recall. But all the rest were either reacquired due to the police action or the leases were converted."

"What do you mean converted?"

"Oh, that means the particular user of the vehicle transferred it into his name and continued the lease," Winston explained.

Dave knew that Bobby kept his BMW after the bust. He knew it had been leased by the drug gang. It had not hit him until right now that Bobby must have converted the lease into his name.

"How many leases were converted?" Dave asked.

Winston hesitated, "Is this an official inquiry, Sheriff?"

"I don't have a warrant, if that's what you're asking, but it could be a great help in an investigation we are working on."

"Let's go into my office," Winston motioned for Dave to follow him.

"Chris, I need to check out another matter. You go ahead and look around," Dave told his son as he followed Winston.

At his desk, Winston began searching through the files on his computer. After a few seconds he said, "Okay, here we are. Of the leases we had outstanding when you so drastically impacted one of my best lease customers, we had eight converted."

"Would it be possible for you to give me the names and addresses of the eight?" Dave asked.

"I'm not comfortable sharing that information without a warrant, Sheriff. Would you excuse me for a few minutes, I need to go to the restroom," Winston said as he turned his computer monitor so that Dave could see it and laid a pad of paper and pen on the desk. He got up and walked out of the office.

Dave looked at the screen in front of him. He quickly scanned down the list. He saw Bobby's name. It showed that Bobby had leased a BMW about a month after the drug bust. It also showed the lease was terminated about one year ago, and the car was returned and resold.

He wrote down the names and addresses of the other seven entries on the note pad. One of the names he recognized as the guy killed in the car crash, his account was still active although he had exchanged cars last summer for a new one. Four of the listing showed as still active, Bobby and two others were terminated. Two of the active listings had current addresses in Bladensburg. Dave folded the sheet of paper and put it in his pocket. He walked back out to the showroom to find Winston talking with Chris next to a bright red Range Rover HSE.

"So, what do you think, Chris?" Dave asked as he gave Winston a thank you nod.

"I think this might be the best option, Dad. It would be more practical than the Corvette for me right now."

Dave glanced at the $127,453 sticker price.

"Should I put a hold on this one, or do you want a different color or option package?" Winston asked. "We have a search program that will find exactly what you want and usually get it here in a couple of days."

"Let's see what the available colors and options are," said Chris.

"Charlie, would you show Chris all of the Ranger Rover options, please?" Winston handed Chris off to a salesman. "So, Dave, any chance I could do business with your other son? I would love to get him whatever he wants, for the best deal he'll find anywhere, guaranteed."

"I'll ask him, Winston."

"Thanks, I appreciate it."

About an hour later, Dave and Chris were on the way home. Chris had spec'd out the Range Rover he wanted. It was orange with a black top and a sticker price of just over $131,000. Winston had given them a 3-year lease price of just under a thousand a month. The search program had found the car at a dealership up state. The other dealer agreed to trade for a blue one Winston had in stock. The car would be here next Tuesday.

Chris dialed his phone, "D, I've decided on a Range Rover, if that's alright. Give me a call when you can."

"Voicemail, huh?"

"Yep, what time is the game today?"

"West coast afternoon game at the Dodgers," Dave answered, "starts at five our time. He's at the ballpark by now. When you talk with him tell him Delagoto Motors would like to have his car lease business too."

"Okay, do you think they will give a package deal?"

"I just bet Winston would do almost anything to be able to say he leases cars to major league ball players. He may even put that on a big sign out front knowing him."

Chapter 19

On Monday morning Dave was anxious to follow up on the information he had gotten from Winston about the possible location of drug gang members. As soon as he sat down at his desk, with hot coffee in hand, he pulled the note paper out of his pocket. He unfolded the paper and placed it on the desk.

He ignored the two names with addresses in Williams County. He knew one of them was dead and assumed the other was the guy Bobby said was going straight. His interest was the two names with Bladensburg addresses.

Dave had never been to Bladensburg, that he remembered, but he thought it to be a small town in Lewis County. Lewis was two counties west of them, about sixty miles away. The two had different addresses. One name was Manuel Soto at 2761 Pike Creek Rd, Bladensburg. The other was Alejandro Diaz at 1218 Miller Rd, Bladensburg. Dave turned to the locator's friend, Google Earth, on his computer. He first typed in the address for Manuel Soto.

The map screen started moving as soon as he pushed the enter key. It flew to the west from Springfield and slowed down just as it got into Lewis County. It landed in a rural area on a country road at what looked to be a farm house. He zoomed back out and saw the small town of

Bladensburg some distance to the north and west. He pulled up the measuring tool. When he ran the line as the crow flies from Bladensburg to Mr. Soto's farm house it told him it was about two and a half miles.

He then went back up to the search bar and entered the address for Mr. Diaz on Miller Road. When he hit enter it flew him right back to the same general area. Again, it seemed to be a farm house on the country road. When he zoomed out, he realized that the two properties were adjoining. Pike Creek Road joined Miller Road at the corner of the Diaz property. The Soto property was the next property to the north.

He grabbed his phone and called George Hoffman at DEA.

"I've got a lead on a couple of guys who were possible Williams County drug gang members, George," he said when George answered.

"Really, I'm listening."

"Manuel Soto at 2761 Pike Creek Rd, Bladensburg, and Alejandro Diaz at 1218 Miller Rd, Bladensburg. I can't say how I learned this, but I have no doubt it is on the money."

"Where the heck is Bladensburg?"

"It's in Lewis County. These two guys live on adjoining properties out in the country. I'm wondering if one of these farms is the new location we've been looking for."

"Have you talked with the sheriff in Lewis County?"

"No, I've met him once, but don't know him. I just got this information and thought you would be the best place to drop it. Remember when they were in Williams County, they had someone inside the sheriff's office, they may have done that again."

"Good point. I'll get with Josh at the State Police and we'll get on this. We'll keep it close to the vest. I'll let you know what we find. Thanks, Dave."

Dave hung up the phone and Bob knocked on frame of his open door.

"Got a second, Chief?" Bob asked.

"Sure, what's up?"

"Brian," Bob answered. "He just had a doctor's appointment and they've released him for light duty. He wants to come in this afternoon. Says he is climbing the walls and wants to do something. I told him to come on in."

"That's great news. Have you got stuff for him to do?"

"I was thinking about seeing if Dan wants him for a while. He always has paper work he needs someone to do. I think Brian would be a great help to him."

"Good idea. As a matter of fact, Dan and I talked about that. Let's go down and talk with him together, I've got some news to share with you guys as well."

The three talked in Dan's office. Dan enthusiastically agreed to keep Brian busy for as long as he was on light duty. Dave brought his guys up to speed on the lead to the possible location of the drug gang. They both thought this to be great news and possibly the break they needed.

"Speaking of the investigation," Dan began, "I've started to put together a list of questions for the clerk and for Cruz. If we are going to reopen the case, I want to be ready to bring the clerk in right away. My reasoning is that SPD may try to get in our way."

Dave got up and walked over and closed the door. He walked slowly over to the window and looked out over the parking lot. Dan and Bob sat quietly, waiting. He turned, walked back over to the side chair he had been sitting in and leaned on the back of it.

"SPD may try to get in our way," Dave repeated, "because they know they didn't do a complete investigation and they are embarrassed. Or, they purposefully didn't do a complete investigation and they don't want us to know why. Is that what you are thinking?"

"Pretty much," Dan said. "If they don't try to get in our way, it would indicate that they have nothing to hide and just didn't follow through."

"But, by the time we find that out, it will be too late under either of the former situations?" Dave continued.

"Right, so I think we need to move based on it not being they just didn't follow through," Dan concluded.

"Why wait to reopen the case? Why don't we just go talk to the clerk. Let's call it an informal follow up, or something. Let's see if he has anything to add. If so, we can always document it and add it to the case file if we reopen," Dave instructed.

"Sure, we can do that," Dan said, "I'll take one of my guys and we'll go talk with him tomorrow. That is if we can find him. The address in the file is hard to read, coffee stains. We'll see if we can catch him at work."

"Good, oh, by the way, Rob Alexander checked the ownership on the house where Flores and Cruz lived. Cruz owns the place, Rob said he paid cash for it, no mortgage."

"I'll put a note in the file," Dan said. "And I'll go talk to Cruz too. At least he will be easy to find, if the jail hasn't moved."

Dave settled into his chair after getting back from lunch. He opened his email and started going through line by line and deleting most without opening. About half way through the list an address from @shelbyco.gov caught his attention. He opened the email. It was from a detective sergeant with the Shelby County Sheriff's office. The email explained that he had looked into Integrity Developmental Consulting as Dave had requested.

The detective told Dave that he was given his request and decided to approach the business as an investigation into unfair rent practices in the area to see what information they may offer about their business.

He visited the Integrity office in an office complex on the east side of Memphis. He found the office to be a single room with one employee. The employee was a woman in her late fifties who was eager to talk, her name was Gwen.

Gwen stated that she had been a full-time employee for just over five years. She identified her responsibilities as mostly accounting and banking for the company. When asked about other employees she responded that she had never met any other employee of the company except the owner. She also said that she had only met him when he hired her and gave her the keys to the office.

She informed that all contact with ownership was via email and phone. The company is headquartered in Grand Cayman. The principal owner is Thomas Brough. They mainly work with for developers who are interested in building in a given municipality. Their main function is to represent the developer in negotiations with the governmental agencies and move the project through the developmental process for the client.

Her job consists of processing invoices and receivables. She also maintains contract files and follows up on delinquent payments. Receivables are sent to the bank in the Caymans. She also handles expenses for owned property and the company plane. She offered that the current client base is in the range of fifteen thousand. She does not know how fees are determined but they average about $200 per month per customer with some as low as $25 and as high as $1000.

She believes Mr. Brough lives in the Caymans, but may also have a residence in Nashville. She thinks he is a studio musician on saxophone as well as running Integrity. This is based on comments he has made about playing sessions with name artists.

She stated that she is paid well with a great benefits package. She processes her own pay checks on a monthly basis. All financial records are sent by email each month.

The detective finished off his email by offering to follow up if Dave needed more information. Dave sent him a thank you and his great appreciation for far more than he was expecting, but most welcome information.

Dave looked again at the average invoice amount and the number of clients. Two hundred times fifteen thousand is three million a month. Wow, he thought, if you make that kind of money, I guess you can afford a plane that isn't used very much. But why keep the plane here in Springfield instead of Memphis, Nashville or the Caymans? Maybe their pilot lives here, it would make sense to have the plane where he is. Dave made a mental note to ask George if that is the reason it's kept here, just for his curiosity.

Brian stuck his head in the door way, "Have you got a minute, Dave?"

"Sure buddy, come on in." As Brian sat down Dave asked, "How're you feeling? You look ready to go, even without the uniform."

"I don't mind the uniform, but this is pretty comfortable. I'm feeling great, still getting back up to normal with stamina and general fitness, but it's coming."

"Good, you okay with helping Dan for a while?"

"Sure, that's fine with me. Hey, the reason I wanted to talk is Bobby was over last night. He says he told you the robbery guys were from the drug gang and that they may have been out to get me since they may not know where he is."

"Yep, we think he may have something there. We're working on it. It seems like a good lead to follow."

"Maybe it is, but," Brian hesitated and looked down at the carpet, "it seems pretty coincidental. I'm not sure it makes that much sense."

"I thought that too at first. But what if the robbery was a set up by them to get you?"

"How could they do that? I wasn't even on duty."

"But you were in the immediate area when the robbery went down. They could have timed it to where you were, knowing you would respond when the call went out."

"No, Dave, there was little chance they could get the drop on me in response to a robbery call. You know that," Brian paused as if he was remembering the day he was shot. "Dave," he said slowly looking up as his friend, "how did that happen? How could I have gotten shot? I wouldn't rush right in. I would be on guard until I was sure everything was secure. You know?"

"I do, I have been trying to figure that out. But other things have gotten me side tracked over and over. I thought you would have been down behind your car door with Flores came out, but I'm no longer sure of that. The only feasible explanation I've been able to come up with is that you were approaching the back door when he came out and shot you. Then Wilson followed him and shot him."

"Maybe, but I would have been ready for that, don't you think?" Brian was still thinking hard, trying to remember. "I just can't figure how he got me."

"Dan is going to talk with Cruz to see if he can fill in more blanks. Let's wait to see what he finds out," Dave suggested.

"Okay, wait, do you think I could go along with him?"

"He'll want someone with him. Why don't you go ask him?"

Brian nodded and left Dave's office.

That evening as they watched the Cubs playing another game in Los Angeles, Jan turned to Dave during a commercial. "The Alzheimer Association is having a benefit ball at the Springfield Convention Center. I bought two tickets and I think we should go."

"No offense to the charity, but I hate that kind of stuff," Dave complained.

"I know you do, but it's for a good cause. They're having dinner, a silent auction and some other kind of entertainment. It may be fun."

"Maybe, but do I have to wear a tie?"

"I'd say yes. It's formal, tux time," Jan smiled.

"Oh, that means you'll be looking fabulous and I sure wouldn't want you there alone, so I guess I'm in," he said with a mischievous grin.

"You're sweet, but who will notice a fat pregnant woman."

"You will be noticed by every single person there. No doubt about it. But especially by me."

"So, you agree to go?"

"Okay, this time."

The ball game came back on and conversation stopped. This particular game the Cubs fell to the Dodgers in a final score of six to two. D played five innings with no errors in the field and two walks and a strike out at the plate.

Dan and Brian came into Dave's office the next afternoon after they got back from doing the follow-up interviews. Bob followed them in and closed the door.

"What did you get?" Dave asked.

"Not sure," Dan answered. "The clerk says that he told SPD everything that was said. When they came in, he saw the guns and hit the alarm. Flores was the only one who spoke, he told the clerk to get back against the back counter and get his hands up. Then he said to Cruz, "you take care of him." The clerk said he thought that meant to kill him since they didn't have masks. Flores went straight to the back of the store and shot Taylor. Then the SPD guys came in and Flores ran out the back. All of the rest followed what was in the report."

"So why didn't SPD put in the report that Flores told Cruz to take care of the clerk?" Dave asked thoughtfully.

"Curious, isn't it?" Dan said.

"That's it from the clerk?" Dave asked.

"Yep, on to what we learned from Cruz, which was pretty much nothing," Dan continued. "Of course, we had to inform his lawyer of our interest to interview his client, so he was there as well. Cruz didn't admit to being in the drug gang when we asked, but he did react to the question. It struck me that he had not been asked about that before. I guess SPD wouldn't have the information we have on that, so they would probably not have taken that line of questioning. He offered nothing about what he and Flores did for a living and would not confirm what was said during the robbery. When I asked him if he knew Brian, he didn't respond and his lawyer said he should not answer any more questions. End of interview."

"Okay, so tell me what you read from him?" Dave asked.

"He's just waiting for the trial and not giving us anything. I do think he knew Brian's name but I don't think he recognized him. Brian had the baseball cap on that hides the injury, so I don't think he had any indication who he was. My read is there is more to him than we know and he just didn't seem as worried about all this as I would have expected," Dan concluded.

"What did you get from it, Brian?" Dave asked.

"I saw the same thing. As Dan said, I was surprised that he seemed so calm. He acted like he was just waiting for this to be over so that he could get back to his life. I also don't think he recognized me, but he knew my name."

"Okay, so, where are we?" Bob asked.

"Still digging, it looks like," Dan exhaled. "But I got a call from SPD while I was out, so there maybe something else to deal with. You want to handle that, Dave?"

"No, let's see what you get from them before I get involved."

Chapter 20

Dave pulled into the drive of the farm that evening instead of going straight home. He found Bobby in the farm office sitting at the desk looking into the computer screen.

"Hey, Boss, sup?"

"How're things, Bobby?" Dave asked.

"Good, 'bout ready to plant. Was just checkin' the herbicide timin'," Bobby said. "Ah think we're good."

"Good to hear. Hey, the real reason I stopped was to ask you something, do you know Manuel Soto and Alejandro Diaz?"

"Manny an Al, yeah, I know em. Theys in deep, if ya run into em, watch em," Bobby said.

"What do you mean?"

"Theys muscle, strong armers. Somebody got outta hand, they took care of it. They still around? Thought they spilt back ta Mexico. They was tight with the bosses down there."

"Well, we think they're still around. You think they could have something to do with the car crash in Williams County and the attempt on Brian?"

"Could be, but they was more fists and broke bones types," Bobby paused, "when somethin' big was up, they'd bring dudes up from down south. Ya know, somebody that'd do the deed and split back cross the border. No trace, ya dig?"

"I dig. Look, I need to get home, thanks for the info."

About a week later Dan came into Dave's office one morning.

"Been playing phone tag with Paul Jacoby for a while. He finally caught me this morning. Sure enough, SPD got the ballistics report and when they told the state's attorney office that they wanted to add it to the file, they were told we had the file," Dan said.

"Did he sound happy?"

"He did not. He wanted a full explanation. I told him that we had found a jurisdictional issue that we were looking into," Dan smiled.

"And he bought it?" Dave asked hopefully.

"Not in the least. He kind of got unhinged and demanded we give everything back to the state's attorney right away.

He said it was their case, they had a full and complete investigation, the case is closed and we had no right to interfere. It didn't get any better from there. I finally told him that it is out of my hands and that he should have his boss call my boss."

"So, I should expect a call," Dave said.

"Yep, I think so. On another note," Dan continued, "we got the report on the guy you ran off the road. Seems he doesn't show up anywhere. No positive ID from any of our sources. The feds are checking with the Mexican authorities to see if he's one of theirs. They expect it to take a couple of weeks."

"Okay, thanks."

Shortly after Dan left, the phone rang.

"George Hoffman, Dave," the voice said when he answered.

"Hey, George, got some news for me?"

"As a matter of fact, I do, Dave. I put a team on those guys down in Lewis County. They have been babysitting them since we talked last. Followed them up to the capital the other day. They witnessed a meeting with a dude in a bar on the westside. My guys couldn't get close enough to hear anything but when the meet was over, they split up and one of them tailed the guy from the meeting. When we ran the plate from his car it came up 4474 Sterling in the capital."

"Your kidding. Really?" Dave said. "That's the undercover car address."

"Yep."

When police agencies need to license vehicles for use undercover, the state registers the plate at a fictious address in the capital. Dave's office has several cars registered to that same address.

"Who's was it?"

"State Police working with the FBI. They set up a sting on a murder for hire gang. Their guy was posing as a rich industrialist who was looking to have his business partner knocked off. Seems our guys may not be into drugs anymore."

"So, where does it stand now?" Dave asked.

"This was the first meet, they said they would be in touch."

"How much we talking for a hit these days?"

"Half a mil," George answered.

"Well that sure fits with what we suspect may be going on down here," Dave said half to himself.

"We backed our guys off, but the state and the FBI are keeping track of them. The FBI side is being run by Special Agent Linda Recter, I gave her a heads up that you have an interest in these guys. I gave her your number. She said she would keep you up to speed."

"Okay. Thanks, George."

Dave hung up the phone and sat at his desk thinking about what he knew and didn't know. Or was it what he thought he knew and didn't know. He knew the drug guys were out to get Brian, or Bobby. He thought something to be amiss with the investigation of the robbery which killed Chief Taylor and wounded Brian. He thought the two events may be connected. He knew the robbery was not for the money. He knew there was a dead hitman who seemed to be connected to the drug guys.

What he didn't know was why the investigation seemed to be hurried? Was it that they just wanted to get it done, and the results were obvious? Was it strictly political, to get it over before the election? And, most importantly, what he didn't know was how to find answers to these questions.

He got up and headed down to the conference room. Dan and Brian were at the table. They were each reading a report. Dan had a legal pad next to him.

"How's it going, guys?" Dave asked as he closed the door and sat in an empty chair at the table.

"We have about thirty questions that we would like to know the answers to," Dan replied. "But nothing jumps out as the reason for our concern. We did get a report from Williams County on the Cruz house search. The only real news from that was the bank statements they found. Seems our robbery guys had millions. They had accounts in banks all over the area."

"So, as suspected, the robbery was not for the money. They find anything else?"

"Not really, a few guns and some cash, everything else was just normal stuff a couple of guys would have."

"Okay, I got some info on the Lewis County guys. They may be running the hit man service. DEA put a tail on them. They followed them right into a State Police and FBI sting operation. The feds have an undercover guy posing as a wealthy industrialist looking to have his partner knocked off. The Lewis County guys say it will cost him a half mil. He told them it will take some time to get the money together and he'll let them know."

"So, what does that do for us?" Dan asked.

"Well, it makes me think the guy I ran off the road was working with them. I don't know where that takes us, but I'm told we will be kept advised. The good news is that they're being watched twenty-four seven, so if they try a hit on Brian again, we should know about it before hand."

"That's good news," Brian said offhandedly.

"If they're the ones?" Dan cautioned.

"Good point," Dave said, "but who else would it be?"

Dan, Brian and Dave looked back and forth at each other as they pondered that.

"Well, let's talk about your questions," Dave changed the subject.

Dan flipped the pages on his legal pad. "Let's start with the things we got that weren't in the SPD report. In the SPD report the clerk said he thought he was going to be shot. What he told us that was not in the report was that when the two SPD cops came in, the sargent, that would be Roger Wilson, told the patrolman, "you take care of these guys while I get the other one." He also said, and I quote: "When the cop took the guy's gun away, he kept it pointed at me. He stood there for a long time holding the gun on me. I thought he was going to pull the trigger but then the sheriff came in and he put the gun down," end quote."

"What?" Dave asked. "The clerk thought the cop was going to shoot him? Who was the cop?"

"That's what he said. Robert Jones was working with Roger Wilson that day."

"Did the clerk tell you he told SPD that?"

"Yep, said he told them everything just the way he remembered."

"Did he have a guess at how long the cop held the gun on him?"

"He said they heard both gun shots out back while they stood there."

"I'm not sure there's anything there. Jones could have just been waiting for Wilson to come back in. The clerk could easily have mistaken his actions. What else you got?"

They continued through the list of items Dan and his team had found. As they talked, Dave looked through the file of photographs taken at the scene. He was looking at a photo taken just east of Flores' body lying on the ground. He could see the area where Brian had been in Bob's lap as he got to the scene that day. It reminded him of how he felt that day having seen his best friend shot in the head, bleeding. He stared at the photo as he attempted to keep his composure, when he focused on a flag on the ground about two feet ahead of Flores body. That's where his gun was.

All of a sudden, like a bolt of lightning it hit him what he had known all along and not seen. It was the gun. Not that gun, but Brian's gun.

"Brian, would you go ask Bob to come in?"

Brian nodded and left the room. Dave continued to stare at the picture.

"You see something?" Dan asked.

"I think I do." He showed the picture to Dan, "you see this flag, that's where his gun was. Right?"

"I think so, what's the number?" Dan said as he pulled out the numbered evidence list.

"Forty-seven," Dave answered as Brian came back into the room followed closely by Bob.
"What's up, Chief?" Bob asked.

"Look at this picture," Dave handed it to Bob.

"Yep, that's the location of the perp's gun." Dan offered.

"That flag is where Flores' gun was when we got there," Dave pointed to the flag in the photo."

"Yep, I remember seeing it but was otherwise occupied," Bob looked at Brian and nodded.

"Yeah, me too," said Dave, "but tell me what you would think of that if I told you Flores was left-handed? Dan is there a picture taken when the gun is still there?"

"There is," Brian said, "I was looking at it yesterday." He started digging through the pile of photos. After a few seconds he found it and gave it to Dave.

"Look," Dave pointed to the gun in the photo, "the gun is pointed toward where Brian was. If a left-handed person had dropped it in that location it would have been pointed to the right."

"How do you know he was left-handed?" Dan asked.

"Both he and Cruz were Jose. Everyone called Flores lefty to tell them apart. Why would they call him lefty?"

"Because he was left-handed," three guys said in unison.

"Right, so how did that gun get there?"

"Roger might have moved it," Brian offered, "but it doesn't say anything about that in the report."

"He was by Flores when I got out there," Bob said, "and the gun was there. I'm sure of that."

"How long after the last shot was that, Bob?" Dave asked.

"My guess would be about thirty to forty-five seconds."

"Okay, let's work on that. But now the big one, the thing that has bothered me since I pulled up on the scene that day." Dave paused and looked at Brian. "Your weapon was holstered. There is no way you would've been in that situation without your weapon drawn. You would have been down behind the door of your car, or if you were approaching the rear door, you would have had your gun in your hand. Of that, I have no doubt."

The room was silent as each man processed the information. They all soon nodded in agreement.

"Remember when you brought Brian's gear into my office, Dan? I said something was wrong. That's what it was, his gun was holstered. We should have been picking it up off the ground somewhere, Bob. Don't you agree?"

"I certainly do," Bob agreed. "How's the memory, Brian? Anything coming back?"

"No, I still don't remember anything at the back of the store. But I agree that I would have had my weapon at the ready, that's for sure." Brian paused, looking down at the photos on the desk, "How long was it between shots, Bob?"

"Ten, maybe fifteen, seconds," Bob answered.

"Why was he still here?" Brian asked.

"What do you mean?" Dave inquired.

"Well, if the guy came running out the back of the store and shot me, why did he stick around? Wouldn't he have kept running? Or, maybe, jumped in my squad and took off? In fifteen seconds, he could have been off the property."

They all looked at Brian and then at each other, processing the questions. The room was quiet.

Dan broke the silence as he pulled a piece of paper out of a file folder. "The report says, and I quote, "Sergeant Wilson went out the back door just as the fleeting robber shot Sheriff's Deputy Rodriguez. Sergeant Wilson returned fire striking the robber in the back. End quote."

"The timing doesn't work," Dave said. "It's a stretch to say even five or ten seconds, let alone fifteen, don't you all agree?"

Everyone indicated their agreement.

"Okay, as far as I'm concerned, we have enough to reopen the case. Let's keep it just with us for now, but we will be doing a reinvestigation of the death of Chief Taylor. I want to grease some skids over at SPD before we move forward. We will want to re-interview a couple of SPD officers at the least but I would rather they not know that just yet. Are we agreed?"

All agreed once again.

"I think we should talk with Chief Taylor's wife too, Dave," Dan mentioned. "I don't find any record of an interview with her. No one confirmed that she left the message for Rod to pick up milk on his way home that I can find. Probably not an issue, but I would like to confirm that. Would you have a problem with me calling her?"

"Not at all, Dan. I heard she moved back home. I'll get you a phone number from Walt. Why don't you, and Brian, start working up a list of questions for Roger Wilson and his partner that day, Robert Jones. I'll see if I can set it up without them knowing it's going to happen, see if stories change with a bit of added confusion."

"We should be ready early next week," Dan offered.

Dave headed back to his office.

"Mayor Wilson called," Cheryl said as Dave walked by. "He requested a call back."

"Swell," Dave said, less than enthusiastically.

Chapter 21

"So, what can I do for you, Mister Mayor?" Dave asked after several minutes of pleasant conversation when he returned the call.

"Well, Sheriff, I've been informed that you have taken custody of the Rod Taylor investigation files from the State's Attorney. We are extremely interested in getting that case to trial and I would not like to see it delayed further."

"I'm sorry, Mayor, I'm a bit confused as to why Walt Regan isn't asking me about that. I would think it would be more of an issue with him than you? Did he ask you to call about this?"

"Walt's a busy man. When I heard about this, I was concerned enough to get right on it and save him the trouble. So, can we get it moving again?"

"I'm aware that you would like to put this all behind you, but no one has ever explained to me the reason for the rush. Would care to enlighten me?"

"Oh, sure, no problem, Dave. We just want to move forward with a clean slate. No skeletons in the closet, so to speak."

"That's it?"

"Of course, we just want it over, what else could there be?" the Mayor's voice sounded a bit stressed.

"I have no idea. I just thought there had to be some significant reason for the rush."

"No, no, no, we just want it done. So, can I depend on you to send it back to the State's Attorney first thing in the morning? He tells me he's ready to rock."

"Well, Mayor, I'm sorry but it's going to be a bit longer than that."

"Why, what are you guys doing?"

"We're looking over the investigation."

"You're reviewing it, you have no right, it's our investigation. It's all been completed and closed. The State's Attorney needs to get the case to court. You have no right to hold it up."

"No, we do have a right. As I explained to the State's Attorney, the crime occurred in our jurisdiction. That gives us not only the right, but the obligation to review and sign off on the case before it goes to court. If we don't, the case could be subject to judicial review at best and at worst have all the charges dismissed on a jurisdictional technicality. You wouldn't want that, would you?"

"What do you mean, you have jurisdiction, it was in the city. The Westside Commons is in the city. We have jurisdiction."

"No, sir, the east half of the Westside Commons is in the city. The west half is not and is in county jurisdiction."

"What?" the Mayor paused as if thinking, "Oh, yeah, I remember now. You're right, the developer deeded property to the city on the west end so that we could place the welcome sign," his voice sounded a bit deflated.

"That's correct."

"Well, regardless, we did a complete and through investigation and there should be no reason for your review to take more than a few hours. You can sign off on it, send it back over and the State's Attorney can get it to trial," his voice sounded more hopeful, and almost pleading.

"We have a team working on it, but there are other things to do. So, it's going to take a bit more time."

"Tell you what. How about we send a couple of guys over to help with your review. I'm sure we could cut a couple of guys loose for a few days to help. We'll have them there tomorrow morning. That should help you out and speed things up," the Mayor insisted.

"I appreciate the offer, but I must refuse your generosity. We have it under control. Nice talking with you, Mayor. I need to go now. Good bye," Dave didn't wait for a response and hung up the phone. He got up from his desk, grabbed his jacket and headed out the door, expecting the phone to ring.

"Going to lunch," he told Cheryl as he hurried past her desk.

"A bit early isn't it?" she said. "No, I won't give the Mayor your cell number."

He left the building. As he opened his car door the cell phone rang. He hesitated, but looked at the caller ID. It was D.

"Hey buddy," he answered.

"Hi, Dad, you got a minute?"

"Sure, just getting in the car. I can sit here and talk as long as you need."

Dave started the car but left it in park as he talked on the phone.

"It'll only take a minute. I just tried to catch Chris, but he must be in class or something. I'm going to be tied up the rest of the day. Could you tell him that the Range Rover is fine, and to get me one too? I'd like a blue one with a white top."

"I can do that. I'll call him this evening."

"Thanks, Dad. Gotta run, bye."

"See you, son."

Dave hung up the phone and backed out of the parking spot. His plan was to just drive around a bit and think. He drove toward the center of Springfield. He needed a plan to move the investigation forward, but had no real idea what that may be. It was obvious that there was something wrong, but what? Why was the Mayor so intent on getting the case to trial in a hurry? Is he trying to cover for someone, maybe his son? If so, what would that say about what happened behind the store?

"I wish Brian could remember," he said out loud.

As he was approaching the next intersection, he saw a gray Honda cross in front of him on the State highway well after it's light had turned red. Even though he seldom made traffic stops anymore, there were times it just should not be avoided.

He hit the button for all the flashing lights and turned to follow the Honda. The Honda driver pulled over to the side of the street about a block later. Dave stopped just behind the Honda with his car about half way out into the curbside traffic lane. This would give him protection as he stood beside the driver's door. Before getting out of the car he radioed dispatch that he was making a traffic stop and ran the plate number through the computer. The report on the car came back clean. As he approached, the driver rolled down the car window.

"Good morning, I'm Sheriff Dave Harbinger. Could I see your license and insurance card please?"

The driver was a woman with dark brown hair. She looked to be about thirty, and had on a thick furry coat. She just nodded and fumbled in her purse. After a few seconds she handed Dave her license and leaned over toward the glove box of the car to get the insurance card.

"I stopped you because you ran the red light back there, Ms. Abbott," Dave read from her license. "Are you aware of that?"

She nodded and frowned slightly as she handed him the insurance card.

"Please wait here," he said and walked back to his squad.

He took out a traffic citation pad from the console tray and began to write out a warning ticket, but was interrupted by the ring of his cell phone. He looked at the caller ID, it was Walt Regan.

"Say, Walt," he said after punching the hands-free button.

"I understand you had a talk with the Mayor a while ago."

"That I did. I don't think I made him happy."

"That's kind of my read as well."

"Say, I'm tied up right now, but can we meet somewhere and talk?"

"Lunch?"
"Sounds like a plan. Mary's Place in about twenty?"

"See you there."

A few minutes later, Dave had released Ms. Abbott with a warning ticket and a stern reminder that being in a hurry could get her or others hurt, or worse. He headed for Mary's Place to continue his thinking while waiting for Walt. He took a table at the back and had a cup of coffee.

"You trying to solve all of the world's problems, or just your own?" Walt said as he slipped into the booth across from Dave.

"Good question," Dave said looking up. "Guess I was spaced out a bit."

"Well, you may have reason to be. Something is going on," Walt offered.

"Why do you say that?"

"The Mayor just read me the riot act over you guys pulling jurisdictional on the Taylor case. He wants me to pull out all the stops and do anything I can think of to get the file away from you. I have no reason why it's such a big deal, but apparently it is."

"Do you think he may have reason to be protecting someone for some wrong doing? Like maybe his son?"

Walt looked puzzled. "What do you know that I don't?"

"I'm just speculating. What if something happened behind that store that could get Sgt Roger Wilson in a lot of trouble? He and Brian have had issues since high school, what if they got into it and Roger took inappropriate action? Brian doesn't remember, but what if?"

"You're thinking Roger ran to daddy and asked him to take care of it?" Walt said, as much to himself as to Dave.

"I really don't know. I'm just trying to make sense of all of this."

"Brian doesn't remember, Flores is dead, so Roger is the only one that knows what happened back there," Walt said softly. "But wouldn't he just keep quiet about it if only he knew? Why would he tell his dad?"

"Maybe he didn't until he found out that Brian didn't die. Maybe he got worried about what Brian would tell if he woke up. He wouldn't have known that Brian wouldn't remember."

"But why would it still be an issue now? Being that Brian doesn't remember and all," Walt reasoned.

"I don't know," Dave admitted. "It just seems that they are trying to sweep something under the rug, and I'd sure like to know what."

The waitress appeared and took their orders. After she had left Dave changed the subject, "So what have you learned about the close watch they keep on the chief's office?"

"I'm thinking it's all about money," Walt offered softly. "The Mayor and Councilman Banks are living far above any visible income they have. My guess was they were skimming a good chuck of change from somewhere, but I haven't been able to figure where. The city books are audited regularly and no irregularities have been noted as long as I've been around."

"What makes you think they have more money than they should?"

"Cars, several trips a year, dress and jewelry that most of us could never afford, you name it, they seem to have it. For example, you may not know that my hobby is watch repair and restoration. I love watches, much the same as you love cars. I have rebuilt several old high-end watches. I have observed that the mayor has quite a collection of expensive watches. Piaget, Cartier, Omega and Rolex are just a few of the brands I have seen on his wrist. We're talking in the range of ten to thirty plus thousand dollars each. I'm guessing the value of his watch collection is over half a million. And, the jewelry of the wives exceeds that."

Dave's brow wrinkled as he considered Walt's comments. Walt waited. After a few seconds Dave spoke softly.

"Walt, do you think Rod Taylor may have had the same concerns you have?"

"I know what you're asking. I've looked through everything in the office for any indication that he may been concerned, but there is no evidence. Of course, being that Alderman Banks' wife, Paula, is my secretary, she could have removed any evidence he left behind."

"There is that," Dave pondered. "If we assume there is something there, how do we find the particulars and prove them?"

"Yeah," was all Walt said as their lunches was placed in front of them.

The two senior police officials began eating quietly. Each rolling over in their minds what might be the proper course of action to prove or disprove the mounting suspicions.

After several minutes, Dave broke the silence. "If there is something amiss that implicates the mayor's son, and possibly the mayor, in Brian's shooting, who would have knowledge of it other than them?"

Walt looked up from his meal, "maybe patrolman Bob Jones? He was working with Roger that day, he's the only one I can think of who may know something."

"That's a good idea," Dave responded. "He may know what was really going on that day. But, do you think he would talk?"

"Probably not, unless he felt there to be a reason that he needed to come clean. Let me work on this a bit, do a little digging, see if maybe I can find an angle."

"Okay, but be careful."

"Yeah, I'm guessing that you and I should be the only ones knowing about this. I'm sure not going to ask my secretary to type up my notes," Walt smiled nervously. "Let's have lunch here next week and I'll let you know if I find anything."

"Sounds good."

After lunch, Dave went back to the office.

"Agent Recter with the FBI asked you to call," Cheryl said as Dave walked past her desk, "the number is on your desk."

"Thanks, did the Mayor call back?"

"No, and I know you're glad of that."

"You're right."

Dave found the slip and dialed the number Cheryl had left on his desk.

"Agent Recter," he heard through the phone a few seconds later. Her voice was very pleasant and sounded a lot like Jan.

"This is Sheriff Dave Harbinger, returning your call."

"Yes, sheriff, George Hoffman said you had an interest in the case we are working on pertaining to the hired hitmen."

"We are. I'm not sure how much George told you, but we have a connection with the guys involved. They're former drug gang members who were previously working out of a neighboring county. We did a bust on them a couple of years back."

"Yes, George filled me in. And, we believe you guys are correct in your assessment that they have changed career paths. I thought you may be interested that we have intercepted a cash flow that seems to be going in your general direction. At least to banks in your area."

"Oh?"

"Yes, there has been a considerable amount of money deposited in banks in Lincoln and Williams counties from the same sources that have paid our guys in Scott county. We got a court order to look into their bank accounts. We found that the money was coming from offshore accounts. We ran a search on other funds from the same sources and found that there were transfers to your area amounting to hundreds of thousands of dollars total in the time frame of the last six months."

"Any idea who the money is coming from?"

"No, and we aren't even sure where it is coming from at this point. All we know is that it isn't stateside. We're attempting to cross reference, but that will take some time. I'm afraid that's about all I have for you right now."

"Okay, thanks for the update. We really do appreciate it."

"I'll be in touch, Sheriff."

The line went dead.

Chapter 22

Dave and Jan had assumed their favorite game watching positions on the couch in the family room with a large bowl of popcorn and a frosty cold A&W Root Beer for each of them. The eighty-two inch, 4k television brought the game to life in front of them almost as good as being there.

The Cubs had played thirty-two games in the season already and D had become a regular starter at second base and leadoff hitter. He had a four-ten batting average and an on base per centage of four-eighty. All in all, it was an amazing start to a big-league career.

The game was scoreless in the third inning at the Cardinals, when D came to the plate with the bases loaded and two outs. He settled into the batter's box, almost on top of the plate as normal. He was batting right-handed against the left-handed pitcher. The first pitch was a hard curve that just barely missed outside as D watched it go by. The next pitch came inside and D just barely got out of the way.

"He's thinking this pitch will be down the middle," Dave said.

"Yep, the pitcher would not want to go nothing and three in this situation," Jan responded.

The ball left the pitcher's hand. Before it was half way to the plate D began to swing. With all the force he could muster, he brought the bat through the strike zone. Bat and ball met right over the plate, center contact with the barrel of the bat sent the one hundred mile an hour fast ball back in the direction it came from with a slight veer to the left. D didn't move. He stood at the plate watching as the ball flew thirty feet over the left field wall. A grand slam.

The Cubs dugout went wild. Everyone jumped to their feet and began yelling at the top of their lungs. Dave dumped the bowl of popcorn as he jumped off the couch in his excitement. Jan jumped out of the way of the flying snow storm and just barely managed to rescue Dave's root beer as it headed for the floor.

"Easy, Tiger," she said, "man alive, someone would think it was your son hitting that ball out of the park."

"Well," he started to respond as his cell phone rang. He looked at the caller ID and punched the pickup button.

"How about that?" he said into the phone.

"Had to be over five hundred feet," Chris responded.

"Yep, he really got a hold of that one. He's doing great."

"Sure is, I talked with him yesterday. He's having more fun than should be allowed. I'm going up to see him this week end. Gonna catch the games on Saturday and Sunday," Chris said.

"Oh, so you're going to drive up to Chicago for the week end. Are you going to be staying at D's?"

"Yeah, looking forward to it. I haven't seen his apartment. He says it's nice."

"Sounds great." There was a pause in the conversation as they both watched D slam both feet onto the plate as the three other players slapped him on the back and high fived each other.

"Then next week end I'll be coming home to pick up the new car," Chris continued. "You don't have a problem with me putting the Malibu in storage in the barn, do you?"

"Of course not," Dave responded. "But I thought you'd be selling it."

"That's the plan, but I want to wait till summer after I've had some time to clean it up so I can get the most from it. I'll spruce it up and make it look new. That is, if I come home for the summer."

"Wait, what do you mean, if?"

"Well, the brain sensory project I've been working on is showing signs of a break through. The sensor I developed with the medical school seems to have promise. We are doing additional testing right now, but if the preliminary findings prove out, there may be an opportunity for a grant funded project that would keep me here over the summer."

"This is the optic nerve sensor you were talking about, right?"

"Right, we've been able to isolate the optic nerve signals by putting a subject into a grounded isolation chamber to eliminate all other electrical interference. We show the subject images through a window and have been able to determine the shape of the waveforms generated by a specific image across a range of different subjects. It's really interesting."

"You mean you can tell determine what electrical impulse is flowing through the optic nerve based on a given picture?"

"That's right, Dad. We use a form of sensor triangulation to zero in on the lateral geniculate nuclei, or LGN, where the synapse occurs between the optic tract and the striate cortex of the brain."

"If I remember biology class, a synapse is some kind of neurological connection, right?" Dave asked.

"Right, a junction between two nerve cells, consisting of a miniscule gap across which impulses pass by diffusion of a neurotransmitter. We can measure the electrical impulses across the gap, feed them into the computer and compare previous data sets to determine patterns. After a time, we can tell what the subject is seeing. By comparing the computer printout, we can tell you when a subject sees a red ball. It's really amazing. Anyway, the medical team has filed a peer review paper and we are expecting input in the next couple of months. We have also filed a grant request along with our patent for the sensor, the computer program and the process. If it all comes together, I'll be tied up here all summer."

"Sounds to me like it may be a career in the making as well."

"Could be, at the very least my graduate study plan is coming together."

"Hey, could this process have an application for brain function in general? I mean in areas other than the functioning of the optic nerve?"

"I guess so, why? What specifically are you asking?"

"Just thinking. You remember the issues Brian is having with remembering what happened when he was shot. Can you identify brain impulses for a specific brain function, like memory?"

"Oh, you're wondering if we could determine why Brian can't remember?"

"Yes."

"Hum," Chris paused, "we could certainly triangulate the sensors to focus on the part of the brain that deals with memory, but for this technique to work there would need to be a related synapse to focus in on. I'm not that familiar with memory function. Let me discuss it with the medical team to see what they think. I'll let you know."

"Okay, just curious."

"See ya next weekend, Dad. Say hi to Jan."

"Sure thing, see you."

"Sounds like number two son may have a career path from one side of that conversation," Jan said as Dave put his phone down.

"Seems like he is on to something," Dave responded as they snuggled back into ballgame watching mode. "He said to say hi."

"Hi, Chris. Did I hear he's going up for the games this week end?"

"Yep."

"How about we go too? Maybe we could fly up Friday night and back Sunday night," Jan offered. "Maybe Kent and Duetta would like to go too. We could stay there."

Dave looked at Jan and smiled as he punched some buttons on his cell phone.

"Hey, Bro," he said after a few seconds, "how are things?"

"Things are good, just sitting in my recliner watching my nephew play ball on TV," Kent responded. "How's Jan and that little one?"

"They're both growing and doing well. Speaking of your nephew playing ball, do you guys have anything on for this week end? The three of us are thinking about coming up to catch a couple of games. If you can put us up, we'll take you guys along, if you want to go."

"That sounds great, and no we have nothing that would interfere with that."

"Okay, well, we're just in the thinking stage now. We still haven't lined up the plane and I haven't talked with D, but we'll get on the arrangements tomorrow and will let you know. What we're thinking is fly up on Friday evening and back on Sunday night. There are day games both days. Chris is driving up and will be staying at D's. Maybe we can all go out for dinner Saturday night."

"Okay, let us know. I assume you'll be coming into DuPage. We'll pick you up there."

"Yep. I'll call you when we get everything set up."

Dave hung up the phone just as D backhanded a hard-hit grounder while moving to his right deep behind second base. Every one of his teammates was also in motion, the other infielders were moving to the bases, the pitcher dived to the ground toward first base, the outfielders were all coming in fast, and the catcher was moving in front of the plate, right foot on the plate with his mitt stretching toward center field just like a first baseman. In a single fluid motion, D came up spinning to his left, pulling the ball from his glove, and firing a strike into the middle of the catcher's mitt. The ball smacked milliseconds before the runner's foot hit home plate, ending the inning with the bases loaded.

"Yes. That was a gold glove play if I've ever seen one," Dave shouted as he threw his clinched fist toward the ceiling.

An inning later the Cubs chalked up another victory with the four to nothing win. As had become the norm, Dave was completely exhausted as he and Jan headed for bed. The emotions he went through watching D play far exceeded any expectations he had ever imaged.

Dave was still living last night's ballgame when he got in his office early the following morning. It was budget time. The County Board had directed no more than three per cent increase in the budget for the next fiscal year. All of the department heads had provided their preliminary budgets and the stacks of green lined paper were on his cadenza waiting for him.

The green bars showed him the proposed budget, the current year budget, total expenditure to date and the previous year totals for each department by line item. His budget director, Craig Jackson, had everything ready and in order, but Dave felt it his responsibility to review each item. He wanted to make sure the amounts proposed were in line with the previous numbers. It also gave him a sense of what was going on in the department and what is being planned.

With coffee in hand, he plopped the first pile of green bars on his desk and began his review. With red pencil in hand, he marked each item he would want to discuss with the department head when he met with them one on one for budget review. He had developed a quick short hand to remind himself of what caught his attention. A plus sign if the number seemed too high or a minus if it was lower than he expected. A question mark if he needed an explanation or a star if he had no idea what the item was.

When Cheryl came in at her normal time, she brought the coffee pot in and refilled his cup without asking.

"Thanks," Dave said.

"You want me to keep you awake, or let you sleep with your budget sheets?" she asked, only half joking.

"Let me sleep, I need the rest."

"Okay, and I'll keep the hounds away, too," she closed the door as she left.

A couple of hours and three cups of coffee later, there was a knock on his office door and Dan stuck his head in.

"Can I interrupt?" he asked.

"Please do, my eyes are starting to cross."

Dan came in and sat down in front of Dave's desk. He had a curious look on his face. Dave put his pencil down and waited for his head of investigations to speak.

"As you know, there was no record in the files of an interview with Rod Taylor's wife. Since she's left town, we couldn't go talk with her, so I tracked down a phone number and gave her a call. She is doing as well as can be expected and agreed to talk with me about the events of that day. You know the report indicated that Chief Taylor had gotten a message to pick up milk on his way home that evening. But his wife tells me that she hadn't left such a message. She said she didn't think much about it. Her idea was that he must have noticed they needed milk when he put it in his coffee that morning and decided to stop on his way home."

"Was the note in the file?" Dave's interest was spiked.

"No, and nothing in the file indicates what happened to it, if there was one."

"Did you ask her if Rod was worried about something around that time?"

"Yes, and she said he seemed preoccupied a lot. It seemed to her that something was bothering him, but he wouldn't tell her what. He said it was just work stuff."

"Will she give a deposition if we need her to?"

"She said she would be glad to assist in any way she can."

"Your assessment?"

"Well," Dan paused for a few second and collected his thoughts. "The milk note is curious, but I'm not sure it means anything. She seemed quite sure she didn't leave the message, but we also aren't sure one existed. So, I'm writing that off. However, the idea that something was bothering Rod may have merit. A wife knows that sort of thing and I'm calling it credible."

"But what does it tell us? May be important or may not be. I'm sure you've already put it in the report, so let's keep digging."

"Yes, sir." Dan left and Dave went back to the budget.

About a dozen budget items later the phone rang.

"Harbinger," Dave said into the receiver.

"This is Agent in Charge Linda Recter, have you got a minute?"

"Sure, what can I do for you?"

"Well, Sheriff, it may be what I can do for you. We've come across some interesting information you may appreciate."

"I'm listening," Dave felt his heart rate pulse up a notch.

"We arrested those guys from Scott County on a murder for hire charge. Seems they accepted payment from our undercover guy and showed up with guns ready to the location the mark was supposed to be."

"Good work."

"Thanks, well anyway, when we shook down their residences, we found phone text records that indicate activity in your area. There was correspondence with Jose Flores sometime back. It seems they were looking for someone named Bobby, no last name, or Brian if Bobby couldn't be found. There was also acknowledgement that the guy killed in your chase, Pedro Gonzalez, was working with them."

"Really?" Dave exclaimed.

"Yep, he was apparently brought up from Mexico to do a specific job, and then high tail it back over the border."

"So, he was here to do a hit and run back south."

"Could be. Also, there was money transferred into their account that may be relative to the same notes, but we can't confirm that."

"How much?" Dave asked.

"A quarter mil at two separate times. Any of that make sense to you?"

"As a matter of fact, it does. I think I know who they are referring to," Dave offered.

"Your deputy who was shot was named Brian, wasn't he? Is that who you're thinking? You think it may have been a hit on him?" Agent Recter asked.

"That's where we found him. Has either of them talked?"

"Not so far, but we're still working on it. They've lawyered up and are not giving us much. But we're working the banks to try to see if we can trace the money. And there is a lot of money involved, we think they were into a few other things as well. I'll let you know when something else turns up."

"Okay, thanks," Dave signed off.

Chapter 23

Dave walked into the conference room where Dan and Brian were busy logging the information obtained from the interview with Rod's wife.

"I just got off the phone with the FBI," Dave began as he sat down at the table, "they've taken the Scott County guys into custody. They got phone text records that confirm Flores and Cruz were working with them as hit men. They also have evidence of money transfers around the time of the robbery and that the guy I ran off the road, Gonzalez, was one of them. So, it looks like the robbery may have been staged to hit you, Brian. They were apparently looking for Bobby, but the texting indicated you were a secondary target if they couldn't find him."

Dan and Brian were silent for a few seconds as they processed what Dave had said.

"Gonzalez was sent to finish the job?" Dan broke the silence.

"Apparently."

"But if I was the target of the robbery, how could they know I would be at the convenience store?" Brian asked.

"Good question. I guess we're back to the idea that they had someone watching you and ran the robbery when you were nearby knowing you would respond," Dave offered.

"Sounds weak," Brian said softly.

"Does the FBI have enough to prove it, or are we speculating?" Dan asked thoughtfully.

"I'm afraid it's just speculation at this point," Dave responded to Dan. "But here's the kicker, even if that's what happened, getting Brian on the scene is only part of it. The real puzzle is how did they get him out from behind the car door with his weapon holstered? That's what I can't figure out."

The three men sat quietly, looking at each other. One by one they shook their heads as they tried to come up with an answer.

"How do you get a seasoned police officer to let his guard down in a high-risk situation?" Dan verbalized what they were all thinking.

"Only by removing the threat," Dave offered, "that clearly didn't happen here. So, where are we?"

"We know what happened, but we don't know how," Brian said slowly.

"Dave, the Judge is on the phone," Cheryl said in the doorway, "you want to take it or call back?"

"I'll take it, you guys let me know if you come up with anything."

"What's new with the best-looking judge in the entire country?" Dave answered his phone.

"That kind of talk will get you a weekend of Cubs watching," Jan responded. "I've got the plane set up for five thirty departure Friday night. Return from DuPage Airport at nine Sunday night. Does that work?"

"That should be fine. I texted with D this morning and he's going to have tickets at will call for the four of us. He's also good with dinner Saturday night. So, I guess we're all set."

"Good. Say do you want to do lunch today?" Jan asked. "I can be out of here in about twenty minutes."

"I'd love to, but I'm meeting Walt Regan for lunch. Sorry."

"Stand me up for lunch means a nice dinner out tonight, you know."

"I think I can take that. See you later, love you."

"Love you, too. Bye."

Walt was already at the table in the back when Dave walked into Mary's Place. There was a cup of coffee in front of him and he was writing in a small notebook as Dave sat down across from him.

"Hey, buddy, how you doing?" Dave asked.

"Good, Dave, and you?" Walt closed the notebook and slipped the pen in his shirt pocket.

"We got some news from the FBI that seems to indicate that Brian was the target of the robbers. Rod may have just been at the wrong place at the wrong time."

"Really, are you sure?"

"No, we're not at all sure, but that seems to be where things are pointing."

Dave filled Walt in on all of the details as related to him by Linda Recter of the FBI. The discussion continued through ordering and meal delivery.

"So, my concern about what is going on in city hall is completely separate from what happened to Rod," Walt speculated as they enjoyed their meals.

"If what we're thinking holds up, it would appear so," Dave offered.

"Okay, that being the case, would you be willing to assist with my investigation of what is going on at city hall?" Walt inquired.

"I don't see why not, what are you thinking?"

"I'm thinking Robert Jones knows something and it seems to be bothering him, if I'm reading it right," Walt continued.

"He was the patrolman working with the mayor's son the night Brian was shot, right?"

"Right, and ole Bob has been spending a lot of time at Mike's of late. Bending his arm far more than he should I hear."

"Mike's is the bar over on the east side, owned by a former SPD cop as I recall," Dave said.

"Right, a lot of the guys spend time there after shift; it's kind of the cop's home away from home, if you know what I mean," Walt confirmed. "Anyway, word is Jones is in there after every shift night till closing. He's called in sick several times in the last few months. Rumor has it that it's due to hangovers. He seems to be on edge."

"So, what do you have in mind?"

"He lives out in the Fox View subdivision east of town. Do you know it?"

"Sure, I patrolled that area at one time in my career."

"I'm thinking if you could pick him up on his way home some night, maybe we could convince him to tell us what he knows, or what's eating at him," Walt paused.

"Oh," Dave rubbed his chin thoughtfully. "Yes, I think I know what you mean. Pick him up on DWI outside the city limits and bring him into our office for a sobriety test."

"Right, and once in your office maybe we can convince him that if he opens up and fills us in on what's bugging him, we'll drop the DWI charges that could get him fired."

"Does he always drive home about the same time?"

"As far as I know," Walt responded. "I'm thinking we can just pick a date and give it a shot."

"Okay, Mike's closes at two. We'll need a vehicle description."

"Of course, I wanted to see if you would help before I dug into the specific. I'll get on it and get the info we'll need."

"Okay, I'll take care of everything on my end. I'm thinking Dan and Brian will help, but let me run it by them. Let me know when you're ready to go."

"Sure thing, Dave, and thanks."

Dave headed straight to the conference room when he got back to the office. Brian was there working. Dave asked him to come to his office, and on the way stuck his head into Dan's office with the same request.

"We going to run a bit of a sting operation," Dave said as they all sat around his desk. "Walt thinks Robert Jones may know what's going on over at Springfield City Hall and with a little incentive may be willing to share. So, based on the fact that he has been drinking quite heavily at Mike's on a regular basis he suggested a DWI shakedown.

I'd like to keep this close to the vest with only the three of us and Walt knowing about it. Are you guys on board?"

Dan and Brian both nodded.

"What's the plan?" asked Dan.

"He lives in Fox View, east of town. Walt will get us a vehicle description. One night when he's on his way home from Mike's we'll pull him over after he gets outside the city limits. We'll bring him back here and see if he'll spill the beans in order to get out of the DWI rap."

"We may also get him to tell us more about what went on the night I got shot," Brian said thoughtfully.

"I think it's a good plan," Dan offered.

"Okay, I'll be talking with Walt over the next couple of weeks and will let you know when I get more info. Thanks for your help guys."

After Dan and Brian left, Dave got back to the budget sheets to continue staring at numbers. He was into the fleet budget now, which was an area of interest to him due to his love of all things automotive. Looking at the budgeted maintenance line, he noticed that the actual amounts spent over the last years was trending downward. Since the size of the fleet had not changed, he judged that the cars must be more reliable.

He turned to the replacement schedule. They normally replaced a squad at 150,000 miles. This happened on average every three years. The criteria they used was based on maintenance costs and the resale value of the cars. Dave reasoned that if maintenance cost is going down, maybe the trade in times could be increased. His red pencil jotted down, "move trades to two hundred thousand," for discussion with the fleet supervisor.

Dave was feeling a sense of accomplishment when the phone rang.

"Harbinger."

"Hi, this is Dan Weatherford from Wapiti County, Arizona. We met at the Sheriff's convention in KC."

"Sure, I remember you, Dan. Great to hear from you. How are things in the desert?"

"Things are a bit curious to tell the truth. Do you remember me telling you about the Shelby my friend has?"

"Sure, the one Jim Morrison owned. You said you would send pictures if your friend said it was okay."

"Well, I didn't ask him. I saw the car at a local shop where he had dropped it off for an oil change. I stopped and took a look under the car while they had it on the rack. Before I say more, what was the number you said your dad stamped on his cars?"

"Four seven four eight," Dave replied, "why?"

"Well," Dan continued slowly, "with my friend's car up on the rack, I took a mirror and stuck it up over the rear end housing. There were numbers stamped on the top of the housing. It was four seven four eight. I think I found your missing Mustang."

Dave was stunned.

"Wait," Dave stammered, "Dan, you said that car has a parchment interior, ours was black."

"I know, they must have changed the interior color. But I assure you, I am not mistaken. I double checked and rechecked again. Then I ran the mirror up over the transmission and the numbers were there as well. I'm convinced it's your car."

"Wow, Dan, I'm speechless. I never thought I'd see that car again. You're sure four seven four eight is stamped on top of the transmission as well?"

"No doubt about it."

"Okay, let me get with the state police and see if they can dig up a copy of the vehicle theft report. I'll get a copy out to you."

"Will the report confirm the stamped numbers?"

"Yes, that was a part of the filing," Dave confirmed.

"Okay, when I get it, I'll turn it over to the state police with the information I have."

"Great, thanks, Dan."

Dave punched the phone buttons for Bob Cooper.

"Bob, can you do me a personal favor," he asked when Bob picked up.

"Sure, Dave, what's up?"

"We had a car stolen from our collection, maybe ten years ago. There was a report filed at the time. Can you ask your contact at the state police if they can run down that report?"

"Sure, Dave. Who filed the report and from what address?"

"Dad filed it, William, and used the address of my farm. Off the top of my head, I don't remember the exact date, but dad died in 2012 and it was a year or two before that."

"That should be close enough. What car was it?"

"It was a 1968 Shelby Mustang, a blue fastback."

"Okay, I'll get on it."

"Thanks, Bob."

On Friday morning, Dave and Jan got everything ready for their trip to Chicago for the weekend. The plan was that Jan would pick up Dave at his office and they would go straight the airport for the five thirty departure. Jan would drive the pickup to her office because they felt better with it sitting in the airport lot over the weekend. They packed their bags and put them in the pickup before heading out for work. Dave would leave his squad parked at the station for the weekend.

"How about we run through a drive-thru on the way to the airport to pick up dinner for on the plane," Jan offered.

"That's sounds like a great idea, unless," Dave paused as he headed for the door, "what does your day look like? Any chance you could get away early so that we would have time for an early dinner?"

"Sorry, sheriff, I've got a preliminary hearing set for three-thirty. It should only take a few minutes, but it's doubtful I will be out of the office before four thirty. That puts me at your office at four forty-five at the earliest, but more likely closer to five."

"No worries. Fast food it is. Call me when you're on the way. I'll be ready."

They kissed at the door, maybe longer than they should have, but if that made them both late for work, it was worth it.

Friday seemed to take forever. Dave was productive and kept focused but was also clock watching all day. When his cell rang at four thirty-seven it was to his ear in record time.

"Can you wait another ten minutes to see me?" Jan asked

"You can't imagine how hard it will be, but I'll give it a shot."

"Okay, see you shortly."

Seven minutes later, Dave wished Cheryl a good week end and headed for the parking lot. Jan was turning off the street as he walked out of the front door. She pulled right up in front of him and he slipped into the passenger seat. She put the pickup in park and leaned over.

"Hi," she smiled brightly and then their lips met.

"I missed you today," he said, refreshed from the kiss. "How was your day?"

"Long," she offered. "I can't believe how excited I am about the games this week end. You'd think I haven't seen D play before. I guess it's just that he is doing so well that I feel like I want to be a part of it."

Dave just looked at her.

She nodded and grinned, "Oh, now you're going to say you feel that way too." She poked him playfully in the ribs as she put the truck in gear.

Chapter 24

As Dave and Jan walked through the hanger, George was walking around the plane parked just outside. The luggage bay was open and George took each of their bags and placed them inside.

"Looks like it's going to be a smooth ride up to the Windy City," George said. "Should have you there in just over an hour, assuming ATC agrees."

"Great," Dave answered. "Say George, there's something I'm curious about. The plane in the next hanger, the mayor's plane, do you know the flight crew?"

"No, not really, they just show up when something is going on over there, just do their thing and leave when they're done."

"You haven't talked with them?"

"Nope, just a "how ya doin?" or a wave is about it."

"Do you think they live around here?"

"Couldn't say for sure, but I kind of have the impression that they don't."

"Why do you say that?"

"When they are here it's for a considerable amount of time. I've never seen either of them just drop in to check on something or pick something up and leave right away. You know what I mean. If they lived close by you would expect things like that to happen."

By now they had boarded the plane and George was closing the cabin door. Jan was already seated and buckled in. Dave took the seat next to her as George settled into the cockpit.

"Everything looks good out there," George said to Loura as he strapped himself in. "You two ready back there?"

"We're belted in and ready to go," Jan responded clutching the Arby's bag with a fish and a beef brisket sandwich inside. George put on his headset and got to work.

Soon after takeoff, the seat belt light went out with a ding. Jan opened the Arby's bag as Dave headed for the drink cooler located just behind the cockpit across from the entry door. He pulled out two Diet Cokes and put one on Jan's tray table as he got back to his seat. He flipped his tray table down after snapping his seat belt and put the other Coke on it. Jan handed him the brisket and concentrated on the fish sandwich in front of her.

"What was that talk about the other pilots?" Jan asked Dave as they enjoyed their dinner.

"Nothing really, just curious."

"No, you're more than curious. Are you investigating the Mayor?"

"Now, Judge, you know everything I know about the Mayor. Why would I be investigating him? I'm just curious about his airplane."

Jan just looked at him and waited.

"Okay, look," Dave hesitated, "I think something may be going on but I'm not sure. How about you give me a little time to work on it before I fill you in?"

"Nope, I think you should tell me now. Bring me up to speed. Telling me all about it may help you put it together. Who knows, I may even be able to give you some direction. After all, we are partners."

He had no response. She had him there. So, as they ate, he began to tell her everything he had learned and was thinking about the Mayor's extravagant life style. Then as he was in the middle of a sentence her eyes grew big and she grabbed her stomach. He stopped talking.

"She kicked me," Jan said with a gasp.

"Are you sure?" Dave threw off his seat belt so he could lean closer. He put his hand on her stomach but couldn't feel anything. She moved his hand to where it had been, but he still didn't feel anything other than her stomach.

The rest of the flight was spent concentrating on the miracle of life that was their baby.

When the plane came to a stop in front of the general aviation terminal at DuPage County Airport, Loura opened the plane door as Dave and Jan collected their things. By the time they got off the plane Loura had retrieved their bags from the cargo bin. Dave picked them up off the tarmac as Loura closed and latched the bin.

"We'll see you Sunday evening," Loura said.

Dave and Jan nodded as they waved and headed into the civil aviation terminal. Just inside, Kent and Duetta waited on a leather sofa in the lounge area. They jumped up as Dave and Jan came in and hugs were administered all around.

"Good flight?" Kent asked as he took one of the bags Dave carried.

"It was, smooth and non-eventful."

They headed out to the parking lot. Jan and Duetta got into the back seat of Kent's Cadillac Escalade. Dave took the shotgun position after he and Kent loaded the bags inside the rear hatch.

"How's Brian doing?" Kent asked as they pulled out of the parking lot on Kautz Road heading south.

"He's doing great. Seems to have fully recovered other than having no memory of the attack."

"Good to hear. Is he back to work full time?"

"Yes, but we still haven't put him back on the street," Dave offered. "He's been working in investigations and doing a great job at it. I may end up leaving him there, but haven't concentrated on the long term yet."

"I've been looking into his memory condition," Kent continued. "Had several discussions with other surgeons and we all believe that he will remember at some point. Our guess is that he is mentally blocking what happened because of the trauma it caused him. We believe some external event or experience, maybe completely unrelated, will snap him out of it just like flipping a switch."

"But you have no idea what will flip that switch."

"Exactly. Also, you may want to warn him that it may not be a pleasant experience. It will probably come with severe anxiety and hypertension, maybe even a panic attack."

"And you think that because of the trauma that caused him to not remember in the first place. Right?" Dave asked hesitantly.

"Yes, for his subconscious to block it out for this long, it must be something of some consequence."

"Okay, I'll be sure to warn him about that."

The next day the four of them took the train into Chicago. It was not what they would normally do to take in a Cubs game since it is a real mess getting back on the train after a game. But since they were going out to dinner with D and

Chris after the game the rush would be well over by the time they headed back out to the burbs. Besides, Jan had never ridden the commuter rail system.

Metra, operating on the Burlington Northern line from Naperville, dropped them off at Union Station on the west bank of the river in downtown Chicago. From there it was about a six- block walk toward the lake to the State Street subway entrance where they could board the Red Line El train to Wrigley Field. They took an early train to give them plenty of time to catch batting practice before the game. All decked out in Cubs wear, including a Harbinger Jr jersey on each of them, it was no problem for anyone to guess where they were going as they walked down Adams Street.

Dave wore his jersey untucked to hide the Sig Sauer P365 SAS automatic clipped inside his jeans in the small of his back. This nine-millimeter weapon had become his favorite for when he was in civilian clothes. It is totally smooth with no catch points to snag on clothes if he needed to get it out in a hurry. It doesn't even have sights on the barrel or the back, since they are imbedded inside the slide. And being small and light weight makes it the perfect weapon for concealment.

When they got to their seats about ten rows up behind the third base dugout the Cubs were on the field taking batting practice. Chris was already there.

"Has D batted yet?" Dave asked Chris as they settled down after all of the greetings.

"Not yet, he's warming up out behind second," Chris answered pointing to the three infielders standing in a group behind second base. Just as he finished speaking the batter hit a sharp grounder to the right of second base. D jumped out from the group, snagged the ball at shoe top level and fired it to first base in one fluid motion.

"He's looking good," Kent said, beaming.

"You're as proud as me," Dave ribbed.

"I am. As you know, I have never been as big a sports fan as you. But now, I can't wait for the next game. It's really thrilling to see D doing so well."

There was a lull in the action on the field as they changed batters in the gage. D trotted to the dugout to get ready for his turn batting. Two batters later, he came out with bat in hand and began swinging in the on-deck circle.

Once D got into the batting cage, he hit about every pitch. He first batted right-handed. He started hitting down the left-field line and continued to hit line drives, moving around the field toward first base. Then he began hitting fly balls and going for the fence. After a while he moved over to the left-side of the plate and went through the process again. When he trotted back to the dugout, he had hit every ball he had swung at, hit to every part of the ball park and hit three out of the park. Dark glasses were advisable to look at either Dave or Kent, they beamed so brightly.

The ballgame against Cincinnati was not what Dave, Kent and the other Cubs fans had hoped for. D played well in the field, but was intentionally walked three times at the plate. The Reds only pitched to him if there was a runner on base, which only happened once and he hit into a double play. The Cubs lost one to nothing.

After the game they all went out to dinner. D had made reservations at a nice steakhouse on Halstead near the ball park. They had a wonderful dinner, even though the talk of the ballgame was not as upbeat as they would have liked. Still, D's career was going great and they were glad to be able to share that with him.

After dinner, D and Chris headed back to D's place. Dave, Jan, Kent and Duetta walked the few blocks to the El station to head back downtown. It was after nine at night when they took their seats on the red line train heading south.

Dave and Jan sat along the wall of the train and Kent and Duetta sat facing them on the first seat perpendicular to the wall. Dave was nearest the door in the middle of the train car. As was his custom, he quickly noted all the other passengers in the car. There were only seven others, two single males of about thirty on each end of the car, one older male directly on the other side of the door, and two couples. One couple was older and sat facing them across the aisle near the far end of the car to Dave's left. The other couple was also across the aisle but in the middle of the car on the opposite side of the doors.

Dave's cop mind saw no threat in anyone in the car, except for the couple just opposite them. They were both in their early to mid-twenties. She had long black and blonde streaked hair, lots of jewelry and a diamond in the side of her nose. She wore cut-off jeans and a bright green top with a small red and yellow pattern similar to flowers. Her shoes were sandals and her feet were dirty. She was staring at a cellphone.

Her partner was a big guy. Even though he was sitting, Dave judged him to be well over six feet, maybe six-five. His day-old bearded face had signs of scars. He didn't have a body builder build, but was in good shape and would tip the scale at over two-forty. His black ball cap was turned backwards. He wore a blue and green plaid shirt with the sleeves cut off at the shoulders. His arms rippled with muscle. His shirt was not tucked in his jeans and was unbuttoned showing a blue sleeveless tee underneath. He had on high top basketball shoes only partly laced.

The item that most attracted Dave attention was meant to be hidden, and it almost was. Only the slightest hint of silver could be seen peaking out from inside of the big guy's plaid shirt. Dave recognized it as the butt end of a pistol stuck down into his waistband. The guy had his head down and his arm crossed over his belly.

As the train started moving, there was a noise at the far end of the car, to Dave's left. He recognized it as the door of the next car closing. He looked and saw a face looking into the car through the window of the door. The hat with the checker board band told him it was a Chicago policeman.

As the cop came into the car, he did the same review of the car occupants that Dave had done, with the same result. He fixed his gaze on the plaid shirt guy. At the same instance, plaid shirt's girl looked very quickly from her phone to the cop and back to her phone. She whispered something too low for anyone but plaid shirt to hear.

Plaid shirt moved his head up and very slightly to the right to glance in the direction of Chicago's finest. He slowly turned back to the left raising his left hand to rub his forehead, as if he had a headache. But as his left hand went up, his right went down to his waistband inside the plaid shirt.

Dave shifted his weight to his right toward Jan, as his right hand slid behind him. His thumb clicked the safety to the off position as his hand grasped the Sig Sauer. He waited and watched the cop walk through the train car. The patrolman seemed to notice no one in the car except for plaid shirt. Although he didn't look directly at him as he walked by, Dave could tell his sole focus was right there.

Plaid shirt still rubbed his head as he looked at the floor. After the officer had walked by, the black ball cap came slowly up and followed him. Dave saw his eyes for the first time as they stared into the back of the cop. The brow above the cold steel eyes furrowed with hate.

The cop was about halfway between Dave and the other door when plaid shirt made his move. He quietly moved toward the cop as he pulled the pistol out from under his shirt. It appeared to be a .38 caliber revolver. He held it at a ninety-degree angle from the norm as he brought it up and pointed it at the back of the cop's head.

When plaid shirt had passed him, Dave went into action. In one fluid motion he got up behind plaid shirt with the 9mm pointed at his back. But as Dave moved, so did plaid shirt's girl, straight toward Dave. In the next instant everything happened at once.

Chapter 25

As Dave saw the tendon for the first finger of plaid shirt's right-hand start to draw the trigger of the .38, he introduced a bullet from the Sig Sauer to the right shoulder blade of the big man. This caused the .38 to jerk upward as the bullet left the barrel, missing its mark. The bullet just grazed the top of the cop's head. The cop's hat went flying up toward the ceiling of the train car as it followed the bullet.

That all happened milliseconds after plaid shirt's girl lunged at Dave. But instead of stopping him, she was met by Jan's right hand in a forceful chop across the bridge of the nose, sending her down onto the floor of the train car. Before she had hit the floor, Kent was moving to make sure she stayed down.

Meanwhile, plaid shirt was pivoting to his right and falling toward the floor. Dave grabbed his gun hand and kept the gun pointed up. Plaid shirt squeezed off another round as he fell. The cop had ducked down and to the left. He turned to his right and also grabbed the assailant's gun hand. As plaid shirt hit the floor of the train car, he had Dave and the cop on top of him, holding him down and pulling the .38 out of his grasp. Together they rolled him over onto his stomach and the cop slapped hand cuffs on him as he protested and bled.

Dave pulled his shield out from his pocket. He flashed it in the direction of the officer as he radioed in.

"Shots fired, suspect down...," the radio call began.

Dave looked back for the first time to the area where he had been seated. He saw plaid shirt's girl on the floor with a bloody nose. Jan and Kent were holding her down.

"Thanks," the cop said to Dave.

Other than the profane protests of the perp, not a single word had been spoken by anyone during the entire ordeal until that point.

"What happened here?" Dave asked as he got back over to Jan.

"Your lady took this girl out when she tried to stop you," Kent offered. "She sure packs a punch for a pregnant judge."

"You okay?" Dave asked, concerned.

"Sure," Jan said sheepishly, "you know how jealous I am. When I saw her going for you, I just snapped."

"You know you could be looking at an assault charge."
"Well, if it comes to my court, I'll be fair and impartial."

The train was held at the next station. No one was allowed to leave until the police had obtained statements and contact information from everyone on the train. Plaid skirt and his girlfriend were taken to the hospital under guard. The police officer was also taken to the hospital although the assessment of the paramedics was that his injury was no more than a scratch. Because it was on the head, it was best to have it looked at by the hospital staff.

Dave, Jan and Kent were asked to go to the police station for further interviews. They were transported in two squad cars along with Duetta.

Once at the station house they were each interviewed separately by an officer who took their statements of what occurred on the train. When Dave finished his statement, he was escorted into an office. As he entered the man behind the desk got up and approached him.

"I'm Dave Wessel, head of investigations for this precinct," the captain said. "It's an honor to meet you, sir." He motioned to one of the chairs in front of his desk. He returned to his high back desk chair. The name plate on the front of the desk read, "Captain David Dean Wessel."

The conversation went right into baseball and how much the entire police force appreciated what D was doing for the Cubs. After a few minutes it shifted to the trouble on the train.

"We appreciate your help, Sheriff. That is one bad dude you took out there, we've been on him for years, but have never been able to get him in the act as you did tonight. Now we can put him away for a long time."

"I was just doing what needed to be done, Captain."

"What you did was stop an execution and bring down one of the leaders of a gang. That cop worked in our organized crime unit for several years. We had to move him to the El duty after we picked up word on the street that there was a contract out on him. He was involved in a drug bust and killed the brother of the guy you shot."

"So, it was revenge?"

"That's our read. We thought he was the one who put the contract out, but certainly didn't think he would attempt it himself. It's just a good thing you were there and ready to take action."

"I'm just glad I was paying attention."

"So are we. We can't thank you enough. My guys tell me we have everything we need from you for now. There may be more questions, but if so, we can do that by phone. The state's attorney's office will most likely want you and your wife to come back for the trial. They always like to have a judge and sheriff as witnesses."

"I don't think that will be a problem. But it would be nice if the trial is during ball season around a stretch of home games, if you can work that."

"Okay, I'll make sure the court knows of your request," Wessel laughed. "Now, just sit tight for a second while I get someone to take you guys home."

The Captain picked up his phone and punched buttons. While he was talking, Dave looked around the office. It was a normal police office, duplicated in station houses all over the country. There were framed awards on the walls, photos of ceremonies, various certificates of achievement and of course family pictures.

Dave was absentmindedly looking around when something grabbed him like a slap in the face. On the wall to the left of Wessel's desk, just below the Bachelor's Degree in Criminal Justice from the University of Illinois, in block letters was a plaque that read, "Remember: you really can't know WHAT happened, unless you know HOW it happened."

Dave's mind jumped back to the conversation he, Dan and Brian had about what happened when Brian was shot. He remembered Brian saying that they knew what happened but they didn't know how. "No, Brian," Dave thought to himself, "we don't know WHAT happened because we don't know HOW it happened."

"Okay, we're all set," Wessel broke Dave's train of thought. "A police van will be at the front door in a couple of minutes to take you all back out to Naperville."

Wessel got up from his desk and walked with Dave back out to where Jan, Kent and Duetta were seated in a waiting area. Dave introduced everyone and there was some light conversation about the evening events and of course the Cubs game. Dave participated, but Jan kept looking at him as if she wasn't sure he was paying attention.

A few minutes later they were in a police van getting onto the Eisenhower Expressway headed west to the suburbs. Dave and Jan in the third-row seat. Kent and Duetta were in the row behind the driver. There was a wire screen between them and the driver.

"Where are you?" Jan asked Dave. "What did you learn in that office that spaced you out?"

"I'm back on Brian's case, and I just learned that we don't know what we think we know."

"How did what happened to us tonight put you there?"

"It really has nothing to do with tonight; it has to do with a saying on the wall in the Captain's office. It said you really don't know what happened if you don't know how it happened. We think we know what happened the night Brian was shot, but we can't figure out the details of how it happened. So, I'm thinking we don't know what happened."

"Hum," Jan said softly, "sounds like it may be time to reinvestigate."

"Thanks, judge," he rolled his eyes, "Now why didn't I think of that?"

She poked him in the ribs playfully which started the touch back shuffle they often found themselves engaged in.

"Kids, settle down," Kent turned around in the seat in front of them. "You don't want me to stop this car do you?"

"Sorry, dad," Jan responded.

The Cubs won the game on Sunday afternoon with a final score of five to two. D played well in general, but was assessed an error in the third inning when his throw to first base sailed high as he attempted a miraculous throw from deep behind second base. It allowed the runner to advance to second as the first baseman ran to recover the ball. But D he was able to make up for his error three pitches later. He grabbed a hard-hit line drive right over second base and stepped on the bag before the runner could get back for an unassisted double play. At the plate he walked three times and had two hits and two RBIs.

After the game, they hung around to see D before heading back out of town. Chris was going to spend another night at D's place before heading back to school the following morning. When D came out of the clubhouse, they went across the street to have a burger as a group.

Even though it was nearly an hour after the game, there were still a lot of fans in the area. Some of them recognized D. Dave felt a great sense of pride at the way D handled his fans. He was very respectful of each one of them. He didn't hesitate to take pictures and he asked each one their name and if they enjoyed the game. In Dave's mind he seemed to be genuinely interested in what each fan had to say.

"You know, D," Jan spoke up as they settled down at a table, "I'm very impressed with your demeanor in dealing with fans. You don't seem to be bothered by them at all."

"Thanks, Jan," D said. "They don't bother me. If it wasn't for them, I wouldn't be able to have so much fun. I owe everything that is happening to them. If I ever get to the point of being bothered by fans, it will be time to do something else."

After a quick meal, they all said their good byes and headed out. D and Chris back to his place and Dave, Jan, Kent and Duetta to the western suburbs and the airport.

As Dave and Kent followed Jan and Duetta across the tarmac toward the plane, Dave turned toward Kent.

"One more question for you Kent," he said. "Do you think there's anything that we can try to get Brian to remember? Like hypnosis or something?"

"I'm not a psychiatrist, and I haven't studied such things, but I see nothing wrong with trying something like that. But on the other hand, if something would come out under hypnosis, I'm not sure you could rely on it. It could just be like a dream that manifests itself through the process."

"So, you're saying that if we put him under and he tells us what happened, it may or may not be real?"

"Exactly. How would you know if you got the truth or just a figment of his imagination?" Kent offered.

"There is that, but if I get information I don't have, I could investigate to determine if it is true or not. As of now, I have nowhere to look."

"I see your point. If it gives you a direction, it may be helpful," Kent said thoughtfully.

"One other question, can a person lie under hypnosis?"

"I wouldn't think so, as we think of the term lie. But remember, the subconscious may perceive something as truth because it has dreamed it be true. It's an area you would need to talk with someone more studied than I."

"I find it hard to believe anyone could be more studied than you, big brother."

"Oh, I've done my share in my field, but I'm by no means on top of the list. I can assure you of that. But what I mean is that you need to put that line of questioning to someone in that field. Let me put you in touch with Big Wall."

"What?"

"Not what, who, Doctor Walter Mazurck. Wally is a good friend and an excellent psychiatrist. He would be far better at answering your questions."

"Did you call him the Big Wall?"

"Big Wall is what he calls himself. He says psychological problems are like hitting a big wall that you can't see. But if you talk with him, he'll help you see your big wall and get over it."

"That's an interesting take on psychology."

"Maybe, but those of us who've known him a long time, believe getting a new idea across to him, or getting him to agree with you, is like hitting a big wall," Kent laughed. "Anyway, I'll give him a call tomorrow and ask him to give you a few minutes of his time. He will surely be more helpful than me."

"Okay, thanks, Kent."

Only about three hours later as Dave and Jan snuggled in bed, he thought about what an eventful weekend they had had and how much he had to be thankful for, as he drifted off to sleep.

Chapter 26

Every morning, when Dave got into his office, he found the log sheet for the previous night on his desk for his review. On Mondays it was for the entire weekend. This Monday was no exception, except for the size of the report. There had been an unusual amount of activity over the weekend. It was the normal stuff, but just more of it. The normal traffic stops for speeding, DUI, and other traffic violations. There were also the domestic violence calls, public intoxication, minor theft, noise disturbances, loud parties and so forth.

Dave had gotten into his office early, before anyone else, and was deep into his report when the office began to fill up. He heard the normal commotion, but was not really paying much attention to it, until his sixth sense told him something was different. He looked up and the entire office staff was standing in his doorway.

"Another drug dealer bites the dust." Cheryl spoke first.

"You heard about that?" Dave asked. It hit him that he had been so caught up in the events of the weekend that he hadn't even given any thought to the fact that the news would have gotten back here.

"Are you kidding," Dan broke Dave's train of thought. "It was the lead report on the Sunday news programs."

"And, the front page of the Sunday paper," Bob said.

"They said you saved a cop's life," Brian added.

"Yeah, I guess I did," Dave responded, "but it was something any of you would have done."

"Maybe, maybe not, but what I do know is that you did it. That made us all proud," Dan said beaming.

"Okay, thanks. I appreciate it." Dave was a bit embarrassed by the accolades. "I really do, but let's get back to work, and from the look of the daily sheets, you all must have plenty to do."

As they started to move back to their respective duties, Dave motioned for Dan and Brian to stick around.

"I want to go back to the conversation we had last week," Dave said as his two investigators settled into the side chairs in front of his desk. "Brian, you made the comment that we know what happened behind the store, but we don't know how. Remember?"

"Sure, Dave, that's where we are, isn't it?" Brian looked a bit puzzled.

"No, I don't think so. I saw a phrase over the weekend that changed my mind on that. In the investigation office up in Chicago was a plaque that read, you really don't know what happened if you don't know how. I'm thinking we need to rethink what we know."

Dan and Brian stared at Dave. The room fell silent. The three just looked at each other.

"I see what you're saying," Dan spoke up after processing what Dave had said, "I think that's valid. All we really know is that Brian was shot. We'll go back to the beginning, start over and let that tell us what we know."

"Makes sense to me," Brian agreed.

"Sheriff, do you want to take a call from a Doctor Walter Mazurck?" Cheryl said in the doorway.

"Yes, I certainly do," Dave said as he waved Dan and Brian out.

"Dave Harbinger," he said into the phone as leaned back in his chair.

"Sheriff, this is Wally Mazurck, Kent suggested you may have an interesting case for me to look into."

"I really appreciate your call, Doctor. Yes, Kent said you may be able to help."

"Please, call me Wally. Just let me begin by telling you how much I have always appreciated your brother's friendship. He's one in a million and I'd do anything I can to help him out, which extends to his brother."

"Thanks, Wally, how much did Kent tell you?"

"We talked about it in great detail. I understand that your friend Brian was shot in the head and he's not been able to remember what happened."

"Yes, and I'm wondering if hypnosis, or some other procedure, could help him remember. We have a case to solve and I'm sure he knows what happened."

"There may be things that we can do, but I would need more information before I could determine what the best course of action would be. Kent gave me Doctor Patel's contact information. I'll talk with him first to get more clinical information about the injury. After that I'll need to examine Brian to determine how to proceed. Do you think he'll be in agreement?"

"I'm sure he will, but I'll talk with him. Would he need to travel up to Chicago to meet with you?"

"I'm thinking it would be best if I come to you. If I can get Brian's permission to publish my findings, I'd be willing to absorb all of my expenses. I think we may have something here, scientifically speaking. I'm thinking we may be able to get this done pretty quickly, if schedules work out."

"Well, I can tell you Brian's available about anytime during normal business hours, because he works for me. When you say, quickly, what does that mean?"

"Let me talk with Doctor Patel first, but if things are as I suspect, I may be in your office later this week or early next. Would that work?"

"That sounds great to me. We'll make it work. Let me get with Brian to make sure he's on board."

"Good, I'll give you a call after I talk with Doctor Patel and finalize my plans." Wally signed off.

Dave headed down to the conference room to bring Brian and Dan up to speed. They both enthusiastically supported his plan and were ready to move forward at whatever speed Wally wanted.

"I think you're right, Dave," Dan said, "what comes out of the back of Brian's mind might not be what actually happened, but it will give us something to work on proving. That's more than we have now."

"I agree," Brian spoke, "I certainly would like to remember and get this all settled." He paused and looked at Dave, "and speaking of settled, Marie thinks someone may be following her. Are we still in the protect Brian and his family mode around here?"

Dan also looked at Dave.

"Well, not officially, Brian," Dave said slowly. "But when we decided the real danger was probably over, some of the guys felt it would be a good idea to make sure. So, your fellow officers have taken it on themselves to maintain the watch on you and your family. They're doing it on their own time, with our support. Dan and Bob have also been putting in some night watch duties."

"Wow," Brian hesitated, "you think there's still someone out to get me."

"If I didn't, I would've put a stop to it," Dave said. "Even though we could no longer justify the budget impact, I still believe someone may be worried you will remember. If something bad went down, you're still in danger. We just can't be sure."

"I think that hit man was after you," Dan spoke. "We're not about to let the next one get you, either. You've had an armed escort everywhere you've gone since Dave ran that guy off the road. Marie, too, so you can tell her to relax, it's the good guys."

"Okay, thanks," Brian said. "I guess I owe a bunch of guys a lot."

"You wouldn't hesitate to do it for one of the other guys," Dave concluded. "It's who you are too. Let's just get this solved so we can get back to normal around here."

"Walt Regan asked you to call when you get a minute," Cheryl quipped as Dave passed her desk on the way back to his office.

"Okay, thanks."

He picked up the phone as he settled in behind his desk.

"I see you had some excitement up in the Windy," Walt answered Dave's call.

"You heard about that, huh?"

"Who hasn't? It's been the talk around here all day. From what I read you must have been on the guy before he could react. What tipped you off?"

"I saw the gun under his shirt when I got on the train. So. I was alert to him. When he pulled it out as he was going for the cop, I was just reacting from that point on."

"Well, reacting or not, it was good work. Everyone here at SPD thinks you did a great job."

"I appreciate that, Walt. Speaking of SPD how are things?"

"Things are great. Everything's running smoothly. The reason I called was to see if you had time for lunch today. so you can fill me in on all the details of the weekend?"

"Sure, Mary's at eleven-thirty?"

"See you there."

Dave hung up the phone and turned to his budget sheets, he needed to get that finished up so that Craig Jackson could finalize the proposed budget to send on for board approval. About twenty minutes later the phone rang.

"Sheriff Harbinger," he answered.

"Sheriff, this is Linda Recter, FBI."

"Agent Recter, how are things at the FBI?"

"Things are good, thanks. I hear that things are better in Chicago thanks to you."

"Word does get out."

"Yes, it does. Great job. I got a call from the Agent in Charge in the Windy, who asked me to pass on their gratitude as well."

"Thanks, only doing the job."

"Anyway, the reason for my call is that we were able to run down more information on those money transfers to the hit men we talked about. Are you with me?"

"Sure, you said there was information about a transfer to the guys in Williams County."

"Right, and we found that the money came from a numbered account in the Caymans. But that's about as far as we can get with that. I'm afraid there is no way to determine who the account belongs to due to the banking regulations down there, or lack of."

"Okay, well that's something anyway. Thanks for the information."

"There is another thing, Sheriff," Recter continued. "We've been leaning on the State's Attorney and I believe we may be close to getting an agreement on dropping some charges if the suspects will provide information about what went on down there."

"Really," Dave's heart rate picked up a notch, "that would be great. Do you think they'll go for it?"

"Don't know, but we think it is worth a try. Besides, they'll still go away for a long time. I'll be in touch."

"Thanks, Agent Recter, I owe you."

"I'll tell you what. If we can get information out of these guys to solve your case, count it as a return for you taking that guy out in Chicago before he could murder a cop. Deal?"

"Deal. Thanks."

Dave hit his speed dial after completing his call with the FBI.

"Hi, Handsome," Jan answered.

"Baby, you make my day just by hearing your voice."

"I'm in court in two minutes, what's up?"

"I need to break our lunch date, Walt wants to talk."

"Okay, I guess I can share you. It looks like I would be pressed to make it anyway. No problem."

"Thanks, you are so sweet."

"Oh, one thing, I dropped your tux off at the cleaners last week. It's ready to be picked up, can you get it?"

"Ah," Dave was taken aback. "The Alzheimer shindig, that's Saturday night. I had forgotten. Sure, I can get it. Thanks for remembering."

"It's my job. Gotta run, love you," she signed off.

Dave got back to his budget sheets.

"It's eleven-fifteen," Cheryl broke Dave concentration some time later. "Don't you have a lunch date?"

"I certainly do, thanks," Dave looked at his watch out of habit.

Walt had not yet arrived when Dave took a seat at a table in the back of Mary's. Only a couple of minutes passed before Walt came in and joined Dave at the table. They talked for several minutes about the details of Dave's weekend encounter. The meals were ordered and delivered before the conversation turned.

"I'm glad you could meet me today, Dave," Walt became serious. "I've continued to dig as much as I can without having anyone know I'm digging, if you know what I mean."

"I understand, it must be difficult," Dave agreed.

"I've discovered that the Mayor's wife was the beneficiary of a rather large estate a few years back. That may explain my concern about the money they have been spending."

"Hum, I didn't know about that," Dave said thoughtfully. "That could very well explain it."

"Yeah, but I still sense something is going on. I just haven't been able to put my finger on it."

"How did you learn about the estate?"

"From the finance director. He and I were talking over lunch the other day. I mentioned my watch hobby. He volunteered that the Mayor has been into watches since his wife got the inheritance."

"That's very good investigative technique, Walt," Dave smiled.

"Luck is the most important part of good investigations, you know that."

"Of course, so how're we coming on the Bob Jones thing," Dave changed the subject. "We still planning on seeing what we can get from him?"

"Yeah, it looks like he's going downhill, mentally. He hasn't been very good on the job, if you know what I mean. The bar visits also continue on a regular basis. I'm thinking if we give it a couple more weeks, he may be ripe for the picking. I'll let you know."

"Okay, we'll be ready. Just let us know when," Dave paused. "So, Walt, any idea when you'll be ready to jump ship and come on board with us?"

"Actually, I'm ready now," Walt looked at Dave. "But if there's something going on at city hall, I don't see anyone else doing anything about it. So, until I convince myself that it's nothing, I need to keep digging. Sorry."

"No need to apologize, buddy," Dave shook his head. "I appreciate your dedication to justice. We can wait."

"Thanks, Sheriff."

On his way back to the station Dave pulled through the drive up at the cleaners. His tux was ready along with six other items Jan had dropped off that she hadn't mentioned. He made a mental note to pull something on her in retaliation as he paid the bill. His next stop was a florist to order a nice corsage of white roses for her to wear on Saturday night.

Chapter 27

D ave spent the most of the following Saturday in the shop working on the car collection. It was getting to be summer cruise season and he was behind on making sure every car in the collection was ready to go. He always wanted the option to take out any car he felt like driving on any given day in the summer. He had always felt that if any of the cars was not ready because of some mechanical problem that it was a direct reflection on him. His dad had instilled in him a sense of responsibility in keeping the collection in top condition.

Jan was okay with him being unavailable since she was busy with appointments and preparation for the Saturday evening ball. She had told him to be ready to go before six, but otherwise he could do as he pleased.

What he pleased was a tune up on the '63 split window Corvette. Although it only had about three thousand miles since the last tune up, it had been almost four years. He had in mind taking it to the Corvette club show next month and wanted it to be running perfect.

As he was tightening the last spark plug on the driver's side, Bobby came into the shop.

"Hey, Boss, how's it?"

"Good, Bobby," Dave said as he moved around to the passenger side of the car. "Planting going well?"

"Yep, almost done. Only got 'bout fifty acres left. Getting the 'vette ready, huh?"

"Yeah, I'm planning to take three of the sixties vettes to the Corvette club show next month. As a matter of fact, I was thinking that you could maybe drive one of them for me, if Chris doesn't make it home."

"Sure, be glad ta. It'd be fun. Which other two?"

"The two '67's."

"Cool, I'm in for sure."

"Great, I'll tell you what, even if Chris makes it home, you plan on going. If Chris is here, we'll add the '64 and take four of them."

"Alright, it'll be cool," Bobby got serious, "say, Boss, 'got word from one a the old homeys. Said somebody lookin for me."

"Really, did they tell them anything?"

"Na, told em I must ta gone south. Ya think they after Brian, too?"

"I think they may be. We're still watching him, and his family. They haven't tried anything, but that may be because our guys are there. We don't know for sure."

"How did your old homey find you?" Dave asked.

"Didn't really, just email. Still got the old account. Got no reason ta think anybody knows where I'm at."

"I hope you're right. Now you be sure to let me know if you suspect anyone finds out. Okay?"

"Sure, boss, I be cool."

After making sure all four Corvettes were ready to go, Dave headed back to the house to get ready for the shindig. It was almost four which gave him plenty of time to shower, get into the monkey suit and be ready well before the six deadline Jan had set for him.

The invitation stated an open bar mixer from 6 to 7 followed by opening remarks, introduction of dignitaries, invocation and dinner. After dinner the schedule said there would be a silent auction for the charity.

"How much do you plan to donate tonight?" Dave asked as they drove to toward the convention center where the benefit was being held.

"I don't have an amount in mind, why?" Jan looked at him curiously as he drove.

"Just curious, you've got no plans for a silent auction amount, or how much I can spend?"

"I don't care how much you spend, that's your money."

"Well, I may not have enough of my money if what I picked up at the barber shop is true."

"What did you hear?" her look became more than curious.

"I heard Winston Delagoto donated a Jaguar XKE. I've always wanted one of those."

"Really, what year?"

"I heard it's a 1967, but I'm not sure that's accurate."

"Hum, it would look good in the garage next to this car," Jan mused. "What do you think it's worth?"

"Depends on what it is. A nice roadster would be over a hundred grand. If it's a coupe probably more like eighty or so. But the two plus two models would top out about sixty. Of course, it all depends on condition."

"Of course," Jan smiled. "Well, sweety, if you want it, go for it. I'll help if you run out of cash."

"Seriously?"

"Yes, but I thought you were planning to reduce the size of the collection."

"The collection, yes, but this is for us," he smiled back.

When they got to the convention center, Dave pulled the XJL up to the front entrance and let Jan out. He parked the car in the nearby lot and hurried to joined her where she waited just inside the all glass entrance. As he walked up to the door his heart skipped a beat as he took in the beauty of his wife in her teal evening gown smiling at him. She took his arm and they headed inside.

Just off the main lobby was the ball room. As expected, it was large and well occupied by a who's who of Springfield and Lincoln County. Just inside the door was a table covered in purple linen with name cards laid out in alphabetical order. At the table sat Cheryl and another woman Dave didn't know.

Dave didn't recognize Cheryl at first. He wasn't expecting her and she was dressed far different than the normal business attire from the office. Her hair was also fixed in a very formal style he had not seen before.

"Hi, Cheryl," Jan spoke first, bringing Dave to full recognition of his assistant, "you certainly look nice."

"Thanks, Your Honor, but I can't hold a candle to you. You look terrific. I love that dress," Cheryl nodded approvingly.

Cheryl handed Jan a tag that read "Judge Jan Harbinger."

The tag had a pin on the back to attach it to clothes. Cheryl handed a similar one to Dave that read "Sheriff David Harbinger."

"Looks like we're all here now," Cheryl said, "Bob and Dan have already checked in. They're seated at table fifteen."

"Thanks, Cheryl," Dave muttered, having not completely recovered and somewhat embarrassed by it. "I knew Bob and Dan were coming, but I wasn't aware that you were part of this organization."

"I'm not really," she turned to the woman next to her, "Cindy, this is my boss, Sheriff Harbinger."

"Cindy is my sister," Cheryl continued as Dave and Cindy shook hands, "she works for the Alzheimer's Association. She suggested I may be helpful at the sign in desk since I know about everyone in Lincoln County."

"I can vouch for that," Dave offered.

"Sheriff," Cindy said, "I have you and the Judge seated at table six. That will be up front just to the right side of the platform. There are place cards to identify your seats."

"Thanks, to both of you, have a good evening," Jan smiled as she and Dave walked toward the bar.

"What would you like from the bar?" Dave asked.

"Just a coke, please."

As Jan waited and looked around the room, Dave got two cokes from the bar just a few steps away and returned. The room was quite large with about fifty or sixty tables spaced around the middle. Each table was set for eight people.

There were four bars set up, two at the back and one on each side of the room. Dave and Jan stood a few steps from the rear bar nearest the entrance. There was a large platform about thirty feet across and twenty feet deep in the center of the front wall. The platform was two steps higher than the table area. The rest of the wall space along the back, both sides and the front of the room were taken up by tables with the silent auction items.

Most of the hundred or so people in the room were moving in sequence around the outside of the room looking at the items to be auctioned. Next to each item was a card with spaces for bidders to put their name and an amount they want to pay for the donated item.

As Dave scanned the room, he noticed a group of people at the far opposite corner of the room that seemed to be surrounding something. He couldn't tell what it was, but he suspected it may be the car he had heard about.

"I think we may want to go check out the far corner of the room," he said to Jan nodding in the direction of the group.

She nodded and they headed in that direction, cokes in hand. Their trip across the room was interrupted several times by greetings from various people. Most Dave knew but a couple he did not recognize. Thus, the dilemma of a politician who everyone knows, but doesn't know everyone that knows them. Dave and Jan were both cordial and friendly as they responded to each voter.

Once they reached the subject group, Dave could see that it was indeed what he had heard about. The sign by the left front wheel identified the 1967 Jaguar XKE donated by

Delagoto Motors. The sign noted several features of the
car and at the bottom said that there was a reserve on the
car and the starting bid was to be eighty-five thousand
dollars.

The car was a series 1 roadster and was dark green, British
Racing Green to be exact. It had a light brown interior that
Jaguar called Biscuit. The hood, or bonnet, was open to
reveal a very nicely detailed engine compartment. Dave
noted the three side draft carburetors which identified the
engine as the 4.2-liter, 265 horsepower option. It had a
four-speed manual transmission and knock off wire wheels.

"Looks to be the hundred grand version to me," Jan
whispered.

"I'm thinking it would be a real steal at that," Dave
whispered back. "I'm thinking it's probably worth about
one forty."

"Are you going to bid on it?"

"Maybe, I'll let you know later on."

Jan was pulled away by one of the clerks from the court
house to meet family members. Dave was continuing his
examination of the car when he noticed Winston Delagoto
standing about fifteen feet off the rear of the car. He went
over.

"Say, Winston, what's it going to take to meet reserve?"

"Why, Sheriff, are you interested?"

"I am, so what can you tell me?"

"Well, I guess there's no harm in telling you what I'm looking for. I agreed to donate the car with the understanding that I will get back what I've got in it, less a five-thousand-dollar donation. Anything over that goes to the charity. I've got ninety-five in it."

"So that's the reserve?"

"I don't know, they set that."

"What did you have the car listed for on your lot?"

"One-thirty."

"I'm thinking it's worth that. Is it as good as it looks?"

"It's perfect. The restoration was completed about a year ago. The owner ran into hard times and needed to get out from under it, so I was able to buy it right. I'd love to see you win it, Dave. It'd certainly look good in your garage next to the XJL Jan took from me," Winston said as another possible bidder pulled him away from Dave.

Awhile later, a distinguished looking man spoke into the mic on the platform asking everyone to find their seats so that the program could begin. Dave and Jan had been separated since whispering about the car, but soon found each other and took their seats at table six.

"Well, did you bid?" Jan whispered into Dave's ear.

"Not yet. But Winston thinks it will take at least ninety-five to meet reserve," he whispered back.

"What are you thinking?"

"I think I'll bid ninety-five and see what happens. You okay with that?"

"I am," was all she said but her look told him she was excited about it.

The welcoming comments included introductions of all the dignitaries present. Jan was introduced along with the other judges present. Dave was introduced with the county officials. The total number of people introduced was in the range of fifty, which took some time. As Dave scanned the room during the introductions, it appeared to him that most all of the tables were completely full.

After the pastor of the Baptist church gave the blessing, the MC introduced the musical entertainment during dinner. It was a local musical group called the School Daze. School Daze had first started playing together when they were in high school and have continued to play a few gigs per year since.

School Daze played a variety of music including jazz, dixie land and pop. Dave knew all of the band members. Ron played trumpet and was a professional musician with a whole list of accomplishments, including TV shows. Greg was on clarinet and was also an accomplished guitarist and artist. Jeff played trombone, Jerry was on drums, Janie on piano, and Glen on bass. But the one that caught Dave attention was Mayor Wilson on sax.

As the combo played during dinner, Dave kept thinking about what the Memphis detective had told him. The owner of Integrity Developmental Consulting was a sax player in Nashville. The firm that owned the plane the Mayor used was run by a sax player. And the Mayor was a sax player.

After dinner there was a presentation about the charity and all the good it has done and hopes to do. The presentation took just over half an hour. After the presentation concluded, it was announced that everyone would have fifteen minutes to look over the items and place new bids before the auction results would begin to be announced. The room was divided into five sections. The section one auction would end first, and so forth every fifteen minutes. The car was in the last group which meant an hour and fifteen minutes until that auction closed.

Dave went over to the car and put his name next to a bid of ninety-five thousand dollars. He out bid someone named R. Arnold by ten thousand. Now all he could do was wait and keep checking to see if he had been outbid.

The auctions closed one by one. Dave and Jan waited patiently for the car auction to come up. Meanwhile, Jan had bid on several items that struck her fancy. She won a gift basket that had several of the makeup items she used regularly. In that win, she paid more than if she had bought the items separately, but it was for charity. She was not the winning bidder in four other bids she had placed.

Just before the car auction was to end, Dave made his way over to check the bidding. R. Arnold had outbid Dave with a posted offer of one hundred thousand dollars. Dave quickly jotted down one hundred five on the bid sheet next to his name and headed back to join Jan at the table.

As he was headed across the room, he saw the Mayor. He approached with his hand outstretched.

"Great job on the sax, Mayor," he said smiling.

"Thanks, sheriff, I really enjoy playing."

"I can tell. You know, the way you play reminds me of Thomas Brough."

Dave saw the Mayor's head jerk ever so slightly, but there was no doubt.

"Who?" he did not look directly at Dave, "I'm not sure I know who that is."

"Oh, he's a gig sax player in Nashville. I thought you might have heard of him."

"A, no, I don't think I have. Excuse me, Dave," he hurried away.

Dave was left puzzling about what had just happened as the MC took the mic to announce the final auction results. He hurried back to the table.

"You upped your bid?" Jan asked.

"Yeah, I had been outbid so I went to one-o-five."

"I watched, after you bid no one else went over there. I think we're in."

Jan was right. The announcement was made that the reserve on the car had been met and the winner was D. Harbinger at one hundred and five thousand dollars. Dave had his first classic foreign car.

On the way out, Dave and Jan stopped by the auction table to pay for their purchases. The woman at the table told Dave the total for them was one-hundred-five-thousand and seventy-five dollars. He handed her his American Express Gold card. She ran it through and looked shocked when she got approval. Jan had picked up her cosmetics basket and Dave was told he could pick up the car at Delagoto Motors the following week.

Chapter 28

Monday morning Dave asked Dan to come to his office shortly after settling in with his first cup of coffee.

"What's up, chief?" Dan asked as he sat in one of the chairs in front of Dave's desk.

"Did you notice who was playing sax with the band Saturday night?"

"Sure did. You think there may be a connection to the consulting firm you discovered?"

"Looks like we both made the same connection. Maybe we should follow up. I'm thinking a trip to Memphis with some mug shots may be revealing."

"You may be right," Dan agreed. "If the Mayor is that Tom Brough character his office manager should be able to pick him out."

"Can you go? I think the doctor may be coming to talk with Brian this week sometime and I want to be here for that."

344 | Glynn Amburgey

"Sure, let me get on it. I'll get a picture of the mayor and a few other suspects of similar age and appearance to show in a lineup type presentation. I may be able to get out yet today and back tomorrow," Dan said getting up. "I'll let you know."

"Thanks, Dan. I'm not sure where it takes us, but one more piece of the puzzle."

After Dan left Dave checked his rolodex for the number for Delagoto Motors and dialed.

"Winston Delagoto please," he said into the phone after a pleasant voice answered.

"Hello, this is Winston," he heard after a few seconds.

"Winston, Dave Harbinger, when can I pick up my car?"

"Hi, Sheriff, and congratulations. You made a great purchase at well below actual value. I just came from out in the shop and they're cleaning it up now. It had lots of finger prints all over it. It will be all ready to go in about thirty to forty minutes. So, any time after that."

"Great, I plan to come by around noon or so."

"Okay, not a problem on our end. It'll be ready to go. See you then."

Dave walked down to the conference room where Brian was typing away on a computer keyboard.

"Hey, buddy, you got any plans for lunch today."

"Nope, why, you buying?"

"As a matter of fact, I am, if fast food is okay. I want to pick up a car I bought and need someone to drive my squad out to the house for me. We'll grab a bite on the way back in. Okay?"

"Sure, what is it this time?"

"Jaguar XKE at the ALS benefit Saturday night. It's at Delagoto's."

"Glad to do it, can't wait to see it."

Later, as Dave worked in his office, he got a call from Dr. Mazurck confirming that he would be down to talk with Brian on Wednesday.

When lunch time came, Dave and Brian headed for Delagoto motors in Dave's squad. When they walked in, Winston was in the showroom waiting for them.

"It's back in the addition," Winston said, motioning for them to follow as he headed toward the back of the building. They walked back through the customer waiting room, across the shop area, through a series of doors and finally into a large addition on the back of the original dealership. There in front of a wash rack, sat the gleaming XKE.

"It looks great, Winston, thanks," Dave said.

"Pete will tell you about it," Winston motioned to a guy in a uniform shirt with "Pete" over the pocket. "I've got the paperwork on the desk over by the door. I'll make sure it's all in order while you learn about your car."

Winston headed toward the desk while Dave and Brian listened to Pete's instructions. Winston was on the phone at the desk when Dave went over after Pete had finished. He motioned for Dave to have a seat in the chair in front of the desk.

"Did you want both names on the title, or just yours?" Winston asked with his hand over the phone mouth piece.

"Jan would need to sign if it's both, so just mine."

"Just David," Winston said into the phone and hung up. "Betty is completing the title work and will bring it right out."

"Okay fine, no problem. So, when did you add this addition, it looks new?" Dave asked.

"Just finished it up about two months ago. We needed the extra covered space for bad weather deliveries and the new wash rack. It's going to be a real plus to our operation."

"I'm sure it will. Tell me, how did you find the city to deal with, permit wise?"

"Wasn't an issue at all. We hired a consultant to handle all that. Once we had the plans, they took care of all the permits."

"Integrity Developmental Consulting?"

"Yep, they did a great job. Have you done business with them?"

"No, just curious. How did you come to hire them?"

"They were recommended by the city when we told them we were thinking of an addition. I don't recall exactly who, but someone in the building department said they worked with them a lot. They gave us their card and we called them."

"Who did you talk with?" Dave curiosity was peaking.

"A lady in their home office. She took my contact information and they contacted me by email."

"Did you ever meet anyone in person?"

"Funny thing, no we didn't, never met a soul, but they did a great job for us."

"If you don't mind me asking, how was payment to the consultant structured. Did you pay a percentage of the construction cost?"

"No, they wanted a monthly fee, based on a percent of expected new revenue. But since our project wasn't expected to increase revenue, they agreed to a fixed monthly fee of a thousand a month for ten years."

"A thousand a month is a lot of money over ten years," Dave said.

"Not really, Dave, if you consider a consultant charging four to five hundred dollars per man hour. Especially when they put two or three people on a project, it adds up fast. And also, since it's monthly, it's just another expense item accounting wise. They gave me options and I chose the guaranteed no permit delay plan."

"How could they guarantee that there would be no delays?" Dave asked. "That doesn't sound reasonable."

"You're right, they can't. The plan was structured in a manner that my fees would be reduced if delays happened. Time is money during a construction project, so it was worth it to me."

A woman walked up behind Dave and handed a file folder to Winston. He opened the folder and took out papers for Dave to sign. A few minutes later the paper work was complete.

Dave and Brian pulled out of the building in the XKE. Dave drove around to the front of the building. He stopped next to his squad and handed Brian the keys as he got out.

As he drove toward home, Dave thought about how much fun it was to drive a true British sports car. It was an entirely different driving experience from any of the other cars in the collection. It had plenty of power, but no where near that of the American muscle cars of the same time frame. His Corvettes, Chevelle, GTOs, Shelby, and of course the Mopars, would all blow the doors off the XKE in a quarter mile. But it was obvious to him that this car was a different kind of car, better handling, better braking and top speed were its finer points.

Then his thoughts turned to the conversation with Winston about Integrity Development Consulting. In particular, why would they be so sure that there would be no permit delays. His brother in law certainly wouldn't guarantee no delays in dealing with the city permit process, he had said so. What edge could Integrity have in that regard? He made a mental note to talk with Walt about that at their next lunch meeting.

After they dropped the Jaguar off at home, Dave and Brian grabbed a quick lunch at the Arby's on the way back to the office.

"Dr. Mazurck will be here Wednesday," Dave told Brian over lunch. "He says he wants to talk with you to determine how to proceed."

"I've got no problems with that. I'd like to get back to normal, whatever that is."

"Kent says it may be difficult on you to remember what you are blocking out. Are you prepared for that?"

"I don't know, but what choice do I have? I'm going to have to deal with it. So, let get to it," Brian said defiantly.

Back in the office there was a note on Dave's desk from States Attorney Tiernan, he dialed the number.

"So, when can I expect to be able to set a trial date, Dave?" Tiernan asked without preamble.

"Sorry, Bob, we've found some things that need further investigation, not sure when."

"What kind of things?"

"Well, for one, the note from Rod's wife? What happened to it and who wrote it? That would be important to put Rod at the store, if it was a hit rather than a coincidence?"

"What do you mean, a hit? Are you suggesting these guys were hit men out to get Taylor?"

"We're looking into that, but I'm not suggesting it. However, if that were the case the note would be important to put Taylor in that store at that time."

"Hum," Bob said followed by a long deep breath. "If what you are thinking is true, Cruz is not the only guilty party here," he said slowly followed by a long pause. "Okay, Sheriff, you've got the ball, run with it. Let's find out what's going on."

"Thanks, Bob, we'll keep you posted," Dave said and hung up the phone.

"Dan asked me to tell you he is on his way to Memphis," Cheryl's said as she came into his office. "He said you would know what it was about. He expects to be back here in the office about three tomorrow if flight schedules hold."

"I do know what it's about, thanks."

"So, you picked up the car. Sam said to tell you he wants to borrow it."

"Not yet, mom always said, "you don't have to share on the day you get something.""

"Then you're saying he can come over and get it tomorrow?" she said as she walked back out of his office.

When Dave walked out of the station at the end of the day, his squad was blocked in by a car sitting crossways behind it. He recognized the car since he had just picked it up from Delagoto at lunch time. Jan was sitting in the driver seat with a smug look on her face.

"Car theft is a serious crime," Dave said as he walked up to the car. The top was down and Jan had on a Cubs ball cap.

"Are you going to arrest me, Sheriff?" she said with a false worried look.

"That depends on if your buying dinner or not."

"If it keeps me out of jail, then yes, I will."

Dave got in the passenger side and off they went with Jan smiling from ear to ear.

"The Superbird is still my favorite," Jan said as she pulled out of the parking lot, going through the gears, "but this one is certainly a lot of fun. It handles so nice."

"Yes, it does. So, you think we made a good purchase?"

"Every garage needs two Jaguars."

They went to Mary's for dinner. Jan parked the XKE at the edge of the parking lot far away from all of the other cars. Dave had liver and onions and Jan had a cobb salad.

"I talked with the State's Attorney today," Dave said between bites. "He gave me the go ahead to continue the investigation. So, it looks like it will be a bit longer before you can schedule the Cruz trial."

"I know, it may have been because of me. Cruz' attorney is pushing to go to trial. I called Bob for an update. He said you weren't able give him a date."

"Not really, we're working an angle that SPD didn't see, or chose to ignore. Anyway, they didn't follow the lead, so we are."

"The idea that it was a contract hit, and Cruz was paid to take out Taylor?"

"Contract hit, yes, but not sure about the target. We think it could have been either Taylor or Brian."

"From the way Cruz' attorney was asking, I got the impression that they're thinking you may be looking into that."

"Really," Dave's interest peaked, "what did he say that gave you that impression?"

"He asked me if the state's attorney suspected there was more to the case than has been uncovered so far? I told him that he will get that information in discovery if there is more to come. But I have not been informed that more has come to light."

Dave thought for a moment. "It does sound like he suspects something. And if he suspects we're looking into other aspects, it stands to reason that he has shared that information with his client, doesn't it?"

Jan nodded slowly and added with a serious and somewhat frightened look, "maybe you should watch your back, sheriff."

Not much was said from that point on. They were thinking of what may be going on in the minds of others. Ones that may be seeing things closing in on them.

Jan reluctantly let Dave drive the E type back to the station to pick up his squad after dinner. At the station, he held the driver's door open for her as she moved around to drive the Jag home. As he was getting into the squad, she stuck out her tongue as she drove away.

When they got home the game was in the middle of the first inning. They had missed D's double to start the bottom of the first and he was on second with one out when they sat down to watch.

As always, once the game was on that was the sole focus and it pushed aside any thoughts of worry. D had a good game with two hits. He scored once in a four to two win over the visiting LA Dodgers. Dave was feeling good as he settled into bed, but that soon faded as he again thought about what hitmen may do when they're faced with possible exposure. He wasn't afraid of Cruz. He was in jail, but there were others involved who were running free.

Chapter 29

Just after nine the next morning Dr. Walter Mazurck walked into the station asking for Dave. The receptionist called Cheryl who escorted Dr. Mazurck into Dave's office.

Dave and Wally talked about Dave's brother, the Cubs, and other general topics as they got to know each other. After about thirty minutes, Wally got down to business.

"Dave, I'd like to spend the rest of the morning talking with Brian, to get to know him and assessing his mental state," Wally said tapping his fingers together. "Then with that knowledge, I'll take the rest of today and tomorrow to review other cases and confer with some colleges before I determine what course of action would be most effective. If, in fact, I determine hypnosis to be the best course of action, we will move forward with that first thing day after tomorrow."

"Sounds good to me," Dave responded. "Let's get to it."

Dave took Wally down to the conference room. He introduced him to Brian and left them alone so that Big Wall could begin his analysis.

"Walt called and asked if you could do lunch today?" Cheryl said as Dave got back to his office, "I told him you would be at Mary's at eleven thirty." She went back to her typing as Dave nodded.

At eleven thirty three, Dave walked into Mary's to find Walt at the table in the back.

"How you doing today Sheriff?" Walt said as Dave sat across from him.

"I'm good, how are things with you?"

"Great, I wanted to talk with you about pulling our little sting. I'm thinking next Thursday night if you guys are available."

The waitress took their orders before the conversation continued.

"Jones seems to be in a regular pattern now," Walt continued, "he has been heading to the bar after every shift. My read is that something is really bothering him. Let's see if we can find out what it is."

"Okay, I think we should be good by then. The doctor is here talking with Brian this week, so there should be no conflict with next Thursday. I'll set it up."

"Good."

"On another topic, Walt, who in the city controls the building permit process?"

"The city council sets policy and the building and zoning department carries it out. Why?"

"Just curious, who heads up the building department?"

"Charles Wilkinson is the Director of Community Development, B and Z falls under him."

"Charley is director level now? When did that happen?"

"About five years ago when Sullivan retired. Charley was assistant and just moved right up. You know him?"

"Of course, he was in my high school class. He was tight with Roger Wilson as I recall. Are they still best buds?"

"Sure are. He and the Mayor's son hang together a lot."

"That's interesting," Dave said as lunch was placed in front of them.

At about four in the afternoon Dan came into Dave's office.

"Not him," Dan said as Dave looked up from the final budget he was reviewing.

"Really? She was sure?"

"Didn't seem to be any doubt at all. She saw no resemblance."

"Humph," Dave murmured, dejectedly, "I was sure I had it figured."

"Apparently not," Dan concluded.

"You don't think she may have been protecting him?"

"My read was that she was fully cooperative and willing to help all she could. She also said that I was the third cop that has questioned her. The local sheriff you sent and one other that sounded like Rod Taylor to me."

"Really?"

"Yep, she said she didn't remember the name, but she thought he was the chief of Springfield."

"Asking about Tom Brough?"

"Yep, and about the business."

"So, Rod was definitely on to it."

"So, are we now back to Rod being the target, not Brian?" Dan questioned.

"I don't know. But we still don't know who Brough really is, do we?"

"No, we don't, but I'm sure it's not the Mayor."

"Did she describe him?" Dave asked.

"About my height, dark hair, nicely dressed was all I really got. It's been a long time since she saw him, over five years."

"A lot happened five years ago," Dave concluded.

Dave's desk phone rang and Dan left as Dave answered.

"Sheriff, this is Linda Recter."

"Hello, Agent, how's the FBI today?"

"Worried. We just got some intel that's disturbing. One of our wire taps on the hitmen gang picked up a directive, and I quote, get someone to Springfield right away. Is something going on there?"

"Not that I know about. When did that happen?"

"We picked it up about twenty minutes ago, so it's fresh."

"How many of these guys are there?" Dave's frustration showed.

"Welcome to my world, Sheriff. We're trying to track down more specifics, but it appears to be a communication to somewhere in Mexico. I'll let you know if I get something else. I'm late for a meeting, but wanted to give you a head's up. Watch your back."

"Okay, thanks." The line went dead.

Dave sat at his desk, thinking. What is going on? Why would the hitman be dispatched right away? Who is Tom Brough? If the Mayor is not Brough, could it be his son, Roger? Or maybe Brough is Charley Wilkinson? Should he send Dan back down to Memphis with some more pictures? Even if we find out who Brough is, what does it tell him? How did Brian get shot? Who is the target for the hitman on the way to Springfield? Brian, or maybe him?

All of this was still floating around in Dave's brain when he noticed the office was empty and it was almost six o'clock. He headed home perplexed.

Over dinner, Dave was still preoccupied. Jan had gotten home early and fired up the grill on the back deck for a nice grilled salmon meal. Dave sensed that she was aware of his mental gymnastics and was waiting for him to tell her what was going on in his head.

"Here's the thing," he began slowly, "Dan got back from Memphis this afternoon and the Mayor is not Tom Brough. I was so sure I had it all figured out, and now I'm questioning what I really know and how to proceed."

"Just relax, it'll all come out eventually," Jan soothed. "I think you're trying too hard to figure it out. There's no real hurry; you've got time. Take it easy."

Dave smiled in agreement. He didn't want to counter her idea that there was no hurry, that would mean telling her about a hitman who may be coming after him. Pregnant women don't need that kind of stress.

"What's your day like tomorrow?" he changed the subject.

"Routine, except for the doctor appointment at eleven."

"You want me to go with you?"

"Nah, just a check on me, no ultrasound or anything like that. I'll be fine. I would be available for lunch after, though. Ya think you could work that in?"

"Sure, where?"

"Let's do Mary's."

"Was there today, but never tired of it. Noonish?"

"Let's say twelve-thirty, late morning appointments are never on time."

"Okay."

The next morning Dave talked with Brian about the interview with Dr. Mazurck. Wally had told Brian that his preliminary assessment was that hypnosis would probably be helpful, but he still wanted to review some information before proceeding. Brian was looking forward to the session the next morning.

About ten thirty, Dave was just returning to his desk with a fresh cup of coffee when his cell phone rang. The caller ID told him it was Jan's cell calling.

"Hi, wonderful lady, how's your morning?"

"Dave, I think I'm being followed," a somewhat frantic voice said.

"What, tell me about it," Agent Recter's words flashed through Dave's mind, get someone to Springfield right away.

"A few blocks from the court house I noticed a car fall in behind me. It's still there."

"Where are you now?"

"On seventh, coming up to Lincoln."

"Take a right on Lincoln. Describe the car."

"Okay, it's a gray Impala, late model, one guy in it. I can't make out the entire license but it ends in three seven four," there was a long pause. "I just turned on Lincoln."

"Did he follow?"

After a few seconds he heard a long exhale, "no, he kept on going. I guess your wife is paranoid, sorry."

"No, no, never can be too careful. You okay now?"

"I think so, I'll be fine when I catch my breath. Thanks for your help."

"No worries. Glad you're alright. See you at Mary's, love you."

"Love you, too, bye."

Dave found it difficult to get back to work. He was glad Jan was safe and that it was a false alarm, but it also made him uneasy about what could happen. He wandered down to talk with Dan and Brian.

"Here's something interesting," Dan said as Dave walked in. "We sent a team to talk with the residents of the condo building across the street behind the strip mall. Brian noticed that nothing in the file indicated that SPD had interviewed any possible witnesses from there. They found a Mrs. Watkins on the third floor who said she had called SPD but no one ever contacted her. She said she saw, wait, let me read it." He picked up a sheet of paper.

"I was watering my plant in the window and I saw a police car behind the store across the street. I couldn't see the officer because he was down behind the car door. What I could see was he had a gun pointed at someone who was down on his knees by the back door of the store with his hands up. Then my phone rang and I talked with my daughter from Dallas for a while. When I looked out again there were police, fire trucks and all sorts of commotion down there."

Dave fell more than sat down in a chair.

"So, a witness saw me," Brian said, "I had Flores on his knees with his hands up."

"Had to be," Dan agreed. "So, what happen after she went to talk with her daughter?"

"Roger Wilson came out the back door," Dave said, half to himself. "That much we know. What we don't know is what he did after he came out."

"I think he shot Flores in the back and then shot me," Brian said starring at Dave. "If I had the drop on Flores, he couldn't have shot me. There's no way I would have let that happen. The only thing that would have gotten me out from behind that car door would have been my believing that all threat was gone."

"Roger shooting Flores would have eliminated the threat as far as you were concerned," Dave continued for him, "and you would have relaxed and left your cover position."

"Exactly," Brian continued, "I would not have expected him to pick up Flores' gun and shoot me. But I think that's what must have happened."

"That would make sense," Dan chimed in.

"And, if he is Tom Brough, and hired the hit, he would surely not want Flores captured," Dave said. "But would it be cause to kill Brian?"

"He just killed Flores in cold blood, of course he would kill Brian to hide that," Dan concluded. "Besides, he didn't have much time to think. It would have been reaction and cover his ass mode."

The three looked at each other as they each processed the information.

"Okay, so we have a reasonable theory, how do we go about proving it?" Dave asked.

"There's the rub," Dan said. "Doesn't matter what we know, or think we know, only matters what we can prove."

"Did the team make contact with every resident having a view of the scene?" Dave asked.

"No, we have three more that we haven't talked with. We left notes on all the doors asking them to contact us. Three haven't," Brian responded.

"Let's try again. Also, pull out those crime scene pictures again, where was Flores' gun found?"

Brian started thumbing through a file.

"What are you thinking, Sheriff?" Dan asked.

"I just figured out something that's been bothered me. Flores was left-handed, his gun should be on his left. I'm thinking I saw it to his right, on the wrong side."

Brian found the photograph he was looking for and laid it on the table. Sure enough, the gun on the ground in the picture was to his right side.

"See," Dave said, "there it is, plain as day. Assuming Roger is right-handed, that gun is laying where he would have dropped it after shooting Brian, not where it would have been if Flores had dropped it."

They continued looking at that picture and others to confirm that the gun placement did in fact fall in line with their current theory that Roger Wilson shot Brian. After several minutes the trio was convinced that they had a workable theory.

Lunch time came, but since Dave was meeting Jan at Mary's at twelve-thirty he continued to theorize about how to prove Sgt. Roger Wilson was the shooter. Finally, at about twelve-fifteen he headed out. As he approached his squad sitting in its regular spot in front of the station, he noticed a note stuck under a windshield wiper. He pulled it out and opened it. His heart stopped.

He pulled out his cell and punched Jan's speed dial. Her cell continued to ring until it went to voicemail. With note in hand Dave ran back into the station. Dan was walking back toward his office from the lunch room.

"Look what was on my car," Dave yelled as he threw the note at Dan.

In his office he hurriedly looked up the number for Jan's doctor and dial.

"This is Sheriff Harbinger, did my wife make her appointment?" he asked frantically.

He dropped the phone when the response was no, and collapsed into his chair as Dan came into his office.

Dan laid the note on Dave's desk.

It said: SEND THE DOCTOR HOME AND GIVE THE CASE BACK TO THE STATES ATTORNEY OR CRUZ WILL NEED A NEW JUDGE.

Chapter 30

It was only a matter of minutes before the entire office was on full alert. Dan, Bob, and Brian were in Dave's office waiting for direction.

"I talked with Jan at about ten-thirty," Dave told them. "She was on her way to her doctor's office and thought maybe someone was following her. She said it was a man in a gray late model Impala with license ending in three seven four."

"Dispatch," Bob spoke into his radio, "put out a want for a gray Impala with last three digits of license three seven four. Report if seen."

"Let's start at the doctor's," Dan offered. "Brian go over there and back-track to the court house to see what you can find. Take someone with you."

"I'm on it," Brian said as he started to leave the room.

"Ask Cheryl to come in, will you Brian?" Dave asked.

Brian left and Cheryl came into the room.

"Close the door, please, Cheryl," Dave said as she came in.

Bob got up so that Cheryl could sit. He leaned on a file cabinet looking out the window.

"Cheryl, you know everything that goes on around here. Who besides us in this room knew Dr. Mazurck was coming to see Brian?" Dave asked.

"Just the receptionist. She met him when he came in, but that's it," then she paused, "but, he asked to see you when he came in. So, she doesn't even know Brian is the reason he's here."

"I see what you're asking, Dave," Dan cut in. "Anyone in the office could have noticed him talking with Brian in the conference room."

"Maybe," Dave said, "but would they have known he's a doctor?"

"You think someone here is tipping off the bad guys. I don't think so, Sheriff, but I'll find out," Cheryl said getting up and heading for the door.

"How is she going to find out?" Bob asked after she had closed the door behind her.

"I really don't know, but I'm sure she will," Dave answered. "Okay, let's get Jan out of this. I think we have some time. They wouldn't dare hurt her if they want me to meet their demands. The FBI told me yesterday that the hitman gang was dispatching someone here. I thought maybe it was to hit me, but this make more sense. If they took me out, it wouldn't stop the investigation, it would increase the resolve of you guys to find them. The best thing to do is pressure me to end the investigation. So, they took Jan to get to me."

"They can't know that she called you and fingered them, so we have an edge if we can find the car," Dan said thoughtfully. "If they are from out of town, they are probably going to be at a motel, so maybe we start with checking all the motel lots."

"Good idea," Bob said, "I'll get the guys on it right away."

"Make it discrete, Bob, make sure our guys know we don't want to share this with SPD if they ask," Dave cautioned. "I don't think we can trust anyone over there to know we have a clue."

"Sure thing, Boss. We'll keep it on the hush hush," Bob said as he headed for the door.

"Dan, I just had a thought," Dave pondered. "If these guys are part of the same group as Flores and Cruz, do you think they may have a key to Cruz' place? Maybe that's their base?"

"You may be onto something there."

"I'll get on the horn to Rob Alexander and see if he can have one of his deputies do a drive-by to check for activity at the Cruz place."

"You should also let the FBI know what's happened. Let me get my guys on the streets," Dan headed for the door.

"Okay, FBI will be call number two."

Dave dialed the Williams County Sheriff's office number.

"Hey, Dave, how's it going?" Sheriff Alexander asked.

"Not good, Rob, my wife's been kidnapped."

"Oh, no. How can I help?"

"We think the kidnappers may be of the same gang as Cruz. If so, they may be using his house. I was wondering if you could have one of your guys do a drive by to check for activity there? I prefer an unmarked car if possible."

"I'll do better than that, Dave, I'll do it myself in my personal car. I'm out the door now, should only take me about forty minutes. I'll call you back."

"Thanks, Rob."

"Agent Recter," Dave next call was answered.

"This is Sheriff Harbinger we think my wife's been kidnapped."

"Oh, no, I'm so sorry. I was afraid something like this would happen. I sent two teams to Springfield yesterday. I can have them in your office within the hour. Any leads?"

"It just happened and we're still assessing the situation. Any help would be appreciated."

"You sound surprisingly calm, under the circumstances, sheriff."

"Believe me I'm not, but I don't think they're going to hurt her, they're using her to get to me."

"Do you think it's the guys I warned you about yesterday?"

"I do. They want me to stop the investigation on Chief Taylor and Brian's shootings. I must be getting too close."

"You may be right. My guys will be right over."

"Thanks."

Just as he hung up his cell rang. It was Brian.

"What's up, buddy?" Dave answered.

"Dave, we have her car. It's in the doctor's office lot. They must have grabbed her as she was getting out of the car because the car is unlocked and her keys are on the ground next to it. We're securing the scene."

"Okay, good. I'll get Dan and the evidence team on the way. Did anyone there see anything?"

"We haven't started talking with people yet. We want to make sure the scene isn't compromised. We'll talk with everyone we can find in the complex as soon as help arrives."

"Be sure to get names of patients or anyone else who may have been there in the ten-thirty to eleven, time frame. Especially anyone who may have left the doctor's office around the time Jan would have arrived, or just before. My guess is the kidnappers were either waiting for her or came in at the same time she did. Let's see if we can get a vehicle description."

"Sure thing, boss. We'll run things down."

Dave hung up the phone and headed down to Dan's office to get him and the evidence team on the way to the doctor's office. As he got back into his office, Cheryl followed him in and closed the door behind her.

"Sheriff, no one in this office has had any contact with anyone about Dr. Mazurck and Brian."

"You're sure?"

Cheryl just stared at him like he was speaking some foreign language.

"Oh, yes, I know you're sure, sorry," he said somewhat sheepishly.

"No apology necessary, I know the stress you're under can cause mental lapses," she smiled. "Now, what else can I do to help find Jan?"

"Would you be able to stay late tonight, if need be? I need someone here to coordinate everything if I'm out. My guess is that Dan, Bob and I will be going in different directions following leads."

"Of course, Sheriff. I'm rooted right here no matter how long it takes. You just tell me what you need and don't hesitate, hear?"

"Thanks, Cheryl, I don't know how I could do this without you."

"I need to go let the FBI in now," Cheryl said heading for the door as Dave's phone rang.

"Dave, it's Rob."

"That was quick."

"Yeah, let's just say I may have broken a speed limit law getting here. Anyway, your hunch may have been right on target. There are two vehicles at Cruz' house. A white van is in the garage and a gray Impala in on the driveway."

"Did you see the plate on the Impala?"

"Yeah, seven alpha charley kilo four three seven four. We ran that plate and it was reported stolen, a couple of hours south of here."

"Bingo, that's the car we're looking for. Where are you now, Rob?"

"I'm sitting on a side street two blocks up from the house watching it. The van is hot, too, Dave. It has Texas plates and was boosted in Brownsville. What do you need us to do?"

"Can you wait there until we can get there?"

"Of course. I'll also get guys a couple of blocks on either side to make sure we can see all sides of the place. If anyone comes, or goes, we'll know it."

"Good, thanks Rob. See you in about an hour."

Dave hit his speed dial for Dan.

"The Impala is at Cruz' house. Rob has it staked out. Let's go, code 3."

"Brian and I will be on the way shortly. See you there."

As Dave hurried out of his office, he saw four guys in suits by Cheryl's desk, and Bob headed his way.

"You guys FBI?" he asked.

They all nodded in unison.

"Good, let's roll. Sheriff Alexander in Williams County found the car we're looking for. It's at the house of the guy we have in custody for the Taylor killing." They all started for the door as Dave continued, "Bob, I don't think we'll need squads with us. Rob will have his guys."

"Okay, Sheriff," Bob said.

"We'll head down there and I'll go in and talk with Rob," Dave instructed. "Find a nearby parking lot or someplace for you and the FBI to marshal until I check it out."

"Got it," Bob and the FBI guys nodded agreement. "We'll be radio tac two."

It was about forty miles from the Lincoln County Sheriff's office to the residence of one Jose Cruz. Dave's speedometer didn't dip below the century mark very often during the trip. The trip would normally take a good fifty minutes to an hour but not this time. Just over thirty minutes later, Dave shut down the siren and drove the last mile and a half with only red and blue lights flashing.

He stopped on a side street two blocks north of the Cruz house and a half block east. He got out of his squad and walked the half block to where a blue Buick sedan was sitting parked at the curb with a man sitting in the driver's seat. Dave opened the passenger side door and got in next to Rob Alexander.

"Quick trip, Dave," Rob said as Dave quietly closed the door.

"Speed laws don't apply today to either of us. Have you seen anything?"

"Not a thing. It's the house on the west side of the street in the middle of the second block," Rob said pointing. "You see the blue mail box? It's the next house, you can just barely see the rear end of the Impala."

"Got it," Dave looked where Rob was pointing.

"I've got guys two blocks away in each direction with binoculars trained on the house. To the east and west, I've got guys with sniper scopes looking at the front and rear of the house. They can see in a couple of the windows but the others have drapes closed. No report of seeing any movement inside. What do you want to do, Dave?"

"How about we take a drive-by so that I can see the place?"

"Sure, we can drive down this street and go one block west so you can take a look at the back of the house. Even if someone is looking out, they wouldn't suspect this car. Let me tell my guys."

Rob picked up his portable radio from the seat beside him and filled his team in. He started the engine and put the car in gear, but before he could take his foot off the brake his radio came to life.

"Hold it, Sheriff," came the radio call. "Someone's coming out."

Rob put the car back in park and he and Dave both stared up the street toward the house just pasted the blue mail box.

"A man is getting into the gray Impala," the radio voice said.

About that time, Dave saw the rear of the car begin to move backward. They watched as it backed out into the street and began to pull away in the opposite direction from them.

"Subject vehicle is on the move south," Rob said into his radio. "Unit seven begin a tail after he passes your location. Units thirty-four and sixteen begin parallel path."

"Let's see where he's headed," Rob said to Dave. "All three of those units are undercover cars so I don't think he will be tipped off."

Dave called Dan on his cell.

"One of the guys has just left the house," Dave told Dan after he answered. "Rob's guys are tailing him. Are you guys all together?"

"Okay, and yes, Bob, Brian, and the four FBI guys are here with me in the Best Buy lot about a mile north of you. We're ready when you decide what you need us to do."

"Good, let's see where this guy goes. I'll call you back when I know more or have a plan."

Dave and Rob sat watching and waiting as they listened to the tactical channel while Rob's guys followed the guy in the Impala. After less than ten minutes, one of the tailing units reported that the Impala was entering the drive thru lane of a McDonald's. A few minutes later the same unit reported the Impala exited the McDonald's and seemed to be headed back to the house.

"Looks like someone was hungry," Rob grunted.

"Yeah," Dave agreed. "How many guys do you think there are in there?"

"Well, we know there are two vehicles, so there must be at least one in the house," Rob concluded.

"I know how we can find out," Dave's excitement level was rising. "If we take the guy in the Impala, the amount of food he got will tell us how many people we're dealing with. Assuming they are getting food for Jan and her kidnappers we can tell how many of them there are. Right?"

"That's a great idea. You want me to have them pick him up."

"Yeah, let's do that. Grab that sucker."

"Unit forty-four, move in and apprehend the gray Impala," Rob said into the radio. "Tailing units be prepared to assist if necessary."

"Ten-four, unit forty-four responding, three blocks away will apprehend."

Rob turned to Dave, "forty-four is a mark squad. Let's see how this kidnapper reacts."

A couple of minutes later, Rob's cell phone rang. Dave listened to Rob's end of the conversation.

"He pulled over without incident? Good. Okay, arrest him for questioning, take him back to the station. Okay, good to know, thanks. Is Jerry there now? Good let me talk with him and you take the perp in. Thanks, good work." There was a pause, and Rob continued, "Yeah, Jerry, do me a favor, look in the perp's car. Is there a drink caddy in there?" Rob paused again, waiting, "good, how many drinks are there? Thanks, Jerry."

Rob turned to Dave, "three large drinks."

"Okay, assuming Jan is in there, and they got food for her, there's only one kidnapper with her."

"Right, but the Impala guy was talking on his cell phone when my guy approached the vehicle. That means he may think we're on to them. So, what do we do now?"

"Good question," Dave paused and thought, "wait, where is the guys cell phone? That gives us the number of the guy with Jan, if that's who he was talking to."

"Right, we need a warrant, but no problem there, it'll just take a little while, maybe an hour or two. You want me to get one?"

"Yeah, that hour will give me time to decide if I want Jan to be a kidnap victim or a hostage," Dave fretted.

Chapter 31

Rob got on his cell phone to request immediate processing of search warrants for the Cruz property and to view the cell phone information of the Impala driver. The stated purpose for each was the suspected kidnapping, and holding at that location, of a Lincoln County judge.

They sat and waited.

After almost an hour, Dave spoke up, "Rob, you say you've got a sniper that can see the front of the house.
Tell me about him. Is he good?"

"He's maybe the best shot I've ever seen in my lifetime. He's young, just over a year out of the academy, but he was a Marine sniper in Afghanistan. He's well trained and as steady as a rock. Yes, he's good."

"I think I want to go over where he is. Let me get a couple of my guys to take this position and we'll relocate. Okay with you?"

"Sure thing, Dave. As far as I'm concerned this is your show."

"Thanks, Rob."

Dave contacted Dan and asked that he and Brian move in to take over the spot. About five minutes later Rob pulled away from the curb as Dan's unmarked pulled into their location. Brian was in the car with Dan. Rob drove around to the north and over two streets to the east before turning back to the south. Three blocks later they parked along the curb two houses north of a gray van parked at a strange angle in a two car drive way. The two sheriffs walked quickly to the van and got in the passenger side double doors.

In the back of the van, over the rear wheel wells, was a table with the top surface even with the back windows. There were several bags on that table that appeared to be filled with sand or some similar substance. Resting on the bags, and pointed out the back window was a military looking sniper rifle with a scope.

A late twenties man with a shaved head didn't look away from the scope as Dave and Rob got into the van. He was wearing a Williams County Sheriff's Deputy uniform.

"Joe, this is Sheriff Dave Harbinger for Lincoln County," Rob said.

"Hi, Sheriff, nice to meet you," the deputy said, again without moving away from the scope. "Forgive my for not shaking hands."

"Understood, and appreciated," Dave responded. "That's my wife in there, I appreciate you keeping her safe."

"Tell us what you see," Rob said.

"I've got a good bead on the garage from here. I'm concentrating on the steps that come down from the door into the house. There are two steps down to the garage floor. If someone comes out, I've got about three steps of clear before they get behind the van out of view. But if they come down the right side of the van, I'm golden all the way to the back."

"Joe, I want you to know that Dave's in charge here. He has full authority and you should follow his orders just like mine."

"Understood, Sheriff. I'm..."

Joe's words were cut off by Dave's portable radio cutting in with Bob's voice.

"Command One, an SPD squad just went by our position headed your way fast. One of the FBI cars is following."

"Ten-four, thanks." Dave said after hitting the send on his radio.

"Command three, get out of there, go west, they could make you. Have Brian get my squad out of there too."

"We're moving," was the hurried response.

All of the sheriff's cars were keyed the same, so Brian could use his keys to move Dave's car.

"What's going on?" Dave said aloud.

They waited.

A couple of minutes later the SPD squad car pulled into the driveway behind the van parked in the subject garage. The driver's door opened and someone got out. It was too far away for Dave to make out any specific features, but not so for Joe.

"Uniformed officer with sergeant stripes," Joe said dryly, "he's armed."

They watched as the cop went in the house through the garage.

"The car's blocking me, I've got to move," Joe said getting up and heading for the driver's seat of the van. Dave and Rob continued to watch the house out the back of the van as it started to move.

"You may need to pay for some landscaping, Sheriff," Joe said as they felt the van rock. A few seconds later, the van shut off and Joe resumed his position at the scope.

"Nailed it," he said as he sighted in. "Not as good as before, but I can still see down the side of the van. I'm only going to have a few seconds clear before they open the side doors if they do."

Dave contemplated the situation. He needed to make a decision. Jan's life may be at stake but he needed to take emotion out of the picture and decide what to do based on good police work. He took a deep breath. What would he do if he didn't know the person being held?

"Okay," he finally said, as much to himself as to Rob and Joe. "We have a hostage situation. We believe there are two suspects with a single hostage. We know one of the suspects is armed and suspect the other may be as well. They don't know for sure that we know where they are, but they think we will soon. So, they are probably going to want to get out of Dodge. That's why the second guy showed up, to help with the move. We have no idea where they may be headed. We won't have a clear view of the hostage once they are in the van. If we try a traffic stop, we have no control over how they treat the hostage. Now may be are only clear chance."

Rob was silent. Joe continued to stare into his scope.

"Joe, if they both come out with the hostage, and you have a clear shot, take 'em out," Dave said softly.

"Confirming," Joe repeated, "I am ordered to fire if they come out with the hostage and I have a clear shot. Both suspects."

"Correct," Dave exhaled.

Dave looked at Rob, he nodded, his expression was dead serious. They sat in the van, two blocks away from where Jan was being held and watched and waited. The level of tension was as high as Dave had ever felt. He could even feel his heart beat in his toes.

Dave almost jumped through the roof of the van when his cell phone rang. He pulled it out and the caller ID told him it was Brian.

"Yeah," he said shakily.

"Dave, was that Roger?"

"I think so, it looks like he's in this up to his eyebrows."

"Are you okay?" Brian sounded concerned for his best friend.

"Not really, I'm a mess, but we have to get through this. Jan's life may depend on it."

"Hang on buddy, it's going to be fine, we'll get her out of there."

"Where are you, now?" Dave tried to calm himself by getting back into management mode.

"I'm in your car sitting on the wrong side of the street two blocks north of the house. I've got a good view, motor running, gun on the seat beside me. I'm ready."

"Is Dan back where we were before?"

"Yep, he's ready too."

"O…"

Dave was interrupted.

"Activity," Joe said calmly.

Boom, Boom! The sniper rifle barked, the noise level in the van was as loud as Dave had ever heard.

He wasn't completely sure he was talking as he yelled into his radio, "Move in." He saw Rob's mouth move into his radio too, but didn't really hear anything.

Dave and Rob were in a dead run to the car. The accelerator was floored before the engine was fully started. They made the two blocks in less than thirty seconds. As they skidded to a stop in front of the house, Dave saw his squad car parked in the yard of the house just outside the garage door, the driver's door standing open. He jumped out of the car and ran as fast as he could into the garage. What he saw was both frightening and exhilarating.

On the garage floor within a couple of feet of each other were two men, one of them in a Springfield Police uniform. The other in jeans and a blue shirt. Both men were bleeding from the head.

On the right side of the garage, against the wall, Brian's arms were wrapped tightly around Jan. Her face was buried into Brian's shoulder, her hands were tied behind her back with a plastic zip tie. She was shaking uncontrollably. On the floor by Brian's feet was a black cloth bag.

When Brian saw Dave, he started walking Jan out of the garage. Jan had her eyes closed, but as they started walking, she opened them, saw Dave and ran to him. He held her close as she exhaled deeply in his arms.

"I knew you'd find me," she said softly, "I never had any doubt."

"Did they hurt you?"

"No, I'm fine. They kept that bag over my head all the time. I never saw them. They threw the bag over my head as they grabbed me when I was getting out of my car at the doctor. They pushed me into that van and held me down and tied my hands. I have no idea where I am, but that doesn't matter now that you're here."

"You're just outside of Jackson in Williams County," Dave offered.

"That makes sense, based on how long it took to drive here."

Brian cut her hands free as she talked. She hugged Dave and kissed him.

"I think she's fine, Dave. She was standing stiff as a board when I got here," Brian said.

"That was terrifying," Jan was regaining her composure. "I was being pushed out here by two guys. I heard the shots and they both let go of me. I had no idea what was going on, I just froze. I couldn't see to run, hide or anything. When Brian took that hood off me, I don't think I've ever felt such complete relief."

"Did they say anything?" Dave asked.

"No, not really," Jan answered. "They spoke only in Spanish, and not very much at that. I think they may have been talking in English a few minutes ago, just before they came in and got me, but they were on the other side of the house and I couldn't hear what they were saying."

"Only one of these two are who kidnapped you. We have the other one in custody. We picked him up when he went out to get something to eat. One of the guys on the floor is Roger Wilson, the Mayor's son. He came down to help move you to another location after we picked up the other guy. We think Roger was the ringleader. The guy we picked up apparently called Roger as he was getting pulled over."

"But what did they want with me?" Jan questioned.

"They were using you to get me to drop the investigation into Roger. If they took me out it wouldn't end the investigation, so they had to get me to drop it on my own. They used you to get to me."

"So, Roger was Tom Brough," Jan put everything together. "He put out the hit on Rod Taylor because Rod was about to uncover his side business."

"Seems so," Dave agreed. "A lot of money was at stake."

By now the crime scene was crawling with uniforms. The FBI was in charge since it was a kidnapping. The four agents Linda Recter had sent down were securing the area and directing the sheriff's deputies as to what they wanted done. Dave was content to let them run the show and leave him to hold Jan and watch.

"Dave," Rob stepped up, "we have the warrant for the cell phone now if that still has interest to you."

"Oh, okay. I guess we know he called Roger, but might as well confirm it. Do we have the cell phone here?"

"Sure do, I had them bring it out to me," Rod handed a phone to Dave. "It's been dusted for prints already so it's good."

Dave took the phone and punched the redial button to see what number came up. He gasped.

"Agent," he yelled at one of the FBI guys in the garage, "can I look at the cop's cell phone?" Dave pointed to the body on the garage floor.

The FBI agent shrugged and moved over to the body. He bent down and began to look for a cell phone. After a few seconds he stood back up with a phone in his hand. He walked over to Dave and handed it to him.

Dan had been assisting the FBI in the garage. When he heard Dave ask for the phone, he came out to where Dave, Jan and Brian stood.

"What's up, Sheriff?" Dan asked.

"Dan, why would Roger even think about coming down here in his squad, rather than in his personal car?"

"Had to, no time to change over, especially if he was on the south side of town when the guy called him," Dan speculated. "Worth the risk of getting caught."

Dave had called up the redial on Roger's phone and was looking at the number.

"Or, maybe there was no risk of being caught," Dave handed the phone to Dan and pulled out his own cell. He punched in a speed dial number.

"Aviation Specialties, Loura speaking," said the voice on the other end.

"Loura this is Sheriff Harbinger, is George nearby?"

"He's out on the tarmac, Sheriff. I can take him the phone."

"Please, thanks."

Dave waited a few seconds as he heard footsteps and Loura's voice telling George who was on the phone.

"Hi, sheriff, what can I do for you?" George answered.

"George is there any activity in the mayor's hanger?"

"As a matter of fact, they just opened the hanger about five minutes ago. Looks like they may be getting ready for a flight."

"How long does it take them to get ready and take off?"

"At least thirty minutes, if they've already filed a flight plan, more if they still have to do that."

"Is there anything you can do to keep them from taking off until I can get there?"

"Not really, but I'll see if I can slow them down, is this official?"

"Yes, thanks."

Dave turned to Dan and Brian, "We're not done yet, guys. Dan take Brian back to pick up his car. Then both of you get to the Springfield Airport, code three. Come on Jan, we have to hurry."

Chapter 32

Dave made sure Jan was securely strapped into her seat belt before he backed his squad off Cruz' lawn out onto the street. He hit the lights, siren and the gas as he pointed the car back north. Dan's unmarked fell in behind him, also with a full array of flashing red and blue.

Dave hit the hands-free dial to his office.

"Sheriff's office," Cheryl's voce answered.

"Cheryl, Jan's fine, she's with me now. What calls did I get today?"

"Good, yes, Dan called and filled me in. You got calls from Linda Recter, Mrs. Adams, Walt Regan, Josh Trubaldi, and a couple of sales types, it's all on your desk. Why, what's up?"

"I'll fill you in later, need to concentrate on my driving. Thanks, Cheryl."

"Command One to dispatch," Dave keyed the radio.

"Go ahead, Command One."

"Do we have an available unit near Springfield Airport?"

"Unit 18, is available about ten minutes from there."

"Dispatch 18 to Aviation Specialties, see George."

"Ten-four."

"Unit 18, see George at Aviation Specialties at Springfield Airport," the radio said after a few seconds pause.

Jan wasn't completely sure what was really going on, but she knew Dave was onto something and was getting the job done. She started to ask, but saw the needle on the speedometer move past the one-twenty mark, and decided to let him concentrate on driving.

Although the high-speed driving had his full attention, his mind also went back over the last few months. It was now beginning to make sense. With what he had just learned, Dave was now thinking back to what he thought he knew relative to what he now knew to be the facts. The words on the wall in Captain David Dean Wessel's office came back to him, "If you don't know how, you don't know what happened." Now he knew how and what.

Roger Wilson wasn't the ring leading master-mind, he was only the muscle. He was sent into the convenience store to clean up after the hit men did their job on Taylor. The hitmen hired by Tom Brough because Rod had figured out what was going on. Of course, the hitmen didn't know Roger was coming, so when Flores saw him, he ran. Brian was waiting in the back and got the drop on Flores as he came out.

Roger had to kill Flores, to cover the hired killer side of the robbery. Because Brian saw him do it, he had no choice but to take Brian out as well. Officer Jones was apparently paid to participate in the clean-up, and is now struggling mentally with what happened. He may be ready to spill more details, "We'll bring him in and see," Dave thought.

Dave continued to put it all together as he thought it through. The fact that Brian didn't die, caused the entire scheme to unravel. They all had to go into CYA mode. They probably wanted to kill Brian in the hospital, but since there was always someone sitting next to him, it couldn't happen. When Brian didn't remember, it gave them a reprieve, but they couldn't take the chance that he would remember, so they hired the hit men again when he got home.

The whole thing was to protect a multi-million-dollar scam on the business owners of Springfield. Tom Brough ran the scam and pushed everything through the city processes. Most likely, handsomely paying off the city officials involved. And on the other end, Roger could shake down business owners if they didn't want to play ball with the IDC payments, after all he was a cop and the Mayor's son.

The money flowed and was most likely split up into Cayman accounts or payments made for services rendered. He didn't think he would have trouble getting court orders to look into local bank records, now that he knew what to look for. The Cayman accounts would be a different matter, but that's obviously where the lion's share of the cash is.

Thinking about it now, it all falls into place, he thought. Most of the people in the city probably had no idea what was going on. The people involved had become adept at running the scheme under the radar. Even though Roger was the enforcer, Dave now could envision that the Mayor, and the council, probably had no idea what was going on.

Tom Brough ran everything smoothly, and kept track of anything that could interfere with his operation. That is, up until Dave got involved. That was something not so easy to control, but thinking about it now, Dave was impressed by how he tried.

As they neared the airport about twenty minutes had passed. Dave again keyed the radio, "Dispatch, Command One."

"Go ahead."

"Contact Springfield Airport operations. Tell them three units are approaching in pursuit of a fugitive and need access to the tarmac via the gate next to Aviation Specialties."

"Ten-four, sheriff."

Jan looked at Dave, perplexed but still silent. A few minutes later, Dave wheeled the squad onto airport property. He drove past the small terminal toward the general aviation hangers. Squad 18 was parked in front of the Aviation Specialties hanger. A guy in an orange jumpsuit was standing by an open gate just past the squad. Dave drove through the gate.

As he came around the corner of the hanger, he saw the mayor's plane sitting in front of the open hanger doors. George and Deputy Allen Gray were talking with a guy in a pilot uniform. Dave stopped his squad about ten feet from the threesome. George walked toward Dave's car.

"Their passengers aren't here yet," George said. "He was told five souls and lots of luggage bound for the Caymans."

"When are they expected?"

"They're late."

"Allen," Dave raised his voice, "go get your squad and bring it around here. George can we put our cars in your hanger, out of sight?"

"Sure, sheriff, you want me to close up after you're in there?"

"No, that's not necessary, I just don't want them to see us and run."

Deputy Gray ran to the front of the building to get his squad. About that time, Dan and Brian came around the corner through the open gate. George waved them into his hanger behind Dave with Deputy Gray close behind. Loura was now standing just outside the door to their offices.

"George, would you mind taking Jan and Loura into the office out of harm's way?" Dave asked as he and Jan came out of the hanger. "I'm not sure how this guy's going to react when he sees us."

"Sure thing, we'll stay in there."

"Are you going to cooperate?" Dave walked back over the other pilot. "Or am I going to have to arrest you?"

"I'm cooperating, sheriff, tell me what you want me to do?" he said shakily.

"Good. Which way will they be coming in? Do they put their car in the hanger or leave it out front?"

"They'll be coming into the hanger through that door," he pointed to a door at the far side of the open hanger. "They'll leave their car out there."

"Where's the co-pilot?"

"He's on the plane."

"Okay, you get on the plane too, and stay there, got it?"

"Yes, sir," he ran up the plane stairs and out of sight.

"Alright, guys," Dave said to Dan, Brian and Deputy Gray. "Let's get out of sight and surround them. I'll take that office over there near where they will come in. After they're all in, I'll step out behind them. Be ready."

Allen Gray went left around the corner of the hanger door. Brian went to the right around the other corner and Dan stooped down behind a tug near the rear of the hanger.

Dave walked across the hanger to the office next to the entry door. The office was small with only two desks and four file cabinets. There was a table along the left wall with some charts and maps laid out on it. The door had a window in it. Dave stood just inside the door, looking out so he could just barely see the entry door just to his left.

About five minutes passed before the entry door opened. In came a young man, about fourteen or fifteen years old. He was carrying two large suit cases in either hand and a smaller one under his right arm. He had a back pack slung over his left shoulder. Everything seemed to be heavy. He started walking across the hanger toward the plane, after holding the door open for someone behind him.

Next through the door was a girl of about ten. She also was weighted down with bags, one in each hand and a computer bag over her shoulder. Like the boy before her, she held the door before moving toward the plane.

An attractive blonde woman came next. She carried two bags and a large purse. She also had a shopping bag hanging off one of the suit cases. Close to her side was another girl of about twelve or so. She only had one suit case and a large shopping bag, but she did have a pink backpack. The door shut behind them as the four moved across the hanger toward the plane.

A few seconds later the door slowly opened again. A man pushed his way backward into the hanger weighted down with luggage. As the man turned and started to follow the others, Dave stepped out behind him, gun drawn.

"Hold it, Walt, that's far enough," Dave said softly. "Or should I say, Tom?"

Walt Regan stopped but he didn't turn around.

"Is that you, Dave?"

"It's me, now drop everything and put your hands on the back of your head. You're under arrest for murder, conspiracy to commit murder, kidnapping, and extortion, among other things."

Dan, Brian and Allen stepped out where they could be seen, guns drawn. All of the luggage burdened family stopped in their tracks.

"What are you talking about, Dave," Walt continued, but didn't comply with the request to give up, "we're just taking a little vacation. I'll be back in a couple of weeks and we can straighten this whole thing out. I haven't done anything."

"Sorry, Walt, your vacations been canceled. Now put the bags down, I'm not going to tell you again," Dave's voice was now forceful and defiant. Full command voice.

"So, you think you've got it all figured," Walt's shoulders slumped a bit as he seemed to deal with reality.

"All figured. You really didn't think you could get away, did you? I may not have put it together so fast if I hadn't gotten familiar with your cell number. That's what put me here ahead of you."

"I had to keep track of what you were doing, Dave. Nothing personal, just business."

"Well, your business is over. Now drop the bags and put your hands up."

Walt still didn't comply.

"Can we do a deal, Dave? There could be a big campaign contribution in it for you."

"That may have worked with the Mayor and Councilmen, but I have no interest in dealing with a murderer."

"The mayor wasn't directly involved. He probably suspected something, but never looked into it. My guess is because he just liked to use the plane. No, it was just Roger and me."

Well it's over. Now, get your hands up. I'm not telling you again."

The teenage boy who had come through the door first, was almost through the hanger when he had stopped. He suddenly dropped all of his load and made a mad dash for Brian who was only about fifteen feet away from him.

"Junior, no," Walt shouted, as he dropped everything and wheeled toward Dave, possibly thinking Dave's attention would be diverted.

But Dave's attention was not diverted, he trusted Brian, Dan and Allen to handle anything that happened on the other end of the hanger. He did not once shift his eyes away from Walt. He steadfastly observed the flinging of the suitcase out of Walt's right hand just before that hand disappeared under his jacket at his belt line. When the hand reappeared, it was clutching a nine-millimeter automatic. As that nine-millimeter came up in Dave's direction, Dave squeezed off two projectiles of his own, center mass.

Walt was falling to the floor before he could get a shot off.

His wife and daughters screamed, dropped all of their luggage and ran to Walt. He was dead before they got there.

Dave didn't move, even though he knew it was all over. He was grief stricken. Ever since he saw Walt's cell number on the Impala driver's phone, he had been trying to convince himself he was wrong. Finding that Walt was the last one to call Roger Wilson devastated him.

It all made sense, now. Walt probably called him early today to see if they had any clue about Jan's kidnapping. When Cheryl told Walt that Dave was in Williams County, he probably got worried. Then when the Impala guy called, he knew they had to get out of there quick. Thus, why he dispatched Roger in his squad to help move Jan.

Dave had hardly moved a muscle, when Jan was suddenly there.

"Are you okay?" she asked softly.

"I am, I just wish he could have found someone else to take him out."

Jan looked puzzled.

"He knew it was all over," Dave said softly, so only Jan could hear. "He knew I would have no choice but to end it for him. So, that's what he did."

"Suicide by cop?" Jan whispered softly.

"Suicide by me," Dave said solemnly. "Come on, let's go home."

Epilog

The Jose Cruz case was moved out of the Court of Judge Jan Harbinger due to a conflict of interest resulting from the kidnapping of the sitting judge. Cruz appeared before a jury of his peers in the Lincoln County Circuit Court of Chief Judge Jeffery Johnson. The jury found him guilty of murder for hire and conspiring to commit murder. He was sentenced to life in prison. The unnamed Impala driver was tried in Federal Court and convicted of kidnapping of a sitting judge. He was sentenced to thirty years without parole.

Dr. Mazurck was able to hypnotize Brian. The result was that Brian remembered exactly what happened the day he was shot. Brian was behind the door of his squad when Jose Flores came running out the back door. At Brian's command, Flores fell to his knees and dropped his weapon. When Roger Wilson came out the back of the convenience store, he shot Flores in the back even though Brian had already apprehended him. Roger picked up Flores gun, as Brian was walking toward him asking why, and shot Brian.

Patrolman Robert Jones turned state's evidence when questioned after the deaths of Roger Wilson and Walt Regan. He admitted to being paid twenty thousand dollars to help Wilson clean up at the convenience store after the hit on Rod Taylor. He confirmed that their plan going in was to kill both Flores and Cruz as well as the store clerk witness. However, when it came down to pulling the trigger, he couldn't do it. Jones was sentenced to thirty years in the state prison.

D was named rookie of the year and National League MVP. He was only the third player in history to do so. The Cubs won the pennant but lost the World Series in six games to the Yankees.

Dave and Jan welcomed a beautiful six-pound seven-ounce baby girl into the world. They named her Katika. She would surely be one of the most spoiled babies ever.

A special note from the author:

Thank you very much for reading R.I.P. Chief Taylor. I hope you enjoyed it. If so, please do me a great favor by posting a review on Amazon. It would be most appreciated.

Thank you and may God bless.

Glynn

Made in the USA
Monee, IL
26 September 2020

42840608R00226